Ruthless Obsession

A Whitmore Elite Standalone

J.A. Owenby

Trigger Warning

Trigger Warning

Please visit https://authorjaowenby.com/about/ruthless-obsession-trigger-warnings-2/ for triggers.

Download Your FREE Book!

SIGN UP FOR J.A. OWENBY'S NEWSLETTER and download your FREE book, Love & Sins. Stay up to date concerning exclusive bonus scenes, updates on upcoming releases, and more. Just click here or visit www.authorjaowenby.com

One wrong decision shattered my soul.
LOVE & Sins
A Love & Ruin Prequel
International Bestselling Author
J.A. OWENBY

Playlist

Oh My God by Adele
Devil by Two Feet
Freakout by Gianni Canetti
Dark Place by Sani Knight
Seventeen by Nane
Masochist by Sophie Ann
That's Rich by Brooke
Love is a Bitch by Two Feet
Sooner or Later by Years & Years
I'm Not a Woman, I'm a God by Halsey

Prologue

My hard-on painfully strained against my jeans as I leaned against the tree. The rough bark rubbing the sleeve of my navy polo shirt as I watched her every move.

A ray of sunshine trickled through the red, orange, and yellow leaves, spotlighting the dark brown highlights in her otherwise black hair. Teagan Mercer was stunning. She was more than beautiful with her toned legs, curvy hips, and perky tits. But her eyes ... those doe-like eyes could melt the hardest of hearts. Except for mine. The only thing I wanted to see were tears in them while I made her beg for mercy.

I rubbed my clean-shaven jaw, then stuffed my hand in my pocket as I watched her frown at her phone screen. My dick twitching at the mere thought of bringing Teagan to her knees.

"Teagan!" A pretty blonde strolled across the lush green Oregon grass. The rain would begin soon, but the last remnants of autumn stubbornly clung to the air.

Teagan's head whipped up, then she stood and hugged her friend,

Ariana Ellison, the daughter of Theo Ellison who owned TechG8. Theo wasn't who I was concerned about interfering with my plan, though. It was Jagger Whitlock, Ariana's stepbrother, and now boyfriend. Not to mention, Jagger's uncle was the prez of a one-percenter MC club, the Dirty Bastards. They were ruthless if you messed with them, and my goal was to stay off their radar.

From my research, Teagan's friends adored and protected her. Fine. Whatever. But taking down Teagan was a different game than messing with Jagger and the club. I wasn't stupid enough to fuck with them, which meant that I'd spent my summer researching everything about Teagan and her peers. Since this was my first semester at Whitmore University, it increased my chances of laying low, since not many people knew me.

Playing football, though, would put me in the spotlight. Under the leadership of Kane Cooper, we were going places. Fortunately, Jagger was playing this year even after a scare with a knee injury. Our team had the potential to be fucking unstoppable.

"Speak of the devil," I muttered as Jagger approached the girls, who were now sitting on a burgundy-colored blanket that Teagan had spread out on the ground. The corners of Jagger's mouth tilted up in a smile as he joined them, then kissed Ariana.

I liked his style. Possessive. Dominant. His reputation preceded him. He was loyal to his friends but a real motherfucker if he didn't like you.

A flicker of jealousy flashed across Teagan's expression. Then she turned away, I assumed to try to disguise her feelings. Her tongue slipped out and swiped over her cherry-red bottom lip. But I saw her vulnerability. Her longing.

I peeked at my phone, checking the clock. Our class wasn't for another hour, but I wanted to arrive after Teagan to strategically choose my seat, which meant that I had enough time to swing by my house and rub one out. My dick was pleading for a release as I thought about all of the ways that I was going to make Teagan pay for ruining my life. I planned to humiliate and torture her until she confessed her sins.

A shiver skated down my spine. I almost felt bad for her, but then I reminded myself what she'd cost me: everything. It was my mission to dismantle her piece by piece until she was completely destroyed. The mere thought nearly made me come in my jeans.

Chapter One

"I really don't want to go." I groaned for added effect while I crawled onto my bed. "Are you sure you can't come with me and visit Theo? Hell, you've never even seen the house other than pictures. You should go." I batted my eyelashes at my best friend, Ariana, while I tugged on my grey, oversized Whitmore University hoodie. As soon as classes were over for the day, I'd hurried home and thrown on some black yoga pants—comfort was everything.

Ari grinned at me before she delivered the soul-crushing no. "Jagger has a big exam on Monday, so being on the road, then spending time with Dad—Theo—isn't ideal." Ari's expression twisted, hurt flickering in her blue eyes.

"It's okay, babe. Like, we don't even have to talk about it. I'm here when you need me." I rolled onto my back, stretching across the full-sized mattress in my room. Gabrielle, Leighton, Everlee, and I shared a place during the school year. As long as our grades were good, the parents covered the costs. The bedroom was smaller than at home, but I didn't have to share it with anyone, which was worth the boring white walls and drab, dark wood floors. I'd tossed up some artwork and bought a bright teal comforter and throw pillows to perk up the space. Oregon winters were grey and wet, which meant my mood tanked unless I took extra precautions to feel better.

Ari tucked a lock of her blonde hair behind her ear and gave me a sad smile while she extended her legs in front of her, crossing them at the ankles. "I'm sure I'll eventually get over the betrayal, but not yet." Ari wrapped her arms around her waist, her cranberry shirt bunching up slightly.

"If my dad did something like that, I would feel the same. Just give yourself some space." I gently squeezed her jean-clad knee. "I'm always here for you to talk if you need me."

Ari placed her hand over mine. "I know, and I love you for it. When are you leaving to go home?"

"Around eleven tomorrow morning, after my class." I pressed my lips into a thin line. "I'm going to surprise the folks, so if you change your mind, you can stay at my place and never see Theo." I grinned at her, realizing I was trying to win a losing battle. I'd made a new playlist for the road to keep me company.

"Speaking of your parents, how are things with your mom?"

"Shit. It's why I'm surprising them this weekend. That way she can't plan ahead and give me a bunch of lame excuses why she can't be in the same room with me." I glanced away, the inescapable pain tugging at my heart. My mom had never been easy, but when I turned fourteen, she changed. At first, I kept my distance, but after witnessing what Ari and Theo had gone through, I wanted to make things right with mom. She was the only one I had.

"You're doing the right thing, Teagan." Ari offered me a supportive smile.

"Well, it won't be the same without you. Guess I'll just have to wait for our girls' weekend and shopping trip. We score in Oregon with no sales tax."

"Not to mention better stores than back home. Usually have to go to Seattle for a good selection." Ari pulled her knees to her chest and propped her chin up. "What about Gabby, Leighton, or Everlee? Could they go home with you?"

I placed the back of my hand against my forehead. "Cheer practice. You remember how it is during football season."

"Every minute of your life is dedicated to the team." Ari's expression softened. "Do you miss it?"

After three years of high school drama and being the youngest person in the history of the Wahlberg Academy team to make captain, I'd had enough shit to deal with for a lifetime. Granted, I did miss the sport and competitions. If I wanted to, I would try out next year. I was at the gym five days a week, staying in shape and continuing to perfect my flips and jumps.

"Part of it. I do *not* miss the bitches." I sat up and twirled a strand of hair around my finger, pondering what I wanted to do for the evening.

Ari stood and picked up her handbag. "I should pick up something for dinner on the way home. You're welcome to join us."

I waved her off. "Nah, I have a suspicion that you and Jagger fuck on every counter of your kitchen." I screwed up my nose in disgust, thinking about eating my food where they'd christened the surface.

Ari giggled and swatted my leg. "We clean and disinfect, thank you very much. At no time have you ever come over to eat and propped your elbows in my ass print."

A heavy sigh slipped through my lips. "I want someone to make ass prints with."

Ari tilted her head. "I have a feeling you're going to find your guy this year. Whoever or wherever he is, he's looking for you, too."

I rose, then hugged her. "If you're right, then I'll pay for a trip to Mexico for the four of us."

"Oh, I'd better get busy finding him then." Ari released me, giggling. "Text me later, bitch. Please be careful on your way to Washington tomorrow, too."

"Always."

I walked Ari downstairs and to the front door. Leaning against the frame, I watched as she climbed into her new blue Audi R8 parked next to my red Audi R8. Our cars were nearly identical except for the color, and mine was a convertible. Ari and I had been sharing and choosing similar clothes and vehicles for years. We weren't biological twins, but we were similar in so many other ways.

A chilly, wet wind whipped into the doorway, and I shivered before I waved and hurried back into the house. It would be nice to have dry weather in Spokane, even if it were only for a few days.

I strolled into the spacious kitchen I shared with the girls and spotted a small stack of envelopes on the table. Everlee was a mail hooch. For whatever reason, she loved to check the secured mailbox daily. Sifting through the pile, I spotted my name. It wasn't often that I received anything, but there it was—a beautiful black envelope with *Teagan Mercer* written in gold calligraphy. I frowned when I realized there wasn't a return address.

Carefully opening the sealed flap, I removed a white card, and my eyes widened as I read the message.

You've been chosen to attend The Viper Secret Society. Use this code to log in for additional information. Come alone and tell no one.

Holy. Fucking. Shit. I'd heard rumors about the King Cobra but had never known anyone that had been allowed to witness it first-hand. From what I understood, it was an honor to be selected, but that was all I knew. Whispers of kinky and group sex had traveled around the college campus, but only a few times. I had no problem with the rumors if they were true. God only knew it had been far too long since I'd been laid.

I sank into the dining table chair, my heart banging against my chest. I glanced at the note again, then shot out of my seat and up the stairs to my bedroom. Gathering my MacBook from the desk, I plopped down on the bed and typed in the website that had been provided on the note. A large King Cobra appeared on the screen with a red 'enter' button on its back.

The snake pixelated, then disappeared. The sound of footsteps thumped through my speakers as a hand reached out and pushed open a door. Riveted by the theatrics, I carefully input the code.

"Hello, Teagan," a disguised voice said. "Thank you for replying. Please join me Thursday evening, October twenty-first, for a night that you'll never forget. Pay attention to the rules."

A white skull mask with black eyes appeared, and strong hands steepled their fingers together. Unable to see the color of his intense gaze, I focused on the details that were scrolling on the screen next to him. I scooped up my phone off the bed and took notes of where and when. Once again, he impressed the importance of keeping the invitation and participation a secret. Honestly, it would be easy not to tell anyone. The girls would fucking freak if they knew, then Ari would tell Jagger, and he would never let me leave the house. He was almost as protective of Ari's friends as he was of her. Almost.

"See you then," the voice said, then the screen faded to black.

Scowling, I grabbed the notecard and typed in the web address again. Nothing. An empty white page with a 404-error message instead.

"Dammit," I whispered, staring into space and trying to decide if I would accept the invitation. At least I had a week to decide. Sex with a stranger might be a lot of fun. No strings, no talking, no accusing stares or awkward conversations.

The sound of the front door opening reached my ears, and my attention darted around my room. I jumped off the bed and shoved the notecard back into the black envelope, then tucked it between a few books on my desk.

"Anyone home?" Gabrielle called out.

"Hey, I'm here," I responded, then descended the stairs to talk to her. Hopefully, I could focus enough on what she said and not what I would most likely be doing next week.

Chapter Two

There were things that I loved about Oregon, but the winter wind wasn't one of them. The rain had pelted against my windshield, my wipers on high as I'd driven out of the state. Within minutes of entering Washington, the clouds cleared, and the sun greeted me.

I yawned, then turned up the tunes, tapping my fingers on the steering wheel to Adele's "Oh My God." It would be interesting to hear a club mix for sure. The beat was solid, and her voice was to die for. I danced in my seat while I kept my eyes on the road.

Singing along with the song, I spotted the Spokane sign. It was only half an hour to the house, and my ass was killing me. Not to mention I hadn't slept much, my mind continually wondering about the Viper Secret Society invitation. I'd bounced back and forth between going or not going. What if it was dark and sinister, and I never left alive? I hadn't ever heard of anything like that happening, but that was the problem. Very little was known about the secretive elite club.

My brain sifted through every possible scenario. There was only one way I would know what happened behind those doors—check my nerves and show up. My pulse kicked into high gear while I chewed on my lower lip. What was more puzzling...why was *I* handpicked out of the thousands of girls on campus? Sure, I was popular, but so were my friends. We all came from extremely wealthy families and excelled at anything we put our minds to. My mother, Allison, said it was because I was well-bred. I was surprised that my parents didn't have a husband picked out for me, but maybe they were waiting to share the news until after I graduated college.

Turning into my driveway, I approached the white mansion and pushed a button on the rearview mirror. The garage opened, and I rolled into my space. Frowning, I realized that neither of my parents' cars were there. I was surprising them, so it wasn't a big deal, but I'd hoped they would be home.

I grabbed my overnight bag and purse, strolled to the door, and twisted the doorknob. "Shit," I muttered, realizing it was locked. I rifled through my handbag and finally located my house key. Seconds later, I let myself in and walked into the laundry area. "Hello?" As I reached the kitchen, the only sound was my Gucci flats smacking against the white marble floor. As usual, everything was spotless, but I noticed the espresso machine and fruit basket weren't on the countertops. I hurried to the foyer, then the living room. I stood, shock resonating through my entire being as my attention swept the space. Empty. Every piece of Victorian furniture, the television, artwork ... all gone.

Dread seeped into my bones.

I ran through the ten thousand square foot home, searching for any signs of life, but each one was empty, including my bedroom. It had been stripped clean. With trembling hands, I pulled my phone out of my purse and called Mom. No answer. Dad was next, but it went to voicemail after a few rings. Were they selling the house and hadn't told me?

I hurried to the front door and opened it, but there was no Realtor's lockbox. What in the fuck was going on? My back scraped against the wall as I slid down until my ass hit the cold, hard floor.

Tears welled in my eyes, and I angrily swiped at them. Were my parents in trouble, and they had to leave quickly? Maybe they couldn't contact me because the call would have been traceable. *That's what burner phones are for!*

My mind scrambled with who to contact for answers, and there was only one person I could think of. I located the number on my cell and tapped the name of my best friend's father.

"Theo?" I asked when he answered the phone.

"Hey, Teagan, how are you?" Theo asked.

"I'm not sure." My words caught in my throat. "Do you know where my parents are? I came home to surprise them and ..." I sniffled. "The house is completely empty."

"I haven't spoken with your father in a few months, Teagan. And what do you mean by empty?" His concern bled through the line.

"No food, no furniture in my bedroom, living and dining areas are bare, and so is the kitchen. Everything is gone." My heart rate quickened, my palms slickening with sweat. "They left without telling me," I choked out.

"I'm on my way, Teagan. Stay inside and keep all of the doors locked," he ordered.

I sucked in a shaky breath, willing myself to hang on until Theo arrived. "The spare key should be near the water hose faucet on the side of the house. Use it to let yourself in. If not, then ring the doorbell."

"Sounds good. I'll be there shortly."

I disconnected the call and rose slowly, attempting to cling to a reasonable answer of where my parents were, but I wasn't finding one. In an emotional fog, I walked through the manor once more, hoping this wasn't my new reality.

I'd lost track of time and was upstairs in my room when Theo's deep voice echoed through the main floor.

"I'm up here," I called out, returning to the top of the stairs.

"Teagan ..." Theo's cheeks drained of color. "I'm going to take a look around. Why don't you come with me?" He waved me down. I wasn't sure if he was worried that someone might be inside, but where in the hell would they even hide?

I joined him, and he slipped his arm around my shoulder. "Who else have you called?" He looked at me, his expression full of compassion.

"Just you. I was hoping I was making a big deal out of nothing."

We walked through the mansion, not speaking as he witnessed the abandoned property for himself. Finally, we stopped in the kitchen.

"Teagan, I don't understand." His grey-blue eyes flashed with worry. "Let me make some calls, but come over to our place. You can use Ari's room for tonight while we figure this out."

"I'll meet you there after I lock up." I massaged my neck, my muscles riddled with tension.

"Okay." His fatherly gaze fell on me. "I'm sure they're safe, hon."

I nodded. With the furniture gone, I had to agree with him. As far as I could tell, kidnappers didn't take them along with all of our belongings. Fear threaded through me, and I reminded myself not to jump to conclusions. Even though it looked like they packed up and moved without telling me, leaving me behind. A lump lodged in my throat as my mother's words assaulted my emotionally battered brain. *It will be nice not to have you around all the time. Why don't you just move out, Teagan? That way, we no longer have to pretend to be a happy family.*

I ground my molars together, hatred for her ripping through me. Once I located my overnight bag, I hauled ass to my car and left as fast as possible.

Theo was waiting by the front door when I pulled into his driveway. The drive wasn't long, but in that short time, my emotions bounced around from shock to being absolutely mortified that my family had left without a word. If my parents hated me so much they could just leave, what had they told Theo in private? What did he think of me?

"Come in and make yourself comfortable. The kitchen is to the left and Ari's room is upstairs." Theo opened the door and offered me a warm smile. "I'm going to contact the police to see if there's anything they can do to help."

"Thank you." Heat rushed up my neck and cheeks. "I'm sorry I involved you in ..." I gulped, "whatever is going on. If it's okay, I'll head to Ari's room. I should call and let her know I'm here."

A flicker of sadness crossed Theo's face. "How is she?"

I pursed my lips together. I don't think Theo meant to put me on the spot, but I was suddenly feeling awkward. "She's good. She's still processing what happened between the two of you, but she's happy with Jagger."

Theo shoved his hand in the pocket of his black slacks. "Good. She deserves all the happiness in the world." He cleared his throat, then said, "I'll reach out to some people I think can help locate your parents." He squeezed my shoulder. "You're not alone, Teagan. You still have family here."

"I appreciate it." I stood on my tiptoes and hugged him before I walked through the foyer toward the stairs that led to the bedrooms. My attention returned to my parents. I would have rather my mother beat the shit out of me with her designer purse full of rocks than be worried about her and Dad. But why would Mom waste the energy when she could mutilate my soul from the inside? A dark cloud of self-loathing hung over me as the agonizing heartache wrapped its fingers around my chest. *They left you.* I sucked in a sharp breath, forcing myself not to think about it for a few minutes. I desperately needed to collect my thoughts.

Reaching Ari's room, I tossed my bag and purse on her bed, then closed the door and leaned against it. My gaze swept the area, finding the blue and white color scheme warm and cozy. The sad part, Ari had never used the room since she'd been shipped off to the academy before Theo bought this house.

I dragged my feet across the room, touched the lamp, then sat on the edge her bed. Once I'd located my cell, I called Ari.

"Hey, did you make it home?" Ari asked without even saying hello.

"Uh ... yeah. The drive was fine." Tears clouded my vision, and I swallowed over the lump in my throat. I was about to voice my worst fear.

"You sound strange. What's going on?" she asked, concern weaving through her words.

"Well, I'm going to keep your unused room company. I'm at Theo's for the night."

"What? Why?"

I could imagine the surprised look on her face, her blue eyes wide.

"When I got home ... Ari, no one was there. I mean everything was gone. There's no furniture. No food. No curtains. Nothing."

An audible gasp escaped her. "What the fuck?"

"Yeah. That's what I thought, too." I blew out a sigh as I flopped backward on the mattress, a blue and white striped throw pillow falling and smacking me on the head. "I have no idea what's going on, Ari. I don't know if they were in some kind of legal trouble and took off, or just moved and left me behind." I choked on my words, crying. "I didn't know who else to call, so I reached out to Theo, and he met me there. When he saw the vast emptiness of the manor, he told me to stay here tonight. I hope you're not mad. I know you and Theo aren't on the best of terms right now."

"Teagan, how in the world could I be upset about you calling Theo? I'm glad he was home and not on a business trip. Even then, he would have called the housekeeper for you. He's always loved you like family." A hint of sadness clung to her words.

I rubbed my forehead, attempting to calm the hot tears streaming down my face. "I just don't want to make it harder on you."

"Bitch, please. You're my best friend, and I'm grateful Theo was there for you. I might be confused about who he is, but in some ways he's still the same father that loved and raised me."

I slipped my hand beneath my head. "He asked about you. I realize that crazy shit went down, but I believe he genuinely loves you, and what happened was a horrible thing to do. But desperate people make desperate choices, babe. After I thought about it, I might have done the same if I'd been in his shoes. I'm not for certain, but that's the twist. Until we live the same or similar experience, how do we really understand what we would do?" I didn't want to say it out loud, but I would be next in line for shit choices if my funds weren't intact, so who was I to judge Theo? I closed my eyes briefly, my emotions fluctuating between anger and depression.

"A part of me understands what you're saying, but my heart hasn't caught up with it yet. I just need more time."

I closed my eyes, willing an answer to appear quickly and explain where my parents were. "Why would they leave me?"

"Teagan, you don't know for sure that's what happened. I can't imagine how hard this is but take a breath. Do you want me to drive up?"

I rolled over onto my stomach and propped my head on my arm. "No, I'll be heading back your way in the morning. Unless my parents show up or call, I have no reason to stay. I'm just glad I have a place to sleep tonight."

"Theo will take care of you. You've always been their favorite." Ari's wistful tone pulled on my heartstrings.

"While I'm here, do you need me to bring anything tomorrow?" I glanced around the room. "Not that there's much here." I attempted a smile even though she couldn't see it.

"I'm good, but can I check with Jagger to see if he forgot anything?"

"Yeah. As long as I can lift and load it in the car, I'll grab it." My tummy growled, reminding me I hadn't eaten since early this morning.

"Okay, he just walked in the door. If he forgot something, I'll let you know. Can I call you back in a few minutes? I want to talk to Jagger to see if his uncle can help track your parents down."

I grimaced. "Ari, I'd rather you not mention the situation about my parents to him. Let me see what Theo finds out, then we can take it from there. I need a day to process this ... whatever this is." I hoped she understood. I just couldn't deal with telling anyone else at the moment.

"I get it. Just remember I'm only a text or call away. Love you, babe," Ari said.

"You, too, bitch." I ended the conversation and laughed out loud at the irony that I was at Ari's parent's house instead of mine. I massaged my temples, wondering how the hell my life had flip-flopped within hours.

After speaking with Ari, I'd checked the credit card that my parents paid for. It had a zero balance, which was good, but as I began to look at my purchases, a message popped up that the account had been closed. Son of a bitch. My parents left without leaving me a fucking dime. No goodbye and no way to cover my bills or eat. Fury rolled to a boil inside me, and I ground my molars. As hard as I'd tried, nothing I ever did was good enough. If I were a few years younger, I would have called the cops and turned them in for child abandonment, but I was nineteen, and no one gave a fuck about an adult who couldn't support herself. I had to find a way to earn some money, and quickly.

An obnoxious growl from my stomach reminded me it was time to eat. I hadn't ever been a stress eater before, the opposite usually, but nothing about my situation was normal. I needed to find some food and talk to Theo. Maybe he'd been able to locate my parents. He and Dad had been golfing buddies for years, but since I was away at college, I wasn't sure if they were still close.

I hopped off the bed, then grabbed my phone and shoved it in the back pocket of my jeans. Hurrying downstairs, I located Theo in his office, and I poked my head in. "Are you busy?"

"Come on in and have a seat." He finished scribbling something on a piece of paper, then set the gold pen on his large, walnut desk.

"Were you able to talk to the police yet?" I sank into the leather chair in front of him. According to Ari, Theo lived in his office more than any other room in the mansion.

"I did, and since their belongings are gone, they're not concerned. They told us to call if there were any additional details, but for now ... I reached out to a private investigator, Teagan. Pierce and Sutton Westbrook own the Westbrook Security firm where I hired Zayne and Vaughn, the bodyguards. If anyone can help, they can."

My leg bounced nervously. "My credit card is closed. There's not a balance, either. I'm suspecting they just moved and didn't tell me."

Theo's forehead creased. "Try not to let your mind visit that scenario. I understand it's difficult, but let's make sure they're safe, then once we have more information ... well, we'll get through it, hon. You always have us, so please don't feel like you're alone."

I clenched my jaw, willing the tears that were building in my eyes not to fall.

"I appreciate it, Theo." I stood, desperately needing to be by myself.

"I'll keep you updated, hon."

"Sounds good." I nodded, then quietly left his office. My heart was torn in different directions, leaving me confused and angry. Regardless of how this played out, I had to remember that I always landed on my feet. Unfortunately, I didn't understand how fast the rug was about to be pulled out from under me.

Chapter Three

By nine the following day, I hugged Theo goodbye. He had packed plenty of food for the road and filled my thermos with coffee. It was more than my parents had ever done. Granted, I'd never had to worry about money, but any caring and nurturing actions on their part were thin. My mother made it clear that she wanted me gone from her life. I just didn't know what I'd done. Her nasty comments about not being good enough and shaming the family over the last several years had cut deep. Not even Ari knew that I was emotionally lying on the floor, bleeding a slow death.

The girls and I had found a fantastic house to rent for the school year, and I slowed as I approached. The early afternoon sunshine blinded me as I turned into the driveway. My pulse stuttered against my wrist as I stared at the house, terrified that I wouldn't be able to pay my part of the rent or food. Even though I realized I should talk to my friends, I couldn't be a burden. I wasn't their responsibility.

Even though Everlee would be irritated, I checked the mail before letting myself in. I wasn't sure who would be here since it was the weekend.

"Dammit." Everlee tapped her foot against the living room's hardwood floor, her hands on her hips. "I was just going out to check the mailbox." She folded her arms, glaring at me.

"I saved you the trip." I beamed at her, pretending that everything in my world was perfect. I set my bag down, then flipped through the envelopes. My heart skidded to a stop when I identified my name in gold calligraphy. Quickly, I shoved the envelope into the back pocket of my jeans, then thrust the rest in Everlee's face, hoping she hadn't noticed that I was hiding a letter from her.

"Damn, Teagan. You don't have to stick the mail up my nose. What's up with you?" She quirked a dark brow at me.

"I'm sorry, I'm just tired from the trip." I offered her a reassuring smile.

"How were the folks?" She plopped down on the couch, clutching the stack of letters to her chest.

"Normal. Work. Plans to travel. Ya know, same shit on a different day." I gave her a half-shrug, mentally pleading with her to drop it.

"No offense, Teagan, and I love ya, but your family is a bit strange." She tilted her head, then a big grin eased across her face. "I have news." She rubbed her hands together, her eagerness to share spilling out of her.

"Yeah? Is it juicy?" I sat on the arm of the chair, careful not to squish the envelope that was burning a hole through my denims.

"Have you seen the new running back for the football team?" She squealed. "He's so fucking hot. I mean cream your panties hot."

I rolled my eyes at her and laughed. "Did he ask you out?"

She shook her head. "No, I was thinking about asking him." She chewed on her bottom lip, waiting for my reaction.

My brows knitted together. "What about Remington? You guys went out once, then you never talked about him again. I take it things didn't go well."

Everlee's expression fell. "It was weird. Like, date with a best friend weird. He's a good kisser though." She giggled, hiding her smile behind her hand. "He asked if he could kiss me goodnight just to see what it was like. I was down with it. I mean, I was curious, too."

I laughed. "Maybe you two simply aren't ready for each other."

"Who knows, but it was a fun evening. We're on the same page, so it's not a big deal. No one got bent out of shape over it. Thank goodness. Hanging with the guys when we're all out together would be awkward as hell."

"No shit." I faked a yawn. "I'm going to unpack and do some laundry. Do you have plans later?"

"Not sure, but most likely yes. I think there are a few parties happening. We should check them out."

"I'll let you know. I need to take care of some things first." I stood, then grabbed my bag and purse near the entrance before heading upstairs. The minute I was inside my room, I quietly closed and locked the door. Pulling the envelope out of my pocket, I stared at it, my heart pounding against my chest. Carefully, I lifted the flap and removed another white card. My mouth gaped while I read the message, my body trembling.

Word has it that you need money. If you think you can handle it, show up at the address you were provided ... tonight instead of Thursday. If you obey, you'll be rewarded with a thousand dollars.

I rapidly blinked, trying to make sure I'd seen the message correctly. Glancing at the clock on the wall, I realized I only had a few hours to shower and mentally prepare for ... what? I didn't have a clue. But I had no choice if there was money to be made. What I didn't understand was how the King Cobra had found out about my predicament. I hadn't said a word except to Theo and Ari. I sucked in a sharp breath. Had Ari broken her promise and told Jagger, then the gossip traveled to the King Cobra? Questions bombarded my mind at rapid speeds, and my head throbbed.

Sinking onto my bed, I located my phone in my handbag. My fingers flew across the screen as I texted Ari.

Someone knows about my parents. Did you tell Jagger? If you tell me now, I won't be pissed.

Black dots bounced on the screen.

What? No! I promised you I wouldn't. Who knows?

Dammit. Now I had to come up with an explanation. Shit. Even though I believed her, I was confused about how someone gathered the information. Chills snaked down my spine as a thought occurred to me. Was a psycho following me?

I'm not sure yet. I just received a message that said they heard I needed money. I added a crying emoji.

That's crazy. How would anyone know?

I could almost hear the panic in Ari's message.

If you figure it out, tell me. I believe you, though.

I stared at the screen, waiting for her reply. Most likely, I rattled her, but I was also shaken. No one should know about what had happened yesterday.

Keep me posted, T. Thank you for believing me. I would never do that to you.

My fingers danced across the keyboard with my reply.

I will.

I paced the room, trying to figure out what in the hell was happening. Anger pumped through my veins. No one had the right to pry into my private life. My fists clenched and unclenched. If the King Cobra wanted to fuck with me, I would give it right back to them. First, I would take the bastard's money.

One thing the King Cobra hadn't required was particular attire. After selecting and trying on a dozen items from my closet, I opted for a form-fitting black dress and black heels. Elegant and classy was always a safe bet. If others were in jeans, then at least I would stand out in the crowd.

Before I left, I scribbled out a note and let the girls know where I would be, then placed it on the desk. My roomies normally didn't come into my room when I wasn't home, but they would if anything happened to me.

Blasting my car's air conditioning on high, I grabbed a tissue from the glovebox and dried my sweaty palms. I slowed my car, eyeing the white numbers on the fronts of the buildings. For some reason, I had it in my mind that my invitation was to a house, not an industrial area. I'd wrestled with my instincts to turn around and run. If it weren't for the money, I would have bowed out already. Not only was it dark, but it was in an isolated area. Nothing about this was smart, but I had a score to settle. No one had a right to invade my privacy, and I wanted answers.

Identifying the building, I turned left into the dirt and gravel parking lot. *Great, exactly what my heels needed.*

I rubbed my chest, where my heart hurled itself against my ribs. The palpitations were full of fear and adrenaline as I searched the area. There were only a handful of cars, and the streetlights were dim.

I shut off the car, then collected my cell and clutch. Climbing out of my R8, I closed the door and waved my hand in front of the handle, the locks sliding into place. Gravel crunched beneath my shoes, my ankles wobbling as I carefully made my way to the sidewalk. The instructions had said to push the red button on the black box near the entrance. I sucked in a deep breath when I spotted the front of the building.

My footsteps slowed, my body trembling as I willed myself to calm down. I gripped my phone tighter, then pulled up the keypad in case I needed to dial 911 quickly. Squaring my shoulders, I lifted my chin, marched to the entrance, then pressed the button. The sounds of chirping crickets and frogs filled the otherwise silent evening. I shifted from one foot to the next, waiting. Nothing. I raised my hand, my finger a mere inch from pushing the buzzer again, when the lock popped open.

I glanced over my shoulder, then grabbed the handle, the cool metal pressing against my palm as I opened it and walked inside. If

I'd had half a brain cell working correctly, I would have wedged a rock between the door and the frame in case I needed to turn around and haul ass. Unfortunately, all I'd seen was pea sized gravel, and that wouldn't do me any good.

The building was dimly lit, but I could easily see. I took a tentative step down the hall, my heels clicking against the white tile floors.

"Last room on the left," I muttered, convinced that I'd lost my fucking mind. "One grand for showing up," I chanted softly, propelling myself forward. My question, though: would I leave here and have an opportunity to spend the money I earned?

I spun around and rushed out of the building, slowing as I wiped my sweaty palms against my dress. Tapping my foot on the sidewalk, I realized that my rent was due in five more days. Until I learned where my parents were, there was no guarantee any of my bills would get paid, which meant it was up to me to take care of my basic needs. I slowly turned, staring at the door. Anxiety spread through my body like a fever, scalding and dizzying me. My parents were gone, and I was too embarrassed to tell my friends. Whose parents moved without telling their own kid? Not to mention that I refused to be a burden to them like I had to my mother. It was time to suck it up and earn some money. I took a deep breath, willing my pulse to calm down. Courage fueled me forward. I could fucking do this.

I narrowed my gaze as I pushed the button again, waiting. Hearing the door unlock, I entered the building once again and made my way down the hall. Gulping, I approached a dark figure standing near the entrance, guarding a room. It turned toward me, and I gasped and stumbled backward.

"Hello, Teagan."

I waved, trying to identify the voice, but it had been disguised once again. The person was tall but well-built, with muscular arms and a broad chest. He was definitely a male. A skull mask like I'd seen in the introduction video hid his face, and his black shirt and pants didn't reveal any hint of skin.

Clearing my throat, I stood straight, facing my opponent. "I'm here. What's next?"

"Eager to learn more, I see." A chuckle filled the air.

I smiled uneasily, unsure of what else to do.

With a black-gloved hand, he reached for the doorknob and opened the door. A thin stream of soft, white light spilled into the hall.

"You may enter."

I glanced at the person, then took my first step into the room that would forever change my life.

Chapter Four

The lock clicked into place behind me, and I gripped my clutch so fucking hard, pain shot through my fingers. My gaze swept the room, noting the black leather couch, matching chair, and a rectangular table.

Gathering my hair off my neck, searching for some coolness after breaking into a nervous sweat, I crept around the small space.

"Hello?" I called out softly.

"Teagan, so nice of you to join me this evening."

My head whipped around, searching for who had just spoken. "Who are you?" I licked my lips and pushed away my nerves, my voice quivering and full of guilt for not telling anyone where I would be.

A dark chuckle rippled through the area, my blood freezing in my veins. A tall figure emerged from what appeared to be thin air, but I knew better. Shit didn't really happen like in the movies, but my mind was screwing with me anyway.

Again, he wore the mask that hid his face and the color of his eyes, but this time, I recognized his hands from the video that provided me with the details of our meeting.

I stood five feet seven in my heels, and this guy cleared me by several inches. His presence was dark and commanding, and I stepped backward. A flicker of white caught my attention, and I gawked at him. Black slacks, black shoes, black shirt ... white collar. Jesus fucking hell. Was this dude a priest?

Unable to speak, I pointed at his clerical collar.

"I see I've caught you by surprise."

I nodded. "You're a priest?" I croaked out my question, my legs wobbling beneath me.

"I'm sure you have questions. I'll answer what I can." He sauntered across the room and placed his knuckles on the table, bowing his head.

"Who are you?" I asked, finding my voice.

He looked up, his gaze peering out of the mask and straight into my soul.

"For obvious reasons, I can't divulge that information. You can refer to me as the King Cobra. This ..." he waved to the area we were in, "is my sanctuary, where I can safely live out my ... desires." He merely kept staring at me, his dark eyes scratching over my skin.

An uncontrollable shiver shot through me, and I folded my arms over my chest, suddenly feeling exposed.

"What do you want with me exactly?"

Walking with great purpose, he approached me. He cupped my chin and tilted my head, causing the hair on my neck to bristle.

"Everything."

I gulped. "Sexual?"

His fingertips lightly trailed down my cheek and over my collarbone, then between my breasts. "You will receive a thousand dollars for tonight. If you wish to return, the second meeting will be two thousand. For each time you come back, I'll pay an additional thousand dollars."

My brows furrowed. "I don't have to come back?"

His thumb traced my nipple through the material of my dress. "You'll be back, Teagan Mercer. They *all* come back."

He'd done this before. Of course he had. He was the King Cobra, and maybe the rumors I'd heard were true. At least some of them. The fact that he was a priest fucking rattled me, though. Badly.

"We've wasted enough time." He sank into the chair and parted his legs, revealing the outline of the erection in his pants. "Remove your dress."

I hesitated. "How did you know I needed the money? If you tell me, I'll do whatever you want, but honestly, you're creeping me out. I just need an answer."

The King Cobra shifted in his seat, and I wondered if he was smiling behind his mask.

"My child, I have eyes and ears everywhere. Nothing you do is a secret from me." He leaned forward, steepling his fingers together. "Drop the dress, and I'll send you an extra five hundred dollars now." He reached into his front pocket and placed his phone on the arm of the chair.

Obviously, he wasn't going to tell me how he learned about my situation, but this wasn't anywhere close to over. "How many years have you been a priest?" I asked, fumbling with the zipper on the back of my dress, shaking. Apparently, I'd lost my damned mind. At least I'd worn a black lace bra and matching thong underneath just in case my clothes came off.

"Long enough." His tone was clipped, unfriendly.

Even though his voice was computerized, I could tell it was deep.

I took the hint and slipped the dress from my shoulders, then pushed it down my torso and hips before it dropped to the floor. Carefully, I stepped out of the heap of material and stood quietly.

The King Cobra rose and circled, stopping behind me.

"So beautiful," he whispered. He opened the clasp of my bra, then he brushed the straps off my shoulders. The black lace landed on my dress, my nipples hardening against the cool air. "Hands behind you."

I did as he asked. He pulled my arms tighter, then he wrapped my wrists with rope and tied a sturdy knot. Struggling against the hold, I whimpered. In spite of my nerves, I had to admit, there was some part of me that loved the idea of sex with a masked stranger who was dominating and controlling. Best of all, no strings attached.

"Kneel." My knees landed in the soft material of my clothes, my pulse kicking up a notch as I waited on pins and needles for his next command.

His fingers wrapped through strands of my hair. A spark of desire rippled through me, reminding me of my deepest, darkest fantasies.

"I'll hear your confession now."

My head whipped around, trying to see him. "What? I'm not Catholic."

He knelt beside me, his breath fanning across my cheek and ear. "You've done things that are unimaginable, Teagan Mercer."

I froze, my brain scrambling for what he might consider unimaginable. He brushed the hair from my shoulder, his touch sending a spark of heat through me. How in the hell could I be so turned on by a priest who was a total stranger?

As if he could read my mind, he asked, "Are you wet for me, Teagan?" He rose and sat down again. "If I were to run my finger over your sweet slit, would you be soaked and ready for me to devour you?"

Jesus. Why was this sexy as hell? I responded with my silence. He'd already talked me out of most of my clothes. I should feel like a whore, but I had to get paid first. If he didn't follow through, then I was just a slut. Shame washed over me, and I chewed on my bottom lip. I would have to deal with my feelings later. Right now, I had a job to do.

"Yes," I whispered.

"Tell me, my child. What is your confession?"

My tongue darted over my dry lips as his shaded eyes shifted with my movement. Thoughts of Ari and Jagger flooded my brain, embarrassment hot on its heels. I loved my best friend, and I hated how I felt about her new relationship. "I'm jealous of my best friend."

"Why?" he demanded.

"She ... she's in a new relationship, and I wish it were me instead."

The King Cobra rose and stood in front of me. "Do you want him for yourself?"

I stared at the bulge pressing against his slacks.

"At one time, yeah, but not anymore. He's perfect for her. I just feel like a third wheel, and I haven't met any guys that are decent dating or relationship material." A weight lifted off my shoulders. I hadn't admitted to anyone how I felt ... but this. He'd peeled back the layers I'd been hiding behind with one confession, exposing me. It was exhilarating and freeing to allow him to see my flaws.

He fumbled with his belt, then flipped open the button on his slacks. The sound of his zipper filled the room, and my heart flip-flopped in my chest. He freed his thick cock, and I nearly moaned, my pussy clenching. How had I been terrified minutes before, but now I wanted him to bend me over and fuck me senseless? My dirty little secret, banging a priest. I was fucked up in the head, but I didn't give a shit at the moment.

He wrapped his long fingers around his shaft and stroked himself. "Open your mouth and stick out your tongue. It's time to receive the penance."

I parted my lips and followed his orders, heat pooling deep in my belly as I watched him jerk off. He grabbed my shoulder with his free hand, digging his fingernails into my flesh as his come shot across my tongue and face. I closed my eyes, his hot fluid dripping from my bangs onto my forehead and down my cheeks. When he'd finished, he lifted my chin and looked down at me. Humiliation flooded me as I realized he'd used me for his own filthy secret. This wasn't fun sex like I'd thought. He'd exploited and shamed me. A sob stuck in my throat. What had I been thinking?

"Do not wash your face. You will leave here with my mark on your skin and in your hair. Once you're home, take a shower. The remainder of your money will be waiting for you in your Venmo account when you're finished." He stepped away and tucked himself into his slacks. Without another word, he untied my wrists, strolled across the room, then out a side door.

I rubbed my tender skin as I struggled to hold back my tears. Collecting my clothes, I hurriedly dressed, then let myself out. Staring at the floor, I hoped the guard couldn't tell that I'd just been disgraced. Until this weekend, I hadn't ever been stripped of my dignity and discarded like trash. First my parents, then the King Cobra. And all for a quick buck.

Slipping my house key into the lock, I quietly turned the knob, hoping no one was in the living area watching television. Before I stepped inside, I removed my heels, then let myself in. Securing the door and bolt, I glanced around. The girls weren't watching TV, but I could hear Gabby and Leighton's voices from the kitchen.

I dashed up the stairs, careful not to make any noise. Once in my room, I flipped the lock, tossed my clutch on the bed, and hurried to the bathroom. Horror ripped through me as my sad brown eyes stared at the mess in the mirror. Come had dried on my cheeks, forehead, and hair. If anyone had seen me, I would have been horrified. Tears clouded my vision as I turned on the shower. In the beginning, I'd considered turning the tables on the King Cobra, but instead, I had slinked away with my tail between my legs. The minute he'd stomped away from me, I knew there wouldn't be a next time. The invite had been meant to shame and humiliate me while he got off, hiding his real identity behind a mask, and lying to the church and people that trusted him. Disgust knotted my gut, nausea bubbling to life in my belly. I repeatedly swallowed, willing my stomach to settle down.

I stepped under the hot spray and rinsed the damage off, cursing his name as I attempted to pull myself together again. No one had treated me that way. Ever.

An hour later, I was showered and dressed in my white and blue sleep tank and matching shorts. I'd scrubbed my face and washed my hair twice, hoping to wash the horrible, degrading feelings down the drain. What in the hell had I been thinking? No amount of money was worth the humiliation. Recalling that I no longer had funds or financial support from my parents, I cringed with how I'd earned some money. At least I didn't have to ask my friends to cover my rent.

My phone pinged, and I grabbed it off my nightstand. I tapped the screen, seeing the Venmo notification. Knots formed in my stomach as I opened the app, then my mouth hit the floor while I gaped at the message.

For a job well done.

Four thousand dollars sat in my account. Before he changed his mind, I transferred my funds to my bank. *Holy. Shit.*

I flopped back onto my pillow and gawked at the ceiling. My mind raced as I sifted through the evening. Was the humiliation worth four thousand dollars? Hell no. I would never put up with that treatment. But if I were honest with myself, as much as it horrified me, it was hot in its own twisted way. I wouldn't admit it to anyone, though.

I hopped off the mattress, sat at my desk, and grabbed my laptop. Within minutes I'd listed my monthly bills, my eyes widening. I had no idea that my parents had paid thousands of dollars each month— rent, food, car, insurance, phone, and my credit card. I nibbled on my lip, trying to think of a way to take care of the expenses on my own. First, I had to make cuts where I could.

I fisted my hands over my face, wishing there was another way to support myself. But desperate people made desperate choices. Finally, I sucked it up and made the decision. It was time for me to own my shit, and not rely on anyone else. The King Cobra could humiliate me and come anywhere he wanted. At least the four grand would help take care of my bills. I breathed a sigh of relief, realizing I would be able to hide my secret about my family for a while longer.

My cell buzzed again, but it was a text.

Next time I want a darker confession. See you tomorrow.

Then the bastard better pay me double. I blinked at the message several times before my mind started to search for my next confession.

Chapter Five

Exhausted from lack of sleep, I dragged my ass out of bed Monday morning for classes. Thoughts of the King Cobra had possessed me, leaving me tossing and turning all night. I yawned as I placed my feet on the wood floors and wiggled my toes. Since I would meet the King Cobra tonight in a dress and heels, I opted for something more comfortable to wear for the day.

A soft knock on my door pulled my attention from my thoughts.

"It's open." I tucked my hair behind my ear, stretching.

"Hey," Gabrielle said, peeking into my room. "I brought you some coffee."

"Ahh, thanks, babe." I beamed at her as she handed me the warm mug full of steaming brown liquid. Taking a sip, I sighed as my body absorbed the nectar of the gods and relaxed.

Gabby sat on the edge of my bed. "These early classes are kicking my ass. I know you had a busy weekend, so I thought I would make sure you were awake. I don't know when you got home Saturday evening, and I crashed out early last night." She arched a dark brow at me.

I shook my head, grinning. "If you're implying that I had a date, I assure you I didn't."

She scrunched up her nose. "Dammit. I was hoping you were having an evening of hot, naughty sex and blowing off some steam."

Careful not to let my expression slip, I stared at the floor, my hair hiding my face. "I haven't met anyone yet. You?"

She crossed her legs. "Have you seen Kane Cooper's friends? We have some new football players this year."

"Are they hot or do they just think they are?" I laughed, then took another sip of my coffee.

"The few I've met hang out with Kane, and they're in one of my classes. Those guys are definitely yummy. You should go to the big party with me on Friday night. Word on campus is that a lot of the football players will be there, including Kane."

I blew on my steaming mug of goodness, then took another drink, desperately needing the caffeine to permeate my system.

Gabby glanced around my bedroom, then stood. "I'd better get ready. Let me know about Friday, and you can meet Leighton and I there after our evening class. I'm not sure if Everlee is going but I suspect she will. We bitches gotta stay together." Gabby winked at me, then left, closing the door behind her.

The party sounded fun. It would be good to meet some new people, drink, and blow off steam. I probably should have been horrified that my first thought about Friday night was the King Cobra. If he needed me again, I would have to work first, then play. Before I got ahead of myself, I should see how the evening turned out. I hadn't felt too good about myself afterward but being able to pay rent had helped soothe my frustration about the meeting.

An hour and a half later, the rain and wind whipped around, chilling me to the bone as I made a mad dash across the parking lot dressed in black yoga pants and a Whitmore University grey hoodie. No matter how hard I tried, I couldn't get warm this time of year. Dodging through several people, I ran up the stairs and inside the building where my calculus class was located.

I carefully wiped the rain from my face with the sleeve of my sweatshirt, then walked down the hall to the last door, my sneakers screeching against the white tile floor with each step. At least I wasn't the only one. Students bustled toward their rooms, chatting and squeaking all the way.

"Annoying, isn't it?"

I glanced over my shoulder at the person who'd spoken. A guy with blonde hair and green eyes flashed me a grin. A dark-haired guy with deep brown eyes bumped him with his shoulder.

"Dude, don't stop in the middle of the hall like that." He reached up and slapped the blonde on the back of his head.

"Fucker," the blonde grunted.

I couldn't help but laugh at them.

"Girls, stop fucking around. It's time for class," the third guy with light brown hair said, placing his free hand on his hip, then swishing his butt as he pranced past me and inside the room.

Biting my lower lip, I noticed how well his jeans molded against his thick thighs and gorgeous ass.

"Are you assholes going to stand there all day blocking the doorway?" Kane asked, elbowing his way through who I suspected were his teammates.

"Hey, Teagan. Excuse the assholes." He nodded behind him, where several guys were staring at me.

"I assume you know them?" I laughed again as the boys continued to cut up. They had no idea how much I needed and appreciated the entertainment.

"Yup. That's Quinn, Hunter, and Reese. You already know Anderson and Sterling from Jagger. The dude you were checking out is Vance."

Heat feathered across my cheeks.

"Do you want me to introduce you?" Kane offered, completely serious.

I had nothing to lose by meeting a hot guy. "Yeah, why not? Thanks. I hear there's a party Friday. Will you guys be there?"

"We wouldn't miss it." Kane's mouth kicked up as he held his arm out to me, but before I could slip mine through his, Hunter checked him with his shoulder, then grabbed my hand instead.

"Milady, allow me to escort you to your seat." He grinned, his smile igniting a spark inside my chest.

I laughed. The girls would love to hear about these clowns. One thing I knew for sure was I desperately needed to have some fun. Shit had been intense lately.

Glancing over my shoulder, I realized Quinn's and Reese's attentive gazes were still on me. I wondered if they would be down for a threesome. I had no idea where these guys were from, but they knew how to grow some fine as hell kids, wherever it was. It would certainly give me something to confess to the King Cobra. If he wanted to hear my sins, I needed to ensure I had some juicy ones.

Hunter cracked jokes until I chose a seat, then he bowed and joined his friends at the back of the class. I was relieved they hadn't sat near me. I wouldn't have been able to concentrate.

For the next hour, I pushed all thoughts of the King Cobra, my parents, and the hot football players behind me out of my head. I had to focus on my future, which looked a hell of a lot different than it had last week.

At nine that evening, I nodded at the guard dressed in black and wearing the same dark skull mask with white around his eyes he had on Saturday.

At least this time, I wasn't so scared that I might puke on his shoes.

"Teagan." His tone was calm and matter of fact while he unlocked and opened the door for me.

"Thank you," I whispered, my manners kicking in even though I had no reason to thank him.

A red light lit the room, and this time the King Cobra was waiting for me. I smoothed my navy cocktail dress. It was a miracle I hadn't been caught slipping out of the house looking like I was about to attend a socialite gathering. I really had to figure out how to lie to my friends if I continued to do this.

"Good evening," the King Cobra said from his chair. "You look stunning."

"Thanks. I was hoping you would like it." I hated to admit that I'd dressed to impress him, but what else was I going to do? I'd even changed my hair, and loose curls hung past my shoulders. This guy, whoever he was, paid me well. As far as I was concerned, it was part of the job.

"Turn around and let me look at you." He made a motion with his finger.

One thing about being wealthy and popular, I was used to being on display. I lifted my chin and did as he asked.

"Did you change your hair for me?" A quizzical tone hung onto his words.

I considered not telling him the truth, but he was a priest. He could probably easily spot a liar.

"Yes. Do you like it?" My voice was soft, shy. I wasn't a shy person, but this was new territory, and I had no idea what to expect.

"Very much so." He paused, his fingers drumming against the arm of the chair. "Pull your dress up and take off your underwear. I want to see your pussy tonight."

Holy shit. Guess he was getting right to business. Luckily, I'd had a Brazilian wax a day before our first meeting.

I set my clutch on the floor and began to step out of my heels.

"Leave them on," the King Cobra demanded.

I gathered the sides of my dress and slowly raised it over my thighs, revealing a white lace thong. He propped his head on his fist, appearing bored. *Great.* I hooked my thumbs beneath the waist and slid them down my legs. He seemed more attentive once I stepped out of them, but it was hard to tell behind his mask.

He stood, then patted the table. "Sit."

The cool air brushed my thighs as I walked across the room, then sat on the edge of the wood surface.

"Spread your legs." The red light shimmered, then turned into a low white, clearly exposing me.

I placed my elbows behind me, then leaned back and parted them.

"Spread yourself apart."

Dammit, this was hot, and I was growing wetter by the second. I wondered if he would fuck me instead of coming all over my face, but I wasn't sure where his limits were at this point. From what I could tell, he didn't have many, or he wouldn't even be here.

My fingers moved to my core, and I pulled myself apart. I gave my clit a little massage. If he wanted a show, I could certainly give him one. I wasn't getting paid to be a good girl.

"Who do you want to fuck, Teagan? Who is on your mind right now?" He folded his hands behind him, focusing on every move I made.

My folds grew slicker as he watched me. "I was wondering if you were going to fuck me, or if I would leave frustrated again."

His chuckle filled the room. "What is your confession, my child? Tell me while you slip a finger into your cunt."

A soft moan escaped me as I did as he asked. "I met some of the new football players today and fantasized about a threesome. One fucking my pussy, the other fucking my ass." My hips lifted off the table, an orgasm stirring deep inside me.

He cleared his throat. "Have you done this before?"

"Yeah. It was so damned good, too. My ex-boyfriend's cousin lived in another state. When he came to visit, we all hooked up. I've never told anyone." My breathing quickened, nearing my peak.

"Enough!" His voice boomed through the room, startling me and I nearly fell onto the floor.

I plastered my hands on the table, afraid to move. The King Cobra strolled over to the chair and sat on the edge. "Bend over my lap." He patted his leg.

I joined him, then draped myself over his knees, my bare butt sticking in the air. His palm slapped my skin, and an unbearable sting ripped through me. I screamed as he continued and hot tears burned down my cheeks, dripping onto his leather dress shoe. Reaching behind me, I attempted to block him, but he moved my arms and smacked my sore ass. Sobs wracked through me, my body shaking. An eternity later, he stopped, and I slid off his lap and onto the floor. I wiped the snot string from my nose and glared up at him.

"You're a bastard," I seethed. "That fucking hurt. Bad."

He unbuttoned and unzipped his black slacks, then freed his dick. "Open your mouth and stick out your tongue. It's time to receive the penance." He stroked himself and gripped my shoulder with his other hand as he rose from his seat.

"You'll mess up my clothes," I snapped.

He fisted my hair and jerked my head back, needles pricking my scalp as he tightened his grip, forcing me to hold still. Within seconds his hot come landed on my skin and marked my face, mouth, and the front of my navy dress. When he was finished, he pulled me up by my arm and slid his fingers between my legs, finding my clit. After a hard pinch, he stepped away. "Bend over the chair."

I glowered at him. "No!"

He spun me around with a quick move, bent me over, and kicked at my ankles with his shoe, forcing my feet apart.

His hand snaked between my thighs again, slickening with my juices. "You come when I tell you to. Not before or after."

"Okay," I choked out as the pleasure began to override the sting of his spanking. He worked his sinful magic on me as he massaged my sensitive flesh. "Oh, God," I moaned, pushing against his touch.

"Come for me, Teagan. But only for me."

I cried out as my release flooded my body, making me forget the pain and humiliation I'd just suffered from the same man who was causing my orgasm.

When I finished, he moved away from my core, and my heart

twisted around itself as he wiped his hand on his slacks as though I were dirty and beneath him.

The King Cobra's footsteps rang through the room as he moved to the door, opened it, then left me alone with my self-loathing thoughts.

Before I stepped back into my thong and tugged my dress down, my phone buzzed from inside my clutch. Grabbing my bag, I retrieved my cell. There was a new notification from my Venmo account. I tapped on the app and barked out a spiteful laugh. Eight thousand dollars was ready for me to transfer to my bank. I moved the money as I calculated how much I'd made in less than an hour total with the King Cobra. Twelve grand. In the past, I would drop more than that in an afternoon of shopping, and I wouldn't even blink an eye. Not anymore. At least I could stand on my own two feet financially and not have to beg my friends for help like the homeless person I was. I might have lost my self-respect in this room, but it was better than admitting I was a complete failure to everyone around me.

I slipped out of the meeting place, hurried down the hall, then exited the building. The cold rain pelted against my skin, and I tilted my face up to the sky, allowing it to rinse me clean. The King Cobra didn't say shit about not washing him off me. Feeling demoralized, I was eager to get the bastard's come off me. I would have to send my dress to the dry cleaners and hope they didn't ask questions. There was no way I was tossing a two-thousand-dollar outfit in the trash. A part of me refused to give him the satisfaction.

An eerie shiver slithered down my spine as my hair clung to my cheeks and shoulders. I glanced around, realizing I'd had an audience. The King Cobra adjusted his mask as he pushed off the brick building wall and began to walk toward me with purpose.

Chapter Six

Istraightened my shoulders, goosebumps traveling down my bare arms as he approached, power rolling off him with every stride. The gravel crunched beneath his black dress shoes. He still wore the disguise covering his face and neck, stopping above his priest collar.

He gripped my arm as the nose of his skull mask brushed my cheek. "There are six things the LORD hates, seven that are detestable to him: haughty eyes, a lying tongue, hands that shed innocent blood, a heart that devises wicked schemes, feet that are quick to rush into evil, a false witness who pours out lies, and a person who stirs up conflict. Proverbs 6:16-19."

I gawked at him, but before I could speak, he continued.

"You, Teagan Mercer, are guilty of all of them, and I *will* watch you fall." He spun on his heel and swiftly walked away.

Rain streamed down my face as I stood rooted in place, shock coursing through me. Whoever the fucker was didn't know me ... at all. Were his words based on our two evenings together? I would be the first to admit that I was selling my body, but he'd offered to pay me, making him guilty of the same things he'd just spouted off.

That son of a bitch had threatened me. He obviously thought highly of himself even though he was a priest breaking his vow. The King Cobra was a liar and coward who hid his true intentions, then had the fucking balls to quote scripture at me.

My skin turned ice-cold, and a rumble of thunder split the sky, my fists curling as white-hot fury swirled in the pit of my stomach. How dare he! I stomped my heel into the ground and released a scream into the night, all the pain and anger from the last week tearing through me. Tears mixed with the plump drops of water, and I wiped my face with my palm.

"If I'm going to fall, then I'm taking you with me, you sick son of a bitch," I swore, then trudged to my car, little puddles splashing around my ankles.

Once I was safely inside my R8, I turned on the engine and blasted the heat. My teeth chattered while I rummaged through the glove box until I located a few tissues that I used to wipe my cheeks and forehead. There wasn't a dry place on my body, and I should've hurried home to take a hot shower and warm up, but I couldn't leave yet. For the next ten minutes, I stared through the dark parking lot and planned exactly how I was going to take the King Cobra down. His scripture whispered through my mind, and I ground my molars together. "Fucking judgmental prick," I said out loud. "See you in hell."

I shifted into drive and pulled out of the parking area, my mind spinning a million miles an hour with how I would take his money and expose him for the fraud he really was. Suddenly, I had a new purpose for living. Pushing the button on the steering wheel, I gave my car the command to call Theo to see what he'd been able to learn about my parents. Maybe this was their sick way of testing me, to see if I had it in me to survive no matter what. Little did they realize, I was about to prove that I could make it through anything, including Mom and Dad being assholes.

Theo's voice came through the car speakers as I turned left onto Division Street.

"Hey, hon. How are you doing?"

"Honestly? I've been better. I understand if you had an update on my parents that you would have called me, but do you have anything at all?"

"You have my word that I'll call you as soon as I learn something concrete. I'm trying not to drag you through every suspicion or share every scrap of information Sutton finds. And, over the last year, your dad and I weren't as close, but I still consider him a friend. I need to understand what happened, too." His tone was low, and concern laced his words.

"It's okay. This time I need an update. What has Sutton found?" I white-knuckled the steering wheel while I waited for his answer.

"There's a credit card trail, but it stopped abruptly, so she's still working on it. The last purchase was in Canada."

My forehead creased. "We have relatives in Ontario, maybe they're going to visit. Theo, I suspect they packed up and left without telling me, but what if I'm wrong? What if they're hurt and laying in a ditch somewhere?" Apprehension poked me in the chest, and I took a long breath, pushing the unwanted worry away. Surely, there would have been signs of foul play.

"I'm not drawing any conclusions, Teagan. You should try not to either. I know it's hard but think through any conversations you had with your parents that might give us an idea of where they might be."

I couldn't admit to him that my mother despised me. At least Dad pretended to like me when I was at home, but he never asked to spend time with me. It was all work, or he was hovering over Mom. Of course, the way Mom went through his money, he had to.

"I promise I'll reach out as soon as I have any significant news. But if you need anything at all, Teagan, call me. Okay? That reminds me: your college is paid for through the year. Hopefully that will take some stress off your shoulders."

The tension in my neck and shoulders eased a little. At least I didn't have to worry about my education. I hadn't forced myself to check with the school since we were beginning the term. Truth be known, I was terrified of the answer. "That's a relief to hear. Thanks again, Theo. I appreciate all of your help. I'll talk to you later."

"Have a good evening, Teagan."

"You, too." I disconnected the call, sinking into the seat. My nerves were shot, and I was ready to curl up in my bed.

Minutes later, I arrived home and parked in the driveway near Leighton's Lexus. I turned off the engine and stared at the light in the living room. It was only nine-thirty, so seeing my roommates downstairs didn't surprise me. Gathering my thoughts and clutch, I opened the car door and hurried to the front porch. I let myself in, hoping my dress was still too damp for the come stains to show.

Giggles filled the air as I realized Leighton, Gabby, and Everlee were all home, watching one of my favorite movies, *The Proposal* with Sandra Bullock and Betty White. My stomach dropped to my toes as I recalled that Betty had passed away only weeks before her one-hundredth birthday. I was grateful she would live forever on the screen, at least.

"Girl, you're soaked," Leighton said, pausing the movie.

"I know. I got caught in the downpour. I'm freezing my ass off, so I'm going to take a hot shower, then I'll be back down to catch up with everyone." I flashed them a wide smile, then walked to the stairs.

"Bitch, hold up," Everlee said. "Where have you been in that gorgeous dress? Did you have a date?" She turned in her seat, facing me.

Eager eyes landed on me while they waited for me to reply.

I cleared my throat. Although I hadn't planned to share any details, I wouldn't lie to my best friends, either. "I don't want to jinx anything since it's too new to say where things are headed."

Gabby's face fell. "No details, then?" She batted her eyelashes at me.

"Not yet, but if I see him again and it goes well, then I'll let you know." I grinned as if I was crazy about the guy I'd seen tonight. Little did they know how much I despised him with every fiber of my being.

"Go shower and hurry your ass back down. We'll pause the movie and make some popcorn. Don't keep us waiting, bitch!" Leighton clapped her hands together, laughing.

I forced a laugh as I hurried up the stairs.

Minutes later, I stepped under the hot spray, my thoughts returning to the King Cobra. I had to find out his identity, but I wasn't sure how. The bigger question was how much I was willing to endure for the money. At least the asshole had gotten me off. After him watching me play with myself, I was horny as fuck. Then, the spanking. My skin was still sore from his discipline. My thoughts traveled to the upcoming weekend and the party. I was definitely ready. I needed to be fucked and worshipped, not belittled. If the King Cobra wanted a confession, I would make sure that I had the best time of my life in order to give him one.

Chapter Seven

The rest of the week passed with no word from the King Cobra or Theo. I'd talked myself out of working for him, then changed my mind once I sat down and looked at my expenses and funds. Since I had no idea where my parents were, I had to make sure I could support myself, and at the moment, I had four months' worth of finances saved, and there were six left in the school year. Even if I applied for a student loan, it wouldn't be available until next semester, and a minimum wage job wouldn't even cover my rent. This was my problem, and I had to deal with it on my own. Becoming a burden to the people I loved wasn't an option, either.

I'd curled my hair for the party, then selected a pair of light wash skinny jeans and paired them with a snug blue and white sweater that clung to my curves. I was determined to feel and look good.

I checked myself in the mirror one last time, then applied gloss to my mouth. Smacking my lips, I shoved the tube in my front pocket. I gathered my phone, then made my way downstairs, my ankle boots clunking against the hardwood steps.

A whistle filled the room, and I laughed as Everlee wiggled her brows. "You look hot." She emphasized the letter T.

"Gabby and Leighton said they'll meet us there," Everlee reminded me.

"Oh, perfect. Our Uber should be here any minute." I beamed at her, genuinely excited about an evening of fun.

"Anyone in particular you're hoping to see tonight?" Everlee nudged me with her elbow. She looked beautiful in her dark wash jeans, thigh-high boots, and black cropped sweater top.

"If you're asking about the guy I had a date with, he won't be there. Plus, I haven't heard from him this week." Fear crept into my chest, and I gave it a firm fuck you. I'd promised myself that I would have fun no matter what. My girls would be there as well as some seriously yummy guys.

"Oh, damn. I was wondering who it was. Obviously, he's not very important if he can't call or text you to say hi." She smirked. "His loss, babe. We, on the other hand, are going to have a blast, get drunk, and get laid. I'm so ready."

She wasn't the only one. The Uber app on my phone dinged, and we locked the house and headed to the driveway. Everlee and I crawled into the back seat, then I rattled off the address one more time to ensure the driver had it correct in the GPS. Within ten minutes, we were dropped off at the massive two-story home a few blocks from campus.

"Now this looks like a party," Everlee said, climbing out of the car. I thanked the driver, then we strolled up the sidewalk.

"Devil" by Two Feet drifted out of the open front door. "Let's find the girls." I grabbed Everlee's hand, and we weaved through the groups until we reached the line of people waiting to get inside. "This is insane. Thank God it's not raining."

"No shit! I would look like a drowned rat by the time we were allowed inside. I'll call Gabby, and you call Leighton. Let's see if they're ahead of us."

Pulling up my favorites in my contact list, I called Leighton. After several rings, it went to voicemail. I frowned, then texted her.

"Oh, good. Can one of you come get us?" Everlee nodded at me, indicating she'd reached Gabby. "Yeah, we're about halfway down the line. Sweet. Love ya!" Everlee hung up. "Gabby is already inside, but one of the football dudes said he would find us and get us in right away."

"Did she say who?" I wondered if it might be any of the guys from my class.

"Teagan?" A deep voice called my name.

My arm shot up, and I waved. "I'm here."

I sucked in a breath as Quinn strolled toward us. He was definitely rocking his well-fit jeans that hung low on his hips. My tongue darted across my lower lip as I sized him up. "I just found who I want to play with tonight," I said in a hushed tone to Everlee.

"Mmm. Yum."

I dropped my hand as he approached. "Hey, I was hoping you would be here." Quinn grinned, his hazel eyes sparkling. "Let me escort you ladies inside."

His pearly white smile nearly melted me on the grassy lawn as he held an arm out to each of us. "If you two are ready for a drink, I'll take you straight to the alcohol."

"Hell, yes. It's been a bitch of a week, and I definitely need to chill." I placed my palm against his bulging biceps, then wrapped my fingers around it and gave a playful squeeze.

"And an intro to your friends?" Everlee asked as we walked to the house, then up the steps and between the two white pillars that accented the grey porch.

"Freakout" by Gianni Canetti thumped through the speakers as we entered. I dropped Quinn's arm and broke out in a dance move, trying not to bump into anyone. The place was packed, but I wanted ... *needed* to dance and shake off the stress and anxiety I'd carried all week. The one thing I missed about being on the cheer team was the additional dance and gymnastic classes that were required.

Following my cue, Quinn slipped his arm around my waist and snuggled up to me, his chest pressing against my back. We fell into sync as if we danced together all the time. He definitely had some rhythm. He twirled me around, then planted his hand on the top part of my ass and pulled me against his muscular body. I squeezed his corded biceps, peering up at him. His eyes darkened, his intentions clear as he moved his hips and pressed his erection against me. Every fiber in my being burned with longing and desire.

"Drinks!" Everlee tugged on my wrist.

My lower lip jutted out, but Quinn just laughed. "We've got all night." He tossed me a wink as Everlee dragged me through the crowd to the kitchen.

"Don't settle yet, girl! We've got plenty of time to choose our prey." Everlee giggled, then she grinned and pointed to our girls. "Bitches!"

We made our way to Leighton and Gabby, who were chatting with a few other football players I recognized.

"Yay! Quinn found you," Gabby said, hugging us as though she hadn't seen us in a year. She raised her red Solo cup, then brought it to her lips and took a gulp before shoving it in my face. "Crown and Coke, babe. Have some."

"What do you want to drink?" Leighton asked, tearing her attention away from Hunter. His green-eyed gaze followed her movements. She definitely had good taste. Hunter was hot as hell with his short blonde hair and sculpted arms. He and Reese had worn their football jerseys paired with jeans, which was typical attire for jocks during the season.

"Whatever is easy to grab," I replied, spotting the empty bottles that littered the kitchen counter and island. When parties were this big, the alcohol went fast.

"What she said." Everlee pointed at me but focused on Reese.

I stifled a giggle as Reese shoved his fingers through his light brown hair, his heated stare traveling over Everlee's body and to her face. So much for waiting longer to select our prey.

"Hey. It's good to see you all outside of class." I flashed them a wide smile. "This is my girl, Everlee. Everlee, this is Reese and Hunter."

She bit her lip. "Nice to meet you. I heard Kane had some new guys on the team."

Everlee could talk football pretty well, and she loved to impress the players with her knowledge. During high school, she would watch games with her dad on Sundays. At first, he would pick apart the game for her, then she caught on.

Leighton returned with our drinks, and I sniffed the dark liquid in my cup.

"Crown and Dr Pepper," Leighton yelled over the music.

"Thank you!" I gave her a loud kiss on her cheek.

Conversation with the guys took place, and I found myself searching for Quinn. I wanted to dance, not stand in the kitchen and talk. I had a plan tonight. Get drunk and get laid. Quinn was hot as hell, and I assumed he got enough pussy to know what to do with it.

"I'm going to go find Quinn. I want to shake some ass," I told Leighton and Gabby, grinning at Everlee, who was full-on flirting with Reese. Hunter and Leighton were also talking, so I felt a little out of place. I took a big drink, then began to wind my way through the crowd, barely avoiding alcohol being splashed on me when I walked past the beer pong table. Cheers erupted, and I grimaced.

I stood at the edge of the living area and swept the room for Quinn. "Dark Place" by Sani Knight reverberated through the speakers.

"Teagan!" A hand waved at me, but there were too many people to see who it was. The sea parted, and Ari's beautiful face lit up with an eager smile. Jagger had his arm protectively around her shoulder.

I hurried toward them, then hugged my best friend. "I'm so glad you're here! I haven't seen you in like ... forever!"

"I'm here now, so we should dance," Ari said. "What's in the cup?"

"Dr Pepper and Crown." I handed it to her, then turned to her boyfriend.

"Looking hot as always." I winked at Ari's boyfriend, then threw my head back and laughed. Even though Jagger had been a complete douche canoe to Ari before they were together, he had been sweet to me. For a while, we flirted, but nothing ever transpired. It all made sense after he admitted his feelings for her. At this stage in life, boys could be such dumbasses sometimes. If I didn't meet anyone soon, I would find a gorgeous guy to fuck, take a mold of his cock, and keep it in my nightstand drawer to use any time I wanted. That way, I could forget about the dating scene, including the no-shows and catfishing.

"Already trying to stir up trouble, huh?" A lopsided smile eased across Jagger's face.

"Always. I gotta keep Ari on her toes, right?" I gave him a brief hug, then searched the area for Quinn. Where in the hell had he gone?

"Here." Ari gave the drink back to me. "Let's shake some booty." She took mine and Jagger's hands, then led us to the corner of the group that was already overflowing with sweaty, gyrating bodies.

The beat thumped through me, and I twirled Ari around. Jagger stood at the edge of the makeshift dance floor, keeping a watch over us. As long as Jagger was here, he would make sure we were safe. I appreciated him for that, but eventually, I wanted my own guy to watch over me.

"You know what we should do?" Ari's blue eyes sparkled with mischief.

I shook my butt to the music, then turned in a small circle. There wasn't much room to move. "Seventeen" by Nane started to play, and Ari grabbed my wrist and led me to the center of the group. Jagger was right behind us, curiosity flickering in his attentive expression.

I swallowed another drink, already realizing what Ari was up to. Giggling, I gave her my cup. After taking a gulp, she placed her palms on my hips as I swayed to the tune. Ari worked her way behind me, and I backed up against her. Ari's hands roamed over my body as we moved in sync. Her fingers trailed beneath my sweater, skimming my stomach and revealing my belly button piercing.

"Jagger is about to shoot his wad," Ari giggled in my ear.

I glanced over at him. It wasn't just Jagger. Quinn had reappeared and was watching, along with several other guys. Leaning my head against her shoulder, I parted my lips as I pretended to be aroused. Leighton, Gabby, Hunter, and Reese also gathered around. Another minute or so, and some guy would start to dance with us. If I were lucky, two hotties would join, and I could take them both for a spin.

Turning to look at my best friend, we mashed against each other, our lips nearly touching. We hadn't danced together in a long time, but it was the best way to get everyone's attention if we wanted to get laid. Plus, we laughed our asses off about it later. Some of the expressions on the guy's faces were fucking priceless.

Quinn was the first one to step out of the crowd. I took my Solo cup from Ari, took a drink, and looked at him. My gaze traveled over his broad chest down to the apparent erection pressing against his jeans.

"I couldn't find you." I polished off the remainder of my Dr. Pepper and Crown, placed my palm on his shoulder, then trailed my nails down his biceps and forearm. "Yum." I popped my lips for emphasis. The alcohol was lowering my inhibitions, and I was horny as hell.

Quinn smiled. "Up for some fun tonight?" His hands moved to my waist, then over my ass.

"Oh yeah. I need to blow off some steam ... but." I sank my teeth into my bottom lip and peered up at him. "Do you have a friend who wants to play, too?"

My panties were wet just thinking about a threesome.

Quinn's mouth dropped. "No shit?"

"No shit."

"Two girls?" Hope weaved through his question.

I barked out a laugh. "Nope. Sorry. Not this time, but if you're really good, then maybe ..." I glanced over my shoulder. Ari and Jagger were dancing and all over each other. They would definitely be having fun later.

Quinn waved to Hunter, pulling him away from Gabby and Leighton, but he didn't seem incredibly interested in hooking up with either of them, which was shocking. Quinn leaned closer to Hunter and said something I couldn't hear. I watched as Hunter's green eyes lit up, and an easy smile slipped into place. His gaze swept up and down my body, and he nodded.

Chapter Eight

A few drinks later, Quinn found a room upstairs for us. I hadn't meant to get as tipsy as I had, but I wanted desperately to forget about the King Cobra and my parents. This night was about me and my needs. And I wanted to get fucked. Hard. Nothing sweet or nice about it.

Quinn closed and locked the door behind us and pinned me against the wall. His mouth crashed on my lips before I even realized what was happening. When his tongue swept over mine, my body stirred to life. My fingertips slipped beneath his jersey, skimming over his smooth skin and muscled abs. He groaned as he groped my ass, digging into my skin. His kisses were hot and frantic, and I wondered how long he would last when he was inside me.

Pushing him away, I peered at Hunter, who had located a desk chair to sit on. I took Quinn's hand and strolled over to him. "Do you like to watch? If so, you and Quinn can take turns."

"Anything you want, Teagan," Hunter responded, his voice low and husky.

I squeezed Hunter's thigh, my breath hitching as Quinn tugged on the hem of my top. I straightened and raised my arms. Quinn pulled it over my head, then tossed my sweater to the floor. With a quick flick of the clasp, he unfastened my pink lace bra and flung it next to my top. He cupped my breasts, rolling my nipples between his fingers. I placed my toes on the edge of Hunter's chair, near his crotch.

Hunter leaned over and unbuttoned my jeans. The sound of the zipper lowering was louder than mine and Quinn's moans. Hunter moved my foot to the floor, then shimmied my pants over my hips and down my thighs. I stepped out of them, my eyes on his as he slid his hand between my legs.

"You're so goddamned wet, Teagan," Hunter whispered. "Let me taste you."

Goosebumps traveled over my skin as he spoke my name. I glanced at the bed. I had no idea who it belonged to, but it was about to get used.

I discarded my matching thong and kicked it to the side. Crawling on the mattress, I moved slowly, allowing Hunter a good view of my bare pussy. I giggled as I lost my balance and rolled onto my back. Quinn's tongue darted across his lower lip as his gaze darkened and remained on my boobs.

"I really want to come on those gorgeous tits," he growled.

"Mm, you should, big boy. Why is your cock still in your jeans?" I tugged on the waistband of his pants.

Quinn fumbled with his zipper, then freed his dick from his black boxer briefs. He straddled me, grabbed his shaft, and eased himself between my lips. I dug my nails into his ass cheeks as Hunter spread my pussy apart. He trailed kisses along my thigh, teasing me. With a hard nip to the inside of my leg, I cried out, but my mouth was too full for either of them to notice. Pain ricocheted through me when Hunter bit me again.

I shoved Quinn off, and he tumbled to the side, confusion flickering in his face.

Bolting upright, I glowered at Hunter. "What the hell? That fucking hurt. Is that what gets you off?"

Without a response, Hunter looked up as his tongue swiped up and down my slit. Apparently, he'd decided to answer me with his actions.

My body trembled beneath his talented mouth, and I flopped back on the bed. "Oh, shit, that's better."

Quinn propped up on his elbow, watching as Hunter licked and sucked my sensitive flesh. Quinn stroked his thick cock as Hunter pushed my legs apart and forced my knees to my chest.

"Oh, God," I whimpered. I looked at Quinn and cupped his balls in one of my hands as my hips arched against Hunter's mouth.

"I gotta fuck your titties," Quinn said. He straddled me again, grabbed my boobs, and pinched my nipples.

I sucked the tip of his dick, focusing on something other than how good Hunter's mouth felt. I wasn't ready to come yet, but I wasn't sure how long I could wait.

"Oh yeah, suck me off." Quinn leaned forward a little, his palms on the mattress on either side of my head as he moved his hips to a steady rhythm.

My body quivered beneath Hunter, my release uncurling in the pit of my belly and rushing over me in exquisite waves of pleasure.

Quinn quickly pulled out of my mouth, his lips parted and eyes hungry as he jerked off, shooting his come all over my tits and face. He moaned as he released, and my jaw clenched when he finished, then his gaze landed on me. My stomach flip-flopped as I stared at his hands and froze, my pulse pounding in my ears.

I pushed him away and scrambled off the bed. Hunter's bewildered expression took me off-guard as I collected my clothes.

"What the hell just happened?" Hunter asked, massaging the back of his neck. "Is that it? I'm the only one that didn't get off?" Irritation flooded his voice.

I snatched some tissues from the box on the bookshelf and wiped

Quinn's sticky, white cream off my boobs. Snorting at him, I stepped into my jeans and wiggled them over my hips. "Sorry. I'm done. You can blame *Quinn*." I located my bra and shirt and dressed in seconds, their eyes on me the entire time. Hurrying to the door, I flipped the lock, then looked over my shoulder at the pained expression on Hunter's face. I really did hate to leave him hanging, but I couldn't stay. "Nice hands, Quinn." I snapped, then I left and ran down the hall. The second my brain had cleared from the orgasm and alcohol, I'd recognized Quinn's hands. I needed air—none of this made sense. My mind traveled to the King Cobra. His fingers were the only part of him I'd had a few glimpses of.

Noting the large crowd downstairs, I realized I would need to escape out the back door in the kitchen. Practically slinking down the curved staircase, I reached the main floor and hooked a right, slamming into Ari as she left the bathroom.

"There you are!" Ari giggled and swayed a little.

I grabbed her arm. "I need to get some air."

Ari's brows knitted together. "Are you sick?" She placed her palm against my forehead as though I were a small child.

Not wanting to talk to her while she was plastered, I nodded. "Yeah. I'll be outside." Hopefully, it wasn't pouring rain. Before reaching the back door, I selected a new cup and made another drink. I wasn't sure if I could deal with life at the moment. My parents were gone, and I suspected Quinn was the King Cobra.

"Excuse me," I said, irritated at the group of guys for blocking my escape.

"Need some help there, babe?" A dark-haired guy made a rude gesture with his hips, and the others laughed.

"Get the fuck out of her way, asshole," Jagger said from behind me.

Without another sideways remark, the guys parted, and I let myself outside. Jagger and Ari were hot on my heels. The rainy wind chilled my hot skin, and I sucked in the much-needed fresh air. Glancing around the area, I noted we were almost alone except for a couple near the pool house. They had their tongues shoved so far down each other's throats, they most likely wouldn't even know we were around them.

"Thank you," I said, on the verge of tears. I took a healthy gulp, welcoming the numbness of the alcohol seeping through me, falsely soothing the pain and betrayal bubbling up inside me.

"Are you okay, Teagan?" Ari took my free hand in hers, and we made our way to the other side of the swimming pool to a few empty chairs. Jagger walked behind us but kept a bit of distance.

"I just need some air." I sank into one of the cushion-less loungers, and Ari sat next to me.

"Teagan, we've been friends for years, and I know when something is wrong. Did someone hurt you?" She brushed my dark hair off my face. "I realize the situation with your parents has been hard, too. You know I love you, right?"

I nodded, then glanced at her from the corner of my eye. If I looked directly at her, I would start to cry, and I couldn't explain to her what had happened with the King Cobra.

"I have a secret, Ari. A big one, but I can't say anything to you yet. I need some time." I leaned my head on her shoulder, hot tears spilling down my cheeks. "Please don't be mad at me."

"Babe, secret or no secret, I have zero room to talk. It wasn't that long ago that I was in your shoes."

I didn't miss the tension in her body. She never talked about her past now that she and Jagger were together.

"Yeah, you had yours for a few years. I haven't had this one long. A week maybe. I want to talk to you about it … I just can't."

Ari wrapped her arm around me and rubbed my shoulder. "I'm not going anywhere." She leaned her head on top of mine as my body trembled, and I finally allowed my emotions to get the better of me. Over the last week, I'd been too afraid to admit that maybe something awful had happened to my mom and dad. It was hell waiting to hear from Theo, but I was grateful for his help.

When Quinn jacked off all over me, my brain immediately went to the King Cobra. Quinn's eyes and hands had been so familiar.

Even though my meetings weren't in a well-lit room, Quinn's mannerisms were so similar that for a fleeting moment, I thought he was the King Cobra, pranking me. I just didn't understand why, or what he would do with the information from our twisted time together. An eerie chill slithered down my spine. What if he used the sessions to blackmail me? But for what? He was the one who offered to pay me. Surely, he wouldn't take the risk of exposing himself, would he?

It didn't make sense. The combination of alcohol and hormones had obviously wreaked havoc on me, and I simply thought that Quinn had resembled the King Cobra. I was seeing shit. My cries calmed, and I took a slow, deep breath, my body shuddering against my best friend.

Ari smoothed my hair, a calm silence surrounding us for a minute. "Why don't we get out of here? Jagger is sober. He can drive us anywhere we want. In fact, why don't you stay with us tonight?"

I sat up and wiped the moisture from my cheeks. We would end up drinking if I did, and I would spill my guts to her. Whoever the King Cobra was, I knew he had a way of finding out shit about me.

"I need some sleep. After last weekend when I realized my parents were missing, I haven't slept well. Like an idiot, I thought getting drunk and playing around with a few hot guys would make me feel better, but it hasn't." I looked at Ari, hoping she would understand.

"Well, I hope you at least had one hell of an orgasm." Ari grinned at me.

I stood slowly. "It was awesome." I giggled, appreciating Hunter. Men never apologized when they left us hanging, but Hunter seemed like an okay guy. I would have to make an effort to catch up with him on campus next week.

My phone buzzed in my back pocket. I pulled it out, foreboding knotting in the pit of my stomach as I read the message. *What the actual fuck?*

I know what you did tonight. It's time to confess. Meet me in an hour. BW

My fear quickly morphed to anger, crashing through me. I had to put the King Cobra in his place and confirm his identity. I refused to live with someone watching my every move. I would happily give that sick son of a bitch a confession, then expose him for who he really was.

Chapter Nine

A little after midnight, I parked near the building to meet the King Cobra. The rain had started to fall again, a soft pitter-patter against the ground while I hurried to the entrance. I pushed the red button, anger simmering beneath the surface as I waited to be let in.

The lock clicked, and I pulled it open. Since the son of a bitch had texted me at the party, I hadn't bothered to change clothes or fix my messy hair after my almost-romp with Hunter and Quinn. He would have to deal with it. My boots slapped against the tile floor as I neared the room where I typically met him. Strangely, no one was guarding the entrance this time. I rapped my knuckles against the wood and impatiently waited.

The door creaked open, a soft light spilling into the hall. Typically, I was nervous, but I was too fucking pissed to give a rat's ass. Whoever was spying on me was violating all kinds of federal privacy laws.

"Teagan," the King Cobra said, his voice still disguised.

"You've got some serious explaining to do." I placed my hands on my hips and pursed my lips. Although I wanted to jump on him and pound my fists into his face, I had to remain logical about my plan. In all honesty, I didn't have one except to find out what his fucking problem was.

The King Cobra adjusted his clerical collar and cleared his throat. My attention stayed glued to his movements, and my heart jackhammered in my chest. Those weren't Quinn's hands. *Fuck. I'd been wrong.*

"How did you know where I was?" I circled him, the plan forming in my mind. This time he was my prey, and I would wrap him in his own web of deceit and lies before I exposed him to the world.

"I told you, I have my ways."

"Seriously? That's the best you've got?" I stood behind him, staring at his butt. Even if he was a priest, he had an amazing ass. His black slacks clung to his muscular legs, and his shirt fit his rounded shoulders and biceps. This guy was built.

"Why do you care if I was at a party? I didn't fuck anyone, but that's none of your business, is it?" My tone was sharp.

He spun on his heel and wrapped his fingers around my throat, forcing me to my knees. "Don't push me, Teagan. You're playing with fire, and you won't like how I deal with you. You were with two guys this evening."

I clawed at his hand while my pulse pounded in my ears. This fucker was crazy.

The King Cobra released me, and I collapsed to the floor, coughing. "You twisted piece of shit," I sputtered.

He jerked me to my knees and quickly unbuttoned his pants, freeing his hard cock. He yanked a fistful of my hair and shoved his dick in my mouth.

Shit, why did I like how forceful he was? I was afraid to admit that he might be my sinful addiction. Reminding myself to stay focused on the task in front of me, I realized distracting him would be my best chance. My fingers hooked through his belt loops, and I tugged his black slacks down to his thighs and cupped his balls. He moaned as he thrust deeper, hitting the back of my throat. My hands traced over his legs and bare ass for the first time, etching every muscle, dip, and valley into my memory.

I licked and sucked him, recognizing the signs that he was close to coming. To my surprise, he pulled out and stepped away.

"Take your jeans and panties off," he ordered.

I rose, then quickly discarded my clothes, calculating the perfect moment to strike. I stared at his long cock, waiting for him to continue. All I needed was for him to be in a compromising position, then I would make my move.

He spun me around and bent me over the table, smashing my cheek against it.

"I fucking hate you," I seethed. "You humiliate and shame me for being a female with a sex drive ... all in the name of religion. The worst part? You get off on it. You're sicker and more twisted than I am."

"Yet you come back every time I snap my fingers." His haughty tone turned my stomach.

The sound of a package opening reached my ears, and I glanced over my shoulder as he rolled on the condom.

"You'll probably shoot your wad as soon as you're inside me." My fury surfaced again while I taunted him.

"Shut up." He pushed on my face, pinning me down. Then, with a forceful shove, he entered me.

I gritted my teeth and waited for him to move his hand. He moaned while he slammed into me, sounds of his heavy breathing filling the room. His fingers slid between my thighs as he toyed with my clit, sending delicious shivers through me. Jesus, for a so-called priest, this guy knew what he was doing. I pushed against him, my desire kicking into high gear and taking over any common sense I'd apparently left at the damn door.

"Your pussy feels so good." He released my head, his touch trailing down my back and to my hips. He dug his fingers into my skin, and all the resentment I'd pressed down over the last week rushed up.

"You're a fucking coward that hides behind a mask," I spat.

His palm smacked my ass, and I yelped. "Yet you love when I come all over your face, feeling my hate and wrath for my little slut."

I dug my nails into the edge of the table. "I fucking hate you." My voice caught in my throat as he pinched my clit, my core tightening around him. "Oh God."

Our moans filled the space, then he pulled out and flipped me on my back. With a harsh tug, he jerked up my shirt and removed my breasts from the cups of my bra. He crawled on top of me, then pushed inside again. His mask hovered mere inches above mine, and I could see the flutter of his eyelashes.

I bucked my hips, seeking my release and not giving a shit about his. Fuck him. He was using me, and I was using him. It was a fair exchange.

Even though I couldn't make out the color of his eyes, I could tell when his lids closed, and his mouth parted. I focused on the mask, excitement and fear pumping through me, triggering an intense release. My pussy clenched around his shaft as I trembled beneath him. His body tightened as he thrust inside me one last time, then he jerked and stilled. He slumped against me, and I made my move.

Gripping the bottom of the mask, I yanked it off, forcing his head up. We both froze as we came face-to-face. He stared at me, shock and horror twisting his handsome features.

Chapter Ten

Hunter

I gaped at Teagan while my skull mask crumpled in on itself, lying on the table. I'd been foolish to screw Teagan, but after tasting her pussy earlier at the party, I had to have her. At this point, I was totally down with a good hate fuck. She willingly spread her legs for me—for a man she thought was a priest. I slammed my mouth shut, my dick softening inside her.

"Hunter?" A thousand different emotions morphed over her beautiful face.

I snarled, frustration thick in my throat. She wasn't supposed to find out who I was. Holding the base of my shaft, I pulled out of her, then hopped off the table. I disposed of the used condom and tucked myself back into my slacks, watching her every move.

"Why?" she shook her head, then she climbed down and stomped over to me, still naked, her perfect little tits bouncing with each step.

I cocked my brow at her. Did she not remember, or was she playing me?

With a quick movement, her fist connected with my mouth, and I staggered backward. Teagan was small, but it turned out she was strong and packed one hell of a punch. Blood seeped from my split lip, my tongue darting over the cut and tasting the tangy substance.

"Bitch." I grabbed her neck and backed her against the wall. My head dipped, her dark hair tickling my cheek as my nose grazed her ear. "If you reveal my identity, I will *end* you." Her doe eyes widened at my threat. I loosened my hold, allowing her a trickle of air.

"You're not a priest." Red dusted her cheeks as she struggled to talk beneath my grip.

I smirked. "And to think I almost believed the rumors about how smart you are." Dropping my hand, I backed away.

She sucked in air, her chest moving, and my cock twitched to life again. Teagan Mercer might be the devil, but she was stunning.

"I don't understand, Hunter. Why the charade as a priest and the King Cobra?" She tiptoed to her pile of clothes on the floor and scooped them up, covering herself.

I threw my head back and laughed. "You certainly didn't have a problem fucking one, so what does that say about you?" I shoved my fingers through my messy hair. From her behavior, Teagan didn't remember me. She sure as hell would when all of this was over, right before I destroyed her for what she'd done.

Tears moistened her eyes. "You spanked me, you stupid bastard! Hard! And you bit me earlier at the party. You piece of shit." Her gaze narrowed as she stepped into her panties and pulled them up. The second they were in place, I was aching to rip them off and fuck her again.

Her small fists balled up, but when she charged me, I was ready. Grabbing her wrists, I stared down at her. "I own you, and I'll do whatever I want. Don't forget it." I pushed her backward, and she landed with a thud on her sweet little ass. "Not one word of this to anyone. If you do, I'll release the recordings of your confessions. Every single moment of them." I pointed at her. She probably thought this was over now that she knew my identity, but we were only beginning. When I was finished devouring her body and obliterating her heart, she would be ruined and begging for mercy. I was no fucking priest, and I had no problem ruining her and laughing my ass off while I did.

I opened the door and left her in the room. My dress shoes slapped against the tile and sounded through the hall as I made my way to the exit and stepped into the rain. The entire evening had gone to hell because I couldn't keep my goddamned dick in my pants. My fists clenched as I pushed down the frustration rising in my gut. What the fuck was I thinking?

The wind whipped around me as leaves rustled across the parking lot. Teagan's R8 was the only car left other than my Porsche 718 Boxster. After the shit went down with my family, the parents thought they could slap a Band-Aid on the hole left in my soul with a fucking car and a fresh start. Little did I know that Teagan and I would attend the same university. Fate had favored me and given her a big fuck you. She just didn't realize it yet.

Unlocking my doors, I climbed in as the heavens opened and the rain poured from the dark sky. I reached for the glove box and located my phone. The screen lit up, and I tapped my Venmo app. I laughed as I sent her one dollar. That's what she got for ripping my mask off and acting like a spoiled little bitch. I started the engine, then tapped out a text to her.

See you in your nightmares.

Before I could toss my cell onto the passenger seat, her reply came through.

Whatever sick game you're playing ... it's over. Fuck off.

I barked out a laugh. Teagan was in for a rude awakening. Seconds later, she left the building and walked to her R8. I shifted, then floored the car, fishtailing as I drove straight toward her at high speed. She would either move or die—her choice.

Terror twisted her expression as she stood motionless. Then the light bulb went off, and she performed a quick tuck and roll. I released a snort. At least her ridiculous cheer training had come in useful for something. I considered chasing her, but I didn't want to mess up my car if I did hit her. Blood all over the grill would be a bitch to scrub off. Besides, I wasn't finished fucking with her yet.

My headlights pierced the darkness as I left the parking lot and turned in the direction of my home. The digital clock numbers glowed, showing me that it was nearly one-thirty in the morning. It didn't matter, though. I was wired and had some planning to do.

Chapter Eleven

Hunter

Monday morning football practice had kicked my ass. The coach had been all over me like a bitch in heat, and no matter what I did, I couldn't shake him. I wasn't sure why he had a hard-on for me, but whatever player pissed him off first suffered his wrath the rest of the day.

Mad and in a foul mood about my performance on the field, I stomped off toward the locker room. I had half an hour to shower and get my ass to calculus. I'd been sitting with the guys in the back of the class, but I would sit behind Teagan today.

"Dude, what the hell?" Remington asked as he jogged up beside me.

"What?" I growled.

"What's up, man? You're usually on your game, but today you sucked ass." Remington smacked me in the arm with his helmet.

"Do you need to get laid, or are you enjoying riding me?" I smirked at him, then blew out a heavy sigh.

Remington chuckled, his hazel eyes flashing with mischief. "I got my cock wet last night. Maybe you should do the same. Blow off some steam."

I rubbed my stubbled jaw. "Who'd you hook up with?" I quirked a brow at him. I'd been so focused on Teagan that I hadn't even realized Remington was there.

"This new chick on campus. The girl's got a goddamned mouth on her. She definitely knows how to suck dick." Remington grabbed his cup through his practice pants.

"Hunter!"

"Ah, shit," Remington muttered. "I'm out of here. Good luck with Kane." He slapped me on the back before he jogged ahead.

Kane fell in step, eyeing me.

I glanced at the locker room, wishing it was closer, so I didn't have to deal with more crap. "I'm fine. I just had an off day. Tell coach to suck my dick." My reputation on the field preceded me, but even the best players had off-days.

Kane's chuckle rumbled through his chest. It was his first year at Whitmore University, too. He'd transferred in but already knew several of the team members from their high school. The guys were tight, but Remington, Kane, Anderson, and a few others welcomed me pretty quickly, which had earned them some sweet perks in the society.

"I overheard him talking to another coach that he and the wife got into a bad argument last night. He was banned to the couch." Kane grinned. "Not sure married life sounds like a good idea if you ask me."

I ran my fingers through my sweat-slickened hair. "No shit. I'll pass."

We slowed as we reached the locker room, and Kane turned toward me. "If you need anything, let me know."

"Right now, I need a shower, then to get to class." I tipped my chin at him as I pulled open the door. The stench of sweaty ass and balls smacked me in the face, and I groaned. I'd been playing ball for years, but I never got used to the smell of the locker room after practice or a game.

My irritation grew by the second as I hovered in the corner of the classroom waiting for Teagan, but she never arrived. Finally, I took a seat with the guys and texted her.

Where the fuck are you? I turned my cell over so no one could see the message when she replied. For some stupid reason, I thought she would respond as quickly as she had when she knew me as the King Cobra. Apparently, I was wrong, and she was blowing me off. I would have to quickly deal with her behavior before it got out of hand.

The last college I'd attended had been on the east coast. The girls were stuck up as hell, and no matter who you were, they wouldn't give you the time of day. They were too busy fucking their daddy's best friends. For my dick's sake, I formed the secret society and became the King Cobra. I recruited ten other teammates I trusted to keep their mouths shut. They also stopped getting laid if they blew it, so it worked to everyone's benefit. It didn't take long to realize the uppity bitches loved to be dominated and fucked by several guys at once. If the girls ever wanted out, we had video and pictures of them while the dudes wore masks. When I returned home and was accepted to Whitmore University, I brought the idea with me. Over the summer, I'd learned that Teagan also attended Whitmore. It hadn't taken long for me to decide exactly how to ruin her.

Then, lady luck kissed me on the mouth when she sent Teagan Mercer my way in calculus.

I quickly learned her schedule at school and the gym. Teagan had religiously kept up with her workouts, so paying a girl to slip into the locker room and bring me Teagan's phone was simpler than I'd imagined. Once I got it, I tapped it, which allowed me to hear her conversations and read her text messages. Technology was amazing.

Needless to say, Teagan was my first invite to the new society. And now ...

I gritted my teeth, still seething from her ripping my mask off. I'd been sloppy and let her get too close.

As soon as class was over, I made up a bullshit excuse with the guys and bolted. Teagan not responding wasn't acceptable, and I needed to remind her who she was messing with.

I shoved the bar on the door and hurried down the steps. The blinding sunshine caught me off guard, and I stumbled down the last step, slamming into someone.

I barked out a laugh as Teagan went sprawling to the ground. Before she had an opportunity to recover and take off, I jerked her up by her arm and dragged her around the corner of the building in order to have some privacy.

"Why didn't you answer me?" I pinned her against the brick wall and placed my palm near her cheek.

"I'm not doing this with you anymore, Hunter. You're a fucking coward for hiding behind the mask." She tipped her chin up in defiance.

"*I'm* a coward?" I shook my head in disbelief, then it dawned on me. I stared at her for a moment before I lowered my mouth to her ear. "You don't remember me, do you?"

Her body quivered, and my cock stiffened with her fear. She might pretend that she wasn't afraid of me, but it was clear that I held the power.

Wide-eyed, she searched my face. "I've never met you. Kane introduced us a few weeks ago, Hunter."

I looked away, attempting to block out the memories of the day when my entire life changed ... because of her.

"When I'm finished ruining you, you'll remember everything you said and did." I pushed off the wall, anger pulsing through my veins. If I didn't walk away, I would hurt her, and I had to stick to my plan.

"Hunter, I don't understand!" Teagan tugged on my arm, and I turned on my heel, pinning her with a heated gaze.

"*You* don't understand?"

"No. What did I do and when? I don't remember who you are." Fear flickered in her big brown eyes. "Tell me."

At eighteen, I had a nose job, changed the color of my hair, cut it short, and buffed up. The changes had allowed my family to leave the Federal Witness Protection Program, known commonly as WITSEC, and move across the country. But if anyone from my past looked hard enough, they might recognize me, so I laid low.

I shoved her away, then stomped off, leaving Teagan to ponder her question. In all honesty, I didn't expect her to remember me.

Chapter Twelve

Teagan

I stared at Hunter as he walked away, wondering what in the hell he was talking about. I hadn't ever seen him before. There was no question in my mind that I would remember if I had. He was mouthwateringly gorgeous with his blonde hair and emerald-green eyes.

My core throbbed as my body recalled his mouth and how he'd fucked me the other night. His touch was rough and dominating, and I'd loved every second. When he'd entered me, I'd struggled to stay focused on removing his mask.

I sank my teeth into my lower lip, attempting to rein in my desire for the asshole. Whatever he hated me for, I wanted to know in order to level the playing field. I hadn't ever been a pushover until recently when I needed money. My parents' sudden disappearance a week ago had left me vulnerable and exposed.

I shielded my eyes from the bright Oregon sunlight. A sunny day during the rainy season was rare, and I certainly wasn't interested in Hunter Calloway ruining it for me.

Locating my cell in my purse, I pulled up Ari's number.

"Hey, what's up?" Ari asked.

"Are you and Jagger available for lunch?" I glanced around at the students gathering in small groups across the lawn.

"Yeah. I'm actually about to meet him for a burger. You should join us." Ari's voice filled with excitement. I rarely interrupted their time together, but I needed some help.

I quickly pondered whether to attend my next class or not. "When and where?"

Ari rattled off the name of the well-known diner, and I agreed to meet them in half an hour. My stomach growled in agreement.

Heading to my car in the parking lot, I allowed my thoughts to spin. How did Hunter know me, and from where? It didn't make any sense. Hopefully, I could find out some answers soon....

I flung open the door to the diner and immediately spotted Ari and Jagger at the corner table. Ari's blonde and Jagger's black hair created a beautiful contrast. She was as loving as he was badass, but they balanced each other out perfectly.

The white and red checked tablecloths were bright against the dark, paneled walls. The diner was old, but the food was yummy. I sidestepped a few French fries on the floor and made my way to my friends.

"Hey." I flashed them a wide smile as Jagger stood, gave me a quick hug, then pulled out my chair for me. I wasn't sure Jagger owned anything besides jeans, hoodies, and T-shirts, but he certainly wore them well.

Ari couldn't hide her grin as he sat next to her. Her blonde hair was swept up in a high ponytail, and she'd borrowed a grey hoodie from Jagger. It dwarfed her, but it was easy to remove if she got too warm. "I'm glad you're having lunch with us."

"Me, too. I actually want to talk to Jagger about something." I smoothed my teal, long-sleeved shirt with the palm of my hand. Although I would be direct with Jagger, I had to be careful not to give anything away.

Jagger leaned back in his seat and slipped an arm around Ari's shoulders. She snuggled up to him while they stared at me in anticipation.

I cleared my throat before I began. "Hunter Calloway. Do you know him?"

A cocky smile eased across Jagger's face. "I know him. Why?"

I quirked a brow at him. "Um, he says he knows me, but I have no idea from where. I can't place him. Since he plays football, I thought you might have some information. I mean, I realize you're not playing this year, but you still hang with some of the players." I reminded myself to choose my words carefully. Even though I was furious with Hunter, I wouldn't blow his cover as the King Cobra. I would save that card for later. Plus, he'd mentioned he'd recorded our confession time. Gritting my teeth, I checked myself in order not to roll my eyes.

"He's one hell of a running back," Jagger said, massaging the back of his neck, his dark gaze searching me. "I don't know him well, but we've talked ball a few times. Seems like a decent guy."

"Is he from Oregon?" I tapped my nails against the top of the table.

The server placed glasses of water in front of us and took our orders. My stomach rumbled as she walked away, and Ari laughed.

"Glad I mentioned lunch." She opened her straw, plopped it into her glass, and sipped her drink. Her nose wrinkled in disgust. "Blech."

Jagger chuckled, then trained his attention on me again. "He and his family are from Texas and moved here a few years ago. They have money. A lot of money. I'm not sure what his dad does, and I think he's an only kid. That's all I've got, though."

My brows knitted together in confusion. I hadn't been to Texas in years. Most of my time was spent between Washington, Oregon, and California. Oregon had some of the top cheering camps in the country, so I was near the Portland area every summer. My brows furrowed in confusion.

The year that Oregon was on fire, the camp had been moved to Texas of all places. The heat and humidity had been unbearable, so most of the two weeks had been inside a school gym. In the late evenings, we grouped up on the bleachers and chatted. I sure as hell didn't recall seeing Hunter in fucking Texas, though. I massaged my temple, attempting to sift through the possibilities. I was coming up with a big fat blank of where I'd seen him before.

"Is he bothering you?" Jagger frowned. "I'll take care of him if he is."

Even though Jagger's words chilled and excited me at the same time, I couldn't help but smile. Jagger would move through life beating the hell out of people if Ari let him.

Leaning back in my seat, I blew out a sigh. "No. He's in one of my classes, and I've seen him around campus. He wasn't here last year, so I was just curious." I glanced at Ari, who was staring a hole right through me. The corner of her mouth twitched, and I realized she had questions but most likely wanted to wait until Jagger wasn't with us. My best friend knew me well, and I would have to work hard to not slip up with details about Hunter. When I was able to find out more, then I would fill her in. Maybe I would ask Jagger to dig into Hunter's background, but I wanted to see what I could learn on my own first. The fewer people in my business, the better.

Once I arrived home, I made a beeline for my room. I grabbed my laptop from my desk and crawled onto my bed. My belly was full after lunch with Ari and Jagger, and my eyelids felt heavy, but the drive to find out more about Hunter propelled me forward.

Opening my computer, I turned it on, the machine whirring to life. I typed in the web address and pulled up my checking account balance. Hunter had been a real bastard and sent me a dollar after he'd fucked me. Apparently, it had been his cheap shot at making me feel like shit, but it hadn't worked. I'd already felt belittled from our other confession times together.

I flopped back on my bed, dissecting our conversations for any hint of why he was so angry with me. Maybe I shouldn't give a shit, but it was nagging at my soul. Finally, I sat up and began a Google search on him and his family. Oddly, there was hardly any information available. His Dad, Noah Calloway, was a technical mogul, but I couldn't find an image of him on the internet anywhere. There was a small blurb about Noah and the business, and that was all. Their house was in a wealthy community on the edge of town, but there weren't any pictures to be found—no images from the sale of the home, no sales price, nothing. Hunter's mom wasn't mentioned at all. Hunter had a free ride for four years due to his football talent, but the black and white photo was taken with his helmet on and a practice jersey. What was even more bizarre was that Hunter didn't have any social media accounts. He wasn't on Snapchat, Instagram, TikTok, or any of the other platforms that I searched. Basically, he was untraceable.

Alarm bells blasted off inside my head. Who the hell were these people? The information was scarce, which was seriously weird. Ari's dad owned a tech company, and he was all over the internet. Something wasn't adding up. I chewed on the tip of my nail, debating what to do.

Climbing off the bed, I grabbed my phone, purse, and coat before going downstairs. It was time to do a little spying of my own. I checked the kitchen for any signs of my roomies, but it seemed like I was the only one home. Since it was Monday evening, an empty house didn't surprise me. Everlee, Leighton, and Gabby were most likely at cheer practice.

The doorbell chimed through the house, and I frowned. Maybe a package had arrived for someone. I flung the door open, then my jaw dropped as my cell clattered to the wood floor. *What in the hell?*

Chapter Thirteen

Hunter

I ran my hand over my still-damp hair as I strolled into my house and turned off the alarm system. I'd sweated my ass off in the second football practice of the day and made a beeline for the shower in the locker room. As soon as I was off the field, Teagan had immediately consumed my thoughts. No matter how hard I tried, I couldn't seem to shake her.

Heading to the kitchen to find something to eat, I called out to Mom and Dad, but only silence responded. I doubted they could hear me across the house anyway, but I didn't feel like searching around for them. Dad worked long hours at the office, and Mom filled her time volunteering at the women's shelter most days. She had the drive to fix people. At least she had found something to fill her time.

I tossed my phone on the white marble kitchen counter and opened the industrial-sized stainless-steel refrigerator. Mom had cooked her delicious beef stroganoff the night before, and as usual, she made enough for me to have for a snack after practice the following day. I removed the glass container, peeled off the lid, and popped it into the microwave. Within seconds, the fragrance of the garlic, onion, and butter tickled my nostrils. My mouth watered as I watched the dish rotate and heat up.

I stared out of the French doors that led to the pool as I waited. Not many homes in Western Oregon had pools, but Dad was a big swimmer, so it was the first addition he'd installed when we'd moved here a little over three years ago. With a push of a button, the outdoor pool became an indoor heated one. I crossed my ankles, leaned on the counter, and watched the drops of water stream down the inside of the glass. Maybe hopping into the hot tub would be a good idea for later. The coach had worked us hard, and my muscles were already screaming at me.

The microwave beeped, pulling me away from my thoughts. I removed the dish and grabbed a fork before I walked through the kitchen and into the family room. Sinking into the grey leather recliner next to the fireplace, I shoved a bite of food into my mouth, then focused on the wooden box with the gold heart in the center that graced the mantle. My dark thoughts wandered, dragging my mind back to the past.

Faster! *Heavy footfalls cracked the twigs, alerting me that they were growing closer. Fear pulsed through me as we ran for our fucking lives. I had to do something. I had to protect us.*

The grandfather clock's chime broke my trance, and I placed my palm against my aching chest, the memories still lingering in my mind. I forced myself to focus on the light beige walls. They offered a nice contrast to the dark wood floors. Winter was gloomy, and it helped that the majority of the house had light colors.

My attention landed on the box again, and I blew out a heavy sigh. "I'm in over my goddamned head," I said aloud. I stretched my legs in front of me and munched on a few noodles. "I wish you were here to help me figure this shit out, but if you were ..." I slammed my eyes closed, overwhelmed with regret and grief that twisted my entire being into a million fucking knots. "If you were, then I wouldn't have a reason to hate that bitch for what she did to you ... to us."

A thick silence was the only response I ever received. It would have freaked me out if I had gotten anything else.

"But tell me this: how could I be into the one girl I shouldn't even be touching? Jesus she's hot, and when I fucked her ..." I swallowed hard, my throat tight and my cock stiffening with the memory of being inside her tight, slick walls. Teagan's petite body had fit perfectly against me, and I was fighting the urge to text her. She might not realize it yet, but she belonged to me. Teagan was mine to possess and mine to destroy.

I finished the rest of the stroganoff and stared at the small box. When we moved, Mom had refused to let it go the entire flight to Oregon. Her arms were tight with tension, and her blue eyes had been rimmed with red for weeks. She hadn't been the same since that day. Hell, none of us had. It was as if we'd buried our hearts right along with ...

I shot out of the chair and scrubbed my face with my free hand, the hatred for Teagan returning full force. If she didn't remember, then I would make sure she would never forget by the time I was finished with her.

Storming out of the family room, I returned to the kitchen, where I rinsed and loaded my fork and container into the dishwasher.

The doorbell chimed through the house, and I glanced at the clock hanging on the wall over the sink. I'd nearly forgotten that I'd invited Kane, Remington, and Quinn over to hang. I suspected that Mom and Dad wouldn't be home until late, so we had the place to ourselves. Hustling to answer before one of them rang the bell again, I plastered on a smile, then answered.

I chuckled when I opened the door to my three friends. One of the perks of summer football practice was that it offered an opportunity to meet my teammates and decide who would be a fit for the society. Since I was the new kid and didn't know anyone well, the summer training had been invaluable. Kane had been the obvious choice. Not only was he the quarterback, but he was also new. However, he had a shit-ton of connections with these dipshits. Once

I'd approached him with the idea, he helped me choose the remaining open slots. The society had made us more than friends. We were brothers that would carry secrets with us for the rest of our lives.

"I came equipped," Quinn laughed, holding up two six-packs of beer.

"Awesome." I took them from him, then stepped out of the way, allowing the guys into the foyer.

"Kane, lock the door for me." I tilted my chin up, watching as he flipped the two deadbolts into place.

"Got it." He finished securing the house, then eyed the chandelier. "I would hate to have to clean that. Do they even make ladders tall enough?"

I chuckled. "We have a housekeeper, so I've never considered it." I blocked everyone's view of the alarm and reset it. Mom and Dad had drilled it into my head to keep the mansion secure even when we were home unless I had a bunch of friends over that were in and out of the house constantly. I would never forget the look on their faces, but when I noticed Mom's legs were trembling, I understood how fucking serious she was. Ingraining it on my brain, I made sure I was diligent with her request.

"Who's ready to get their ass kicked?" Remington asked, rubbing his hands together as though he were itching to deliver a final blow in a fight. The dude loved to win. Loved it. If he weren't cool about losing, I couldn't hang out with him. But, surprisingly enough, he was a good sport.

Quinn smirked. "Dude, I fucking buried you last time."

The corner of Kane's mouth kicked up in a grin. "All talk, man."

The guys continued to razz each other as I led them upstairs and to the game room. I popped open four beers, then stashed the rest in the well-stocked refrigerator next to the loaded bar.

We had our pick of pool, ping pong, or video games on the large 4k television mounted to the wall.

Once we selected our cue sticks, I racked the balls and got down to business. I removed my wallet from the back pocket of my jeans and pulled out a crisp one-hundred-dollar bill. After I waved it in front of them, I placed it on the bar and set a glass on it. I took a long swig, the flavor of the beer flowing over my tongue. I rested my elbow on the back of a chair and waited for the guys to pony up.

"I was thinking about having a party," I said, leaning over the table and lining my stick up to the cue ball. With a quick hit, the balls spun in different directions.

"I know who you *don't* want to fuck," Quinn chuckled as he selected the solid colors.

I sat at the bar and wrapped my fingers around the cold, green bottle. To my surprise, Quinn had brought the topic up quickly. "Nah, I totally will. That bitch owes me." It wasn't any of their business, so I wouldn't share that I'd already fucked her.

Kane took his shot, then quirked his brow at me. "Who are you talking about?"

"Teagan Mercer," Quinn replied, lining up his next shot. "She left our man high and dry." He snickered, then sank his ball into the far-left pocket.

Remington rubbed the back of his neck and sank into the seat next to mine. "Dude, that's some shit. And there are a ton of other chicks out there. Why are you messing with her?"

"She's always been cool with me," Kane added, waiting for his turn.

My hand tightened around the bottle, wishing it was Teagan's delicate neck. Big heart my ass—more like selfish fucking bitch. "As I said, she owes me."

"I'd make her pay up," Quinn said, with a devilish grin. "Slip a little something into her drink, then you're guaranteed that she'll cooperate."

I shook my head and laughed. "Yeah, well, the bitch knows I'm the King Cobra, too."

A horrified hush fell over the room as everyone's attention landed on me.

Kane's eyes widened. "No shit? Dude, how the fuck did that happen?" He leaned against the wall, clearly concerned.

There was no need to worry that Teagan knew my secret, but the guys didn't have the information yet. "Don't freak. I've got enough pictures of her naked and my come all over her face. She won't say shit. It would destroy her."

Remington released a low whistle. "You marked her, man?"

"Yup. Multiple times. She's fucking mine." I shot Quinn a stern look just in case he got any ideas about her.

Disbelief twisted Quinn's features, and he tossed up his hands in surrender. "I had no fucking idea. You haven't said shit until now. I won't mess with her anymore."

"I was in the room with you, asshole, I know what you did. It would have been different if I hadn't been there," I ground out my response.

Kane returned to the table to take his shot. "What's she to you?" Kane sank the ball into the pocket, then lined his stick up again.

Anger bubbled in my chest at the thought of Quinn coming all over Teagan's tits. I'd been forced to keep my mouth shut while we were in the room together, but I wanted to make it clear to all of them. "A gorgeous bitch with a hot, tight pussy," I quipped. It wasn't anyone's business that it was purely revenge-driven need and desire.

"Maybe tell the other guys she's marked, so it doesn't cause an issue. Vance is definitely interested." Kane shot me a questioning glance.

"Yeah, I know. It wasn't a problem until recently, so I'll deal with it." I took another drink of my beer. "Anyway, I'm thinking about throwing a party here on Saturday. My parents will be gone, so as long as I have shit cleaned up by Sunday night, it's all good. They couldn't care less if I have people over, but if I want that to continue, I have to make sure the house is spotless afterward."

"Can't lose that opportunity, for sure," Quinn said, sinking his last ball into a pocket. His hands shot up over his head, and he performed his victory dance.

I rose, adrenaline pumping through my body as I prepared to kick his ass. "So, it's settled. The party will be here on Saturday night. You fuckers can help me clean shit up on Sunday."

"I'm in," Kane responded. "Figure if I make the mess, I should pitch in."

My attention bounced between Remington and Quinn. "You guys down?" I racked the balls again as they eagerly agreed.

"Excellent, then let's spread the word." I nodded at Quinn to take the first shot, the toe of my tennis shoe impatiently tapping against the hardwood floor. A plan began to form in my mind of exactly what I wanted to take from Teagan that night. Funny how the taste of revenge could boost my mood. The beautiful thing was that Teagan had no clue where I lived, since I was new to the university, but she would learn soon enough, and I looked forward to every torturous second of it.

Chapter Fourteen

Teagan

My heart jumped straight to my throat as I stood at the front door with my jaw on the floor.

"Dad?" I nearly knocked him over as I threw my arms around his neck and sobbed into his navy dress shirt. I had no idea what was about to pour out of his mouth, but I wasn't sure I could let him go.

"I'm here now, sweetie." Dad rubbed my back until my cries subsided.

I stepped away and wiped my damp cheeks. Dark circles cast shadows under his eyes, and it seemed like he'd dropped a few pounds since I'd seen him last. Dad didn't need to drop any weight, which told me he was super stressed. He'd always taken care of himself, but his appearance at my house twisted me in knots. I noticed several additional silver streaks threading through his dark hair, too. He'd also shown up at my door, wearing nice but casual jeans. I typically saw him in a suit or slacks, but rarely jeans.

"Hi, honey." He gave my shoulder a gentle squeeze. "I'm so sorry

I scared you, Teagan. There were several days that I didn't have a cell signal, and for whatever reason, I never received any messages or texts from you. Theo finally reached me and provided an update about you. He chewed my ass, too."

Good! Thank you, Theo! I stared in disbelief as my father's eyes glistened with tears.

"I won't tell you that it's okay because it's not, but I'm glad that you're safe. And what in the hell happened? Where's Mom?" I stepped outside, searching for Mom in the passenger seat of Dad's car. Not only was she not there, neither was his Lexus. Instead, a black Infinity had parked next to my R8.

"Where's your car?" I folded my arms across my chest, unease pooling in the pit of my stomach.

"I flew in, so I got a rental. Why don't we get something to eat and talk?" Hope flickered in his dark brown gaze.

"I was leaving when you rang the doorbell, so I'm ready to go." My pulse pounded inside my head as my anxiety kicked up a notch. I had no idea what the conversation would look like, and I was terrified this might be goodbye. I wasn't sure my heart could handle it.

I smoothed my top and ran my sweaty palm down the thigh of my jeaned leg. "Let's go." I squared my shoulders as I joined him on the porch, then closed and locked the door behind me.

Silence cloaked us as we walked to the Infinity. Once Dad had unlocked the doors, I slid into the front passenger seat.

"Do you like this car?" I asked in an attempt to spark a conversation.

"It's okay. I think I prefer my Lexus." He pushed the button, and the engine purred to life. Dad shifted into reverse and backed out of the driveway. "How about some Chinese tonight?"

"That's fine. I'm more curious about where you and Mom disappeared to than eating." A clip of anger worked its way into my words.

Dad rubbed his chin as he drove. "I'm sorry, Teagan. I had no idea you were coming home for the weekend." Sadness laced his tone, causing me to face him.

"I thought you left. Packed and vanished without a word." I clenched my jaw in order to check the tears that were building.

"No. Teagan, I would never do that to you." He glanced at me. "I can see why you thought that, though. The furniture, right?"

I nodded, not trusting myself to say anything. Rude shit I could never take back dangled on the tip of my tongue.

"We're remodeling the house—replacing all of the flooring, painting the walls, installing new cabinets in the kitchen and bathrooms ... the full works. We put everything in storage."

My mouth formed an O. "That makes sense, but it looked ..." I blew out a sigh. "Why didn't you tell me?"

"At the time it wasn't important. You weren't due home until Thanksgiving, and you're not known to surprise us." Dad flipped on the turn signal, then turned right.

"That doesn't explain why Theo couldn't reach you. Both of us called several times." A wall of defense slammed into place, protecting my heart. Whatever Dad needed to tell me, it had better be good, or I would be the one taking off without a word. Even though Hunter wouldn't pay me anymore, I still had enough funds to live on for a while. I'd figured shit out when I had to, and I would again. In a twisted way, I'd gained some confidence in making my own money. It was the *how* that messed with me.

Dad eased into a parking space at a little hole-in-the-wall Chinese restaurant. It was the small, family-owned places that offered the best food. The outside of the building was a dingy white with green and red trim around the roof.

I climbed out of the car, then followed Dad inside. Once we were seated in a booth in the back corner, a server brought us glasses of water. I suspected that I would need something much stronger to drink by the end of the evening.

Dad remained silent until we ordered, then he folded his hands on top of the table.

"How's school? The girls?"

I barked out a laugh. "Cut to the chase, Dad. We can catch up later if we're still speaking to each other." My knee bounced beneath the table, the silverware shaking. I crossed my legs in order to calm my jitters. This shit had better be good because explaining away dropping off the face of the earth ... there just wasn't a reasonable explanation as far as I was concerned.

Dad's lips pursed, then he began to speak in a low tone.

"Again, I had no idea you were coming home. Everything changed so fast. I had to make some tough decisions quickly." The muscle in his jaw clenched. Whatever he was about to say was obviously hard for him, but my parents leaving without a word had been difficult for me as well.

"Your mother." A sad smile eased across his face. "When you turned fourteen, she started changing."

I breathed slowly, kneading my shoulders, hoping to loosen the tension twisting my muscles into painful knots. "Yeah, she became mean and short tempered." I took a sip of my water, my throat suddenly dry. "I never knew what I did to make her change." My hands fell to the booth seat, and I dug my fingernails into my palms.

"It wasn't you, honey. You didn't do anything wrong." He reached for me, and I allowed him to. "I didn't realize you thought it was your fault. I should have talked to you about it. I just wasn't sure what was happening, or how to articulate my concerns."

Relief rushed over me. I hadn't ever told Dad that I thought the change in Mom was my fault. It was calming to hear him explain I hadn't done anything to cause her moodiness. "Then what was it? Were you two having problems?"

"Yes, but because of her change. It seemed the older you got, the worse she became. I begged and pleaded with her to talk to me, but she just shut me out. When you left for school this year ..." Dad patted the back of my hand. "She had a breakdown, or so I thought. I'd worked late one evening, and when I walked through the front door, I could sense that something was wrong. What I saw when I reached the kitchen ..." Dad leaned back against his seat. His gaze traveled from me to the window, and a faraway, sad expression overtook his handsome features.

He looked at me again. "I'm sorry. I know you need answers, Teagan. Please be patient with me, this is very difficult to talk about."

"What happened, Dad? You're scaring me." I breathed my fear into the room. "Is Mom dead?" I covered my mouth with my hand, muffling my cry.

"No. She's safe." He slammed his eyes closed momentarily. "But ..."

Chapter Fifteen

Teagan

Everything inside me wanted to scream at him to hurry the fuck up and tell me what was going on, but I couldn't. Whatever had happened was breaking my father in front of my eyes and tearing my heart out of my chest. Dad had been absent for most of my cheer competitions, dance recitals, and gymnastics performances, but he had been a good provider. If something was important and I needed him, he always made time. I didn't realize he'd been managing Mom all of those years.

Dad took a drink of his water, then cleared his throat. "Your mom had thrown all the packaged meat from the freezer onto the floor along with every item from the refrigerator. She'd dumped out the casseroles, peeled the fruit and threw it onto the marble, and poured out the milk. Everything, Teagan. Food had splattered all over the stove, island, and the walls. Your mom had removed the cabinet doors with a screwdriver, too. When I found her, she was sitting in a pile of eggs mixed with rice and pancake mix. She was crying and her makeup had streamed down her cheeks. Her hair was a mess, and she was saying the Lord's Prayer over and over while rocking back and forth."

I gasped in horror. My mother never had a hair out of place, and she sure as hell would never throw away perfectly good food. "Why?" I managed to ask.

"At the time, I had no idea what was happening, Teagan. We're just now receiving much-needed answers. It's part of why I'm here." Dad stared at his lap, then continued. "As hard as I tried, I couldn't get through to her. I was afraid if people learned of her condition that the rumors and gossip would ruin us."

"You mean destroy your professional reputation." I was old enough to understand how devastating that could be, but he should have called me. I would have come home to help.

"Yes, plus it would create backlash on you and your mom. It wasn't just about the company, honey. It was about *my* girls. I had to protect you both. It was almost two in the morning when I was able to get her into the shower and calmed down. I gave her something to sedate her, so I could clean up the mess and reach out to her family in Canada. I realized that I couldn't do this on my own. I needed help."

Tears pricked my eyes. "Why didn't you call me to help, Dad? You know I would have dropped everything to be there for you both."

Dad offered a sad smile and pointed at me. "Because I didn't want you to worry or miss school. Your education is incredibly important. I was determined that this would be a stress-free year for you. You had decided not to cheer this season, which spoke louder than any words could have. I know my daughter. You're strong, beautiful, and smart as hell, but even the strong people need to take some time to recover. Even though you tried to hide it, I understood the demand of the sport and ... well, excuse me, but the bitches you cheered with had finally gotten to you. Those girls were mean, and I suspect you stood your ground, but you walked away from something you loved with all of your heart. It was troublesome to watch. My job as your father is to protect you. It backfired on me concerning your mom, though."

"It was hard to quit the team, but I value my sanity." I sank my teeth into my lower lip, realizing what I'd just said. It wasn't the best choice of words after Dad had told me Mom had a mental breakdown.

"About your mom. Grandpa Ray and Grandma Judy said they would help with your mom if I brought her to Canada. Unfortunately, I had to drive because I was worried your mom might freak out on the plane. That trip was the longest days of my life, and your mom's, too. It took me twice as long since she continued to have episodes."

"I'm so sorry, Dad. I can't imagine how hard it is for both of you. Is she getting treatment?"

Dad nodded, but before he could continue, our food was delivered. Even though it smelled heavenly, I needed to know what else had taken place. Dad must have sensed my anxiety, because he didn't touch his dinner.

"Ray and Judy helped me check your mom into a mental health treatment center. Judy explained the facility treated a lot of celebrities and was known to keep its clients safe and the information confidential. No one would ever know that she was there. After speaking with the staff, I admitted your mom. The first few days were all about tests and evaluations. They wouldn't allow her to talk to anyone or have visitors. It was only yesterday we learned the diagnosis."

"What's wrong with her? Can they help?" I shifted uncomfortably in my seat, scared of his next words. I swallowed down the fear that had clawed its way up my throat. I had to be brave for Dad.

"Your mom is bipolar, hon. It's treatable, but it's going to be a long ride. She's been cycling since you were a teenager. Once they explained the illness and treatment, it all made sense. Every mood swing, the highs, depression, the days and nights she couldn't sleep, and destroying the kitchen. I remember accusing her of using meth. I had no clue what was really happening. Then, she would level out, but the sadness followed. For a while, I was able to hide it from you, but you got caught in the crossfire. All I wanted to do was protect you, but ... I failed, Teagan. I'm so sorry." Dad's shoulders slumped forward, and he covered his face with his hands. His body shook with muffled sobs.

His words squeezed my chest, a sharp, piercing stab to my heart. "Oh, Dad." I slid off my seat and sat beside him. Wrapping my arms around him, I leaned my head on his shoulder. "I love you. Thank you for doing your best. That's all I could ever hope for. You're my hero for taking care of Mom ... and all of us."

The server stopped by, and I offered her a smile. "Can we have some boxes so we can have the food to go, please?"

I turned back to Dad. "We're going to eat at my house, where we can talk and cry privately." I planted a kiss on his cheek, then helped box up our food. I planted a kiss on his cheek, then helped package up our food as my mind raced with rampant thoughts. Was bipolar hereditary? How did Mom get it? What were the signs? Could I also be bipolar? My pulse hammered against my wrist with the unanswered questions.

Thirty minutes later, Dad and I were settled in at the kitchen table. I didn't expect my roomies to arrive home any time soon. At least, I hoped they wouldn't. Dad and I needed to finish our conversation.

I opened a bottle of pinot noir and collected two wine glasses from the cabinet next to the refrigerator. Mom and Dad had never cared if I drank as long as I stayed put for the evening and didn't drive. They felt as though alcohol was more enticing when it wasn't allowed. "You're staying here tonight, Dad, so have a drink to knock the edge off. You can take my room and bathroom. I'll sleep in Gabby or Leighton's bedroom. Everlee snores and kicks like a two-year-old, so she's fired." I cracked a grin, attempting to lighten the mood before we dove into the deep waters of our conversation again.

Once I warmed our food, I scooped it from the to-go containers onto plates. I grabbed some silverware, then sat down. Trying not to gulp my wine, I forced myself to sip it. I couldn't let Dad know how badly this had fucked me up.

"Where were we?" He speared a piece of his Mongolian beef, then took a bite. His eyes nearly rolled to the back of his head. "Damn, that's good."

"Right? I think of all the fine dining we've experienced, yet this is the best Chinese food I've eaten in my nineteen years." I picked at my sweet and sour chicken, then opted for a few bites of my fried rice. "Is bipolar hereditary? How did Mom get it?" I wrapped my fingers around the stem of my wine glass, then took another drink.

"It's hereditary. Grandma Judy mentioned that her sister, Gretchen, was bipolar."

I blanched. "What? How did we not know this?"

"Well, we're not close to Gretchen, but I got the impression that Judy was trying not to fill anyone's head with ideas. Apparently, eighty percent of bipolar cases are passed down in families."

I gasped, knocking my fork off the table. It clattered to the floor, and I leaned over and picked it up. I was grateful for the opportunity to hide my expression for a moment, too.

Standing, I tossed the fork into the sink and chose a new one from the drawer. "So, I could have it, too?"

"I haven't seen any signs, Teagan. Please try not to worry. Most of the time it's diagnosed in the late teens or early twenties. I'm not concerned about any mood swings. Yours are pretty normal. Plus, when I asked her doctors if it was hereditary, they explained there's only a ten percent chance that you are. In your mom's case, she has what the professionals refer to as late onset bipolar. It was there for years. I just didn't catch all of the symptoms. Not only that but, I think your mom grew skilled in hiding it from me."

I nibbled on my sweet and sour chicken as I sifted through this information, mentally assessing my moods and sleep patterns over the last several years.

"What's next for Mom?" My stomach growled, reminding me to eat.

"Therapy, medication, and whatever other support she needs to find a balance." Dad wiped his mouth with a napkin from the holder in the middle of the table. "I've had some time to ponder the situation, and I think some counseling would be beneficial for me as well. I'm out of my depth with the entire situation, and ..."

"You have to take care of yourself, too, Dad. You're just as important as she is. Please don't lose sight of that. I'll help in any way that I can." Surely there was some good information online, but I also had to be careful what I read. I popped another piece of chicken into my mouth, then my eyes widened. Chewing quickly, I swallowed, then said, "Dad, my credit card was paid in full, then canceled. I haven't had funds since you disappeared."

A mixture of confusion and shock twisted his handsome features. "What?"

His reaction ensured me he had nothing to do with it.

"Do you think it was Mom?"

Dad's cheeks heated, anger flashing in his gaze. "Most likely. I'm not sure it will help to confront her about it, so I'll open a card in your name first thing in the morning. You and I will be the only ones that will have access. First, is your rent taken care of? Car insurance? What else do I need to pay while I'm here?"

"I just paid my rent, and car insurance for the next six months. I'd set some money back in case of an emergency." *Liar!* I busied myself with my food, avoiding looking at my dad.

"I'll take care of your coverage for another year. I don't want to forget again. I'm sorry, Teagan. You have my word that we'll talk on the phone once a week. I don't want you to ever think you're not loved or cared for. You're my daughter, and I couldn't be prouder of you. Mom loves you, too. Hopefully, she'll get leveled out on the meds quickly and you two can begin to reconnect."

Tears clouded my vision, then slipped down my cheeks. "I would like that. We used to be close, then it changed so fast."

The front door opening caught my attention, and I leaned closer to Dad. "The girls don't have a clue that any of this happened, and I would rather not say anything yet."

Dad nodded before he kissed me on the cheek. "Just a dad visiting his favorite girl." He flashed me a sincere smile as Everlee bounced into the kitchen.

Hugs were exchanged, and I excused myself to the bathroom. I needed a minute to breathe and wrap my brain around everything I'd learned. Once I was alone, I texted Theo a huge thank you and to let him know that Dad was here. I also asked him to thank Pierce and Sutton for helping track him down.

Theo's reply came quickly, reminding me to let him know if I needed anything at all. Even though he and Ari had fallen out, he'd been an immense comfort to me.

I sank onto the edge of my bed, my concerns bouncing from Dad to Mom to Hunter. For some stupid reason, I was suddenly sad that I wouldn't have time with the King Cobra anymore. It was clear that I was fucked in the head for missing that asshole. Embracing the thoughts of him, I welcomed the diversion from my conversation with Dad. Maybe Hunter would be the perfect distraction after all.

Chapter Sixteen

Hunter

Dark clouds filled the sky as I waited for Teagan to arrive for calculus. Since it hadn't started raining yet, I'd decided to watch for her from the corner of the building where she couldn't spot me. If I strolled into class after she did, I could sit directly behind her.

Teagan's teal sweater and brown boots caught my eye. Apparently, my dick located her too because he was saluting her at the moment. I shifted, not wanting to walk into a room packed with students while I had a fucking boner.

My attention traveled over her beautiful body, then rested on her face. Dark shadows had settled beneath her big brown eyes. Instead of the smile she usually wore, her full lips were pressed into a thin line. A flicker of worry danced across her expression. For the first time since I'd been following her, she appeared sad—almost depressed. Curiosity reared its head, and I reminded myself it wasn't my job to give a fuck about her. But if that were true, why was I fighting the urge to pull her aside and ask if she was okay … and mean it? Guilt nudged me in the side, and I scolded myself for giving a shit. I didn't, not really.

Once she entered the building, I followed her at a safe distance. I spotted the guys in the back of the room and smiled as Teagan sat down. The seat directly behind her was open, and I nonchalantly made my way there. Excusing myself, I shuffled past the three people on the row, then sank into the chair. The scent of Teagan's strawberry and vanilla shampoo reached my nose, and I inhaled deeply. Damn, she smelled good. I licked my lips as she busied herself with her book and prepared to take notes.

I leaned forward, my chin brushing against her long, dark hair. "Have you missed me?" I whispered.

She spun around so fast she nearly head-butted me. I jerked back, grinning.

"What?" she hissed.

The professor joined us, and I nodded for her to turn around and listen to the lecture. She scowled at me before she turned toward the front of the room. Luckily, I had a good friend who was also in this class, and I knew she could help me with notes if I needed them. Hell, I'd slept through calculus in high school and passed with an A. Math came easy to me, so I wasn't too concerned about listening to the lecture.

Attempting to ignore the annoying fact that all I wanted to do was bury my cock inside her, I shifted in my seat. Why shouldn't I take what she'd so freely given? She was mine.

Removing my phone from my back pocket, I shielded the view from the person on my left and tapped out a text to Teagan.

Meet me tonight at our normal place. 9:00 p.m. Don't be late.

I stared a hole into the back of her head, waiting for her to reply. It was obvious when she received the message because I could almost see her bristle.

Fuck you. I don't need your money anymore.

My brows shot up, confused. What the hell had happened in a few days? *Goddammit!* My cock agreed. I was ready to force her to her knees, then fuck her until her sweet little pussy was raw. I pulled my shit together and messaged her again.

Maybe not, but you still want me. Besides, there's no going back once you're with the BW. I have the ability to ruin you with the videos and pictures.

I smirked as I stretched my legs out in front of me. Blackmail wasn't beneath me. Neither was taking what I wanted from her. She either met me tonight, or I would take Quinn's suggestion when she arrived at the party Saturday evening. Kane had already invited her, and she said she'd be there. Whether she realized it or not, how she got fucked was her choice. Willingly or unwillingly.

She spun around in her seat, and hate radiated from her. "You wouldn't dare." Her eyes narrowed.

I leaned forward, a mere inch from her. "I absolutely would, and I think you already know that about me."

"Miss Mercer, is there something you would like to share with the rest of us?" Professor Smith asked, clearly irritated that he had to stop the class to address juvenile behavior.

I hid my chuckle behind my fist.

"No, sir." She shifted in her seat and bowed her head.

The professor continued, then my cell vibrated. I glanced at the message, anger simmering beneath my calm exterior.

Play with fire, Hunter. You'll get burned. I promise. I know you have dark secrets, and I will find out what you're hiding.

My hand shook with fury as I saw her use some of my own words against me. Even worse, that bitch had been digging into my past where she didn't belong. It was up to me when and how I told her. Fuck! She was threatening me. My resolve to destroy her returned with a vengeance.

Although I pretended to pay attention to the rest of the class, I was too furious to give a shit.

Finally, we were dismissed, and I filed out before Teagan even stood. I already knew the path she would take once she was outside, and I would be waiting for her.

The wind whipped around me as the sideways rain pelted against my skin. I jerked up the hood of my North Face jacket, then hurried to the building where Teagan had her next class.

I opened the door and stepped inside, wiping the water off my cheeks with the back of my coat sleeve. Rounding the corner, I leaned against the wall and waited for her. She would regret her text soon enough.

Teagan entered the building a few minutes later, then made a mad dash to the women's restroom. Even with a coat and hood, wisps of her hair were plastered to her cheek.

I tapped my toe against the white tile floor, willing her to hurry the hell up. My heart jumped in my chest when she rounded the corner and walked my way. Anger fueled my actions, and the moment she was about to step into her next class, I grabbed her wrist and pulled her to the side.

"What are you doing?" She seethed at me.

Despite her protests, I easily dragged her into the empty classroom a few doors down and shoved her against the wall. I covered her mouth with my palm and closed the door behind us. I took her books and purse and tossed them on the floor, the slap against the tile echoing loudly.

"You, little girl, should have never threatened me. You have no idea what you're getting yourself into." My palm slipped from her mouth to her throat with one quick movement. I squeezed until her face turned red. "Now that I have your attention. You have a choice. Meet me tonight, or I'll fuck you here. I don't need your permission. You've already spread your legs for me willingly. By how hard your pussy clenched my cock, I know that you liked it." I loosened my hold on her enough to allow her to breathe. "Never mind. I just chose for you."

I fumbled with the button and zipper on my jeans and freed my aching dick. Placing my hands on her shoulders, I shoved her to her knees. Teagan gritted her teeth together and shook her head.

"You're not thinking this through. I have pictures of you with my come all over your tits, of you sucking my cock, of me spanking you, of my shaft buried in your pussy. At no time was my identity revealed. Not only will this ruin you, but you'll also be expelled from school, and dear ol' dad's business will take a plunge because he can't control his slut of a daughter."

Teagan winced as if I'd slapped her. She parted those pretty lips, and I slid my shaft into her mouth. She might pretend she didn't want me, but she was sucking like she loved every inch of my fat dick within seconds. I fisted a handful of her hair, smiling as she gazed up at me with tears in her eyes. I eased my cock to the back of her throat and choked her.

"That's a good little slut." I fucked her mouth, watching her every move. My balls tightened, and I shoved her away. I pulled her to a standing position, then fumbled with the button and zipper of her jeans. With a quick jerk, I tugged her pants and panties down to her ankles, then smacked her pussy. Hard. I slapped my palm over her mouth as a cry escaped her. "I bet you're soaking wet." I reached between her legs, running my fingertip over her slit. "Do you want me to fuck you, Teagan?" I gave her clit a pinch, and she gasped against my palm. I massaged her tender flesh, watching her.

She moaned and closed her eyes.

"Yeah, my little slut loves to be fucked. Make no mistake about it, Teagan. You belong to me. I own you."

Her eyelids flew open, and she glowered at me.

"Do you hate me?" I slipped another finger into her while rubbing her bundle of nerves with my thumb.

She nodded, her chest moving as she neared an orgasm. I moved away from her pussy, then quickly turned her and bent her over the seat, her perky ass in the air. I held her down, pressing her face into the desktop. I'd had enough practice, I could easily remove a rubber from my pocket, tear open the package, and roll it on with one hand. I was always ready to get laid.

Seconds later, I shoved my long dick into her slick walls. A muffled moan escaped her as I fucked her hard, loving the sound of our bodies slapping together. I used her pussy juices to slicken my finger, then I slammed it into her tight asshole.

"Jesus, my little slut loves that don't you?" I jerked her head up. "Answer me," I demanded.

"Yeah," she whimpered. "Fuck me harder, Hunter."

My name on her pretty lips nearly made me come, but I focused on the pictures of Jesus, Gandhi, and Buddha hanging on the wall at the front of the room. Dammit, I'd forgotten this classroom was for religion and history. My focus dropped to my cock, slamming into her. Her pussy clenched around me, and I realized she was close to her release.

"Do you want to come, Teagan?"

"Please." A moan followed her heavy breathing.

With one more deep thrust, I clenched my teeth in order not to make any noise as I came. Once I'd regained my senses, I eased out and removed my hand from between her legs and laughed.

I found a tissue in my jacket pocket and wrapped the condom in it. I would toss it in the trash when I reached the locker room for football practice. I slapped her perky ass, and she yelped, then straightened.

After I tucked myself into my jeans and fastened them, I pulled hers up her toned thighs and over her hips, stopping long enough to lick her pussy. She shuddered against me and clutched the back of the seat.

I gripped her chin, leaving her pants undone. "I will see you tonight. Don't wear any panties." I nipped at her lower lip, drawing blood.

She reached up and slapped my cheek, and I grabbed her wrists.

"Why are you doing this?" She trembled beneath my heated gaze.

"Because I can." I shoved her away from me and chuckled as I left her. Hate sex had never felt so good, but I wouldn't be as nice to her this evening. My dick twitched in agreement.

Chapter Seventeen

Teagan

What in the hell was wrong with me, and why did I think that was the hottest sex I'd ever had? Hunter had dominated and fucked me, then tossed me to the side like his used condom. Holy shit. I needed my brain examined because I'd loved every second. There was no way I would ever admit that to him, though. I straightened my jeans and fastened them, ensuring I'd pulled myself back together before I left.

Just as quickly as I had admitted I loved the sex ... my feelings flip-flopped, and hate boiled up inside me. I dug my fingernails into the palms of my hands, wishing it was his damned face. That asshole hadn't even gotten me off, but I was well aware that my fury had nothing to do with the lack of an orgasm. It was all about the power he had over me. Hunter knew damn well I would cave to his demands once he mentioned that I would be expelled, and my family humiliated, if he shared the images. Dad had enough to deal with, and I would never forgive myself if I caused him more pain.

Thank God Dad had left for Canada. He was a master at reading my expressions and would know something was off the moment he laid eyes on me. He would be mortified if he knew that I'd fucked some random dude in a classroom.

Pushing against the door, I stepped into the dreary weather. I'd pondered slipping into my class, but then I remembered the professor wouldn't allow students to enter once she'd started her lecture.

I shuddered against the cool wind and rain as I hustled across the campus to my car. After settling into the driver's seat, I turned on the engine and blasted the heat. Placing my forehead against the steering wheel, I realized what was happening with me concerning Mom and Hunter. My emotions were teetering on a rocky cliff, and I was afraid I'd plunge into the darkness with one wrong move. I couldn't handle this on my own.

Grabbing my purse, I located my cell and called Ari. She was probably in class, but I could at least leave her a message.

"What's up, bitch?" Her giggle filled the phone, and my shoulders relaxed.

"Too much to tell you without drinks." I fiddled with a black string hanging on the corner of my jacket.

"Lucky you, Jagger just left for the day, and I have the house to myself. What's your poison?"

Tears welled in my eyes. Why hadn't I realized I needed Ari sooner? I suspected that she had struggled when talking to me about Chuk, Johnny, and Jagger, too. Love for my bestie bubbled up in my chest.

"Screwdrivers? Shots? Hell, at this point, I'm not picky." I grinned, relieved to hear Ari's cheerful voice.

"I'll see what we have. Jagger likes to keep a well-stocked cabinet. Remember when I was staying with him in Washington, and we drank his bottle of vodka?" Ari giggled.

I placed the call on my Bluetooth, then shifted into reverse and carefully eased out of my parking space at the university.

"How could I forget? You two had just hooked up. Finally." I dragged the last word out for emphasis.

"And you totally busted me." Ariana fell silent for a moment. "I'll wait for your answer since you'll be here in a few minutes, but I've been concerned about you since your parents packed up. I need to know how you're doing. And no fucking sunshine shit either. Talk to me like we always do, heart-to-heart."

Ari had a sixth sense. She instinctively knew when I was about to fall apart. She'd been the glue to hold me together in the past, and I'd been the same for her. I was struggling to adjust to her being with Jagger so often, and some girl time was definitely needed.

"Yeah, I need to clue you in on some big shit. I'll see you in ten."

"Byyee." Ari laughed before she hung up.

I stretched my neck, the popping sounds reaching my ears. Pushing the play button on my steering wheel, "Masochist" by Sophie Ann trilled through the speakers. I sang along, realizing how much I identified with the lyrics. Since I'd fallen into the web of the King Cobra, I'd questioned a lot about myself.

My mind wandered back to Hunter. His demand for my presence that night had me reeling. A part of me wanted every inch of him as often as possible. The other part hated him for treating me like his slut. Maybe he was my addiction, and I was getting used to playing rough and being ravished. Hunter might despise me, but his body didn't. My greedy core throbbed, and I chewed on my lower lip with the memories of his cock in my mouth, then fucking me, and leaving me hanging. Every hormone kicked into overdrive, and I fought the urge to text him, but I had to stay strong.

I snapped out of my lust-filled thoughts as I rolled into Ari and Jagger's driveway. Before I shifted into park, Ari flung open the front door, smiling at me as if she'd just won the lottery.

My heart did a happy dance. I'd missed my girl more than I'd realized. Grabbing my phone and handbag, I climbed out of the car, locked it, then made a beeline to the entrance. A gust of wind blew my hair into my face, and I struggled to see. I loved Oregon, but the winter days fucking sucked sometimes.

Ari reached for my wrist and dragged me into her house. "Holy shit, that wind is insane today."

"Aren't you glad Jagger isn't on his motorcycle?" I shed my coat and hung it on the rack near the entrance. I unzipped my calf-high boots and slipped them off, not wanting to track mud all over her clean, dark wood floors.

A few pieces of artwork adorned the cream-colored walls, and a coffee table and brown leather recliner sat next to the matching couch. White, floor-length black-out curtains hung over the shades, brightening up the room. Ariana did a fantastic job decorating.

Ari pulled me in for a big hug, then she took my purse and tossed it on the sofa. She looked gorgeous in her pink sweater and dark wash jeans. In my opinion, Ari was the prettiest of our group, but she didn't realize how beautiful she was, which made her even more attractive. "Drinks and snacks first. You look like you've lost weight, so I'm going to feed you."

My brow arched in question. "I'm not sure ice cream will work well with vodka."

Ari snickered and wrinkled her nose. "We just have to eat the ice cream first, but that's not what I have."

When heavy shit was going down, Ari and I would share a pint of Ben & Jerry's Chubby Hubby.

Ari slipped her arm through mine and led the way to the kitchen. It was smaller than my place, but it was perfect for two or three people.

I barked out a laugh when I spotted the tray of crackers, meat, cheeses, nuts, and drinks. "How did you put all of that together in ten minutes?"

She gave me a lopsided grin. "It was originally for Sunday afternoon when we'll all hang out, but I'll replace it." Ari winked at me, then picked up two screwdrivers and shoved one in my hand. "Drink up, bitch. I have a feeling the shit that's about to come out of your mouth is going to be juicy."

I stared at the glass, grief and guilt bubbling up inside me. Even though Mom was alive, I'd lost her when I was fourteen. All the years of thinking something was wrong with me boiled over, and I started to cry. I couldn't hide it from Ari anymore. My heart had been ripped out of my chest and trampled on. It was a relief as well as agonizing to hear Dad explain Mom's illness.

"Babe! Oh, my God." Ari took my glass and set it down on the counter. She wrapped me in her arms while I blubbered all over her shoulder. "Let it out, Teagan. Whatever it is, we'll fix it."

After my cries slowed, I wiped my damp cheeks.

"Let's go to the couch. There's a box of tissues on the end table." Ari collected our drinks and followed me to the living room.

I sank into the soft leather of the cushion, grabbed a Kleenex, and blew my nose. Ari's concerned gaze tracked my movements as if she were waiting for me to fall apart again.

"Sorry. I didn't mean to lose my shit on you." I reached for my glass, then downed half of it in a few gulps.

Ari sipped hers, then set it down on the coffee table. "Don't even think twice about it."

"I love you, Ari. And ... I miss you so bad." More stupid tears welled in my eyes. I looked away from her, attempting to get a hold of my emotions that were clearly taking me on a wild rollercoaster ride.

"I miss you, too. I know it's been a big adjustment for both of us. Now that we're back in a routine at school, I say we have a girl's night or day once a week. Just us. Then, we can all hang with the girls, too. Jagger will spend some time with Gunner and the MC in a few weeks. I say you stay here with me. He'll be gone for three days. I would *love* to have you."

"Really?"

"Hell yeah. If he gets a guys' weekend, we get to have a girls' weekend." She winked at me.

"That sounds so nice." I sipped my drink, my hand trembling slightly.

"Now that we've figured that out, what else is going on, Teagan?" Worry flickered through her blue eyes.

Anxiety pulled and tugged at my insides. Even though I realized that Ari would never judge me, my nerves were on tiptoes. I inhaled deeply, then plunged ahead.

Chapter Eighteen

Teagan

"My Dad visited Monday evening."

"Oh, shit! And *why* haven't you told me until today ... oh." She tapped her finger on her chin. "It's Wednesday." Ari squeezed my shoulder, then tucked her legs beneath her and stared at me, waiting for me to continue.

"I'm sorry. I've had a lot to process, but I'm telling you now. My parents didn't ditch me like I thought. The house is getting remodeled, including the floors, and all of the furniture is in storage."

Ari's hand flew to her chest. "I knew there was a good explanation. At least I'd held out hope that there was one. Even with the crap between you and your mom, I just couldn't imagine them packing up and abandoning their only kid. It wasn't adding up."

"I'm glad you held out hope. After all the shit my mom has said to me over the years, it was the only reason I could piece together. Thankfully, I was wrong. Horribly wrong." I tucked my long hair behind an ear. "Mom had a breakdown while I've been at college. Dad had to act quickly and make some tough decisions. He didn't call me because he was concerned that I would be worried and flunk out of school. Or worse, drop out to take care of Mom while he worked."

"I really want to share my opinion, but I'm going to keep my mouth closed and let you continue." A wistful expression crossed my friend's face.

"Yeah, I had a lot to say at first. But the more he talked I realized that he made his decisions to protect me." I cleared my throat, my nose stuffy from my tears. "Mom ... Mom is in a treatment facility in Canada."

Ari's blonde brows shot up. "Drugs?"

"No. She's been diagnosed with bipolar disorder. My grandparents are helping Dad with her care. Once Mom was settled in the center, Dad flew out to see me for an evening. Theo had continued to call him until he answered." Even though Ari hadn't said anything, it was still strange thinking of Ari referring to Theo by his name and not as her dad. Hopefully, they would be able to work things out soon.

"Holy shit." Ari shifted in her chair, frowning and probably mulling over what I'd said. "I've studied a little about bipolar in my psych class, and from what you've told me about her sudden mood changes and depression, it makes sense."

An unbearable ache clenched my throat as I fought to speak the following words. "It's hereditary." My voice cracked, revealing my fear.

Ariana shook her head. "No. Nope. No. I learned enough in psychology that I would have noticed, Teagan. Plus, I would have plopped your cute little ass down for a chat. Trust me on this. I've never seen any signs of mental illness, babe. I swear to you."

A tidal wave of relief washed over me. "I needed to hear that. Dad said the same, but he would sugar coat shit in order not to scare me."

Ari harumphed. "I won't. Not ever. I'll be kind because I love you, but I'll never lie or pretend something isn't a big deal."

I slid down in my chair, using the worst posture possible. "My poor Dad is going through hell, and I don't know what to do."

"Let him be the adult and manage shit with your mom. I realize we're almost twenty and capable of helping, but he took her to get treated and reached out to your grandparents. Your dad is a smart guy. Love on him and open communication, but you can't fix this, and neither can he."

I nodded, realizing she was right. "He didn't want me to drop out of school to come home and help."

"Good. You're going to have to trust that he'll talk to you when he needs to. Take a breath and lean into the fact that your mom is getting treatment and ... what if you two are able to rebuild your relationship and be on good terms again?" Hope flickered in her expression.

"I would love that. I've missed her so much over the years. At least I understand that I wasn't the cause of her mood swings." I straightened and tucked a leg beneath me while I took another drink of the screwdriver. "These are yummy."

"Of course they are." Ari smirked, then grinned. Seconds later, her smile faltered. "Is there anything else you wanted to talk about?"

No! I wasn't ready to tell her about Hunter yet. Plus, he would ruin me if he found out I'd shared any information about the King Cobra. I couldn't take that chance.

"No, that was the big news."

"Okay, I just wanted to make sure." She eyed me suspiciously.

I eyed her right back. "I know that look on your face, Ariana Ellison. What gives?"

She picked up her drink and gulped it down. My gaze narrowed. Something was off.

"So, don't be upset, but after you were asking about Hunter, Jagger took it upon himself to check him out."

Shit. Shit. Shit. I cringed. "Ari, I didn't mean for Jagger to start snooping around in Hunter's business. I was just curious about him."

"Well, as of right now, Jagger hasn't been able to learn much ... and that's the problem. He thinks some shady shit might have gone down with his family. Jagger is torn because from what the football players have to say, Hunter is a good guy. At the same time," Ari gave a half-shrug, "I think Jagger is still concerned."

So, I wasn't the only one that couldn't find any details on Hunter. Even though it was nice to know I was still internet savvy, Jagger wouldn't stop if he thought there was a problem, and not being able to dig up any information online was definitely an issue.

"I don't think it's a big deal. Jagger has other things to do than hunt down Hunter's life history." I laughed at my play on words.

Ari grinned and rolled her eyes. "We both know that's not how Jagger works. He's protective of you because you've been my bestie for years. I get it. I'm uber protective of you as well. You're my family, Teagan."

I reached over and hugged her. "You're mine, too. I appreciate Jagger making sure I'm safe."

Little did he realize what was happening behind closed doors. I'd fucked who I thought was a priest and made thousands of dollars. Unfortunately, I was still confused about why Hunter had chosen me. He obviously thought he knew me from somewhere, but he was wrong. I hadn't met him until we were both at the university.

"He thinks he knows me," I blurted before realizing it. "I'm not sure from where, but he swears he does."

Ari chewed on her manicured thumbnail. "Maybe he saw someone he thinks is you, but she's actually your doppelganger? That shit really happens."

I finished off my drink. "I hadn't thought about that. I bet that's what it is! I'll talk to him and see where he thinks we met. You're probably right, though. But it's been seriously messing with me."

"Hell, it would mess with me too." Ari gathered our glasses and rose from the couch. "Refill time." She winked at me as she left the room. "By the way, did you hear about the party on Saturday night? It will be after the football game, so I thought we could all go together."

"I'm definitely in for the game. I think kick-off is at three?" I grabbed my handbag, which had wedged itself into the corner behind me and rummaged around for my cell. A text had come through, and I opened it up.

A not-so-friendly reminder to meet me at nine. Be there or else. BW

I tossed my phone on the coffee table and placed my purse on top of it. Hunter might have fucked me senseless in the classroom, but he would have to wait it out alone tonight. I had plans with my best friend, and since I no longer needed his money, I called the shots. Hunter would have to get that through his thick skull, and I was about to help him.

Chapter Nineteen

Teagan

My phone had blown up the rest of the week with scathing, cruel messages from Hunter. I continued to ignore him since Dad had taken care of the credit card issue before he'd returned to Canada to be with Mom. Apparently, Hunter wasn't used to being told no.

Each day, I ensured there were no open seats around me in calculus class, either. At least I could block off his access to me while I was trying to concentrate and not flunk out. When we were dismissed, I strategically struck up conversations with a group of girls, and we all walked out together, blocking Hunter once again. My inner self cackled with glee when I spotted him standing at the back of the room, wearing a stormy expression. *Checkmate, motherfucker.*

Although I enjoyed mind-fucking Hunter, it had rattled me that Jagger was looking into him. At the same time, I felt safe with the extra layer of protection in case things got out of hand. Hunter had a short fuse, and I suspected that I was the lighter that could set him on fire.

Arriving at the football game, I waved at Gabby, Leighton, and Everlee, who were on the sidelines, looking hot in their cheer uniforms. I trudged up the football stands where Ari was waving wildly at me. Since she had located a parking space before I had, she'd secured our seats. The crowd's energy was infectious, and I suddenly missed being close to the field and cheering with my girls.

I hugged Ari, then settled in next to her.

"This is going to be one hell of a game," she said, loud enough that I could hear her above the noise in the stands. It was packed shoulder-to-shoulder. The late fall weather was cold, but at least it wasn't raining.

"I'm excited! If our guys win, then we've clenched a spot in the playoffs." I clapped my gloved hands together. Even with a coat, scarf, gloves, and calf-high boots, I would eventually freeze my ass off. However, it was worth it.

The spokesperson began to speak, his voice carrying through the stadium as he announced the starting lineup. My belly flip-flopped when Hunter was introduced, and I ingrained his number eighty-eight into my brain. His broad shoulders filled out his football jersey even without the pads. My gaze swept over him, and I chewed on my bottom lip, my attention glued to his tight ass. Hunter held his helmet and waved as the crowd cheered. He had quickly become a star player along with Kane, Jagger, and Quinn. For just a minute, I forgot how much I despised him for threatening to expose me in the videos if I didn't obey him, and I appreciated every hard, muscular detail of his body.

A girl behind us squealed as the referee flipped the coin, and Whitmore received the football first. Ari threaded her arm through mine and pulled me into her side.

"I hope we win, or the party tonight will suck," she giggled.

"No shit. The guys will all be in a foul mood." I watched as Kane threw the ball to Hunter, and he ran his ass off down the field, dodging the enormous defensive line that Nelson University was known for. I hopped to my feet and began yelling as an opposing team member charged at our running back. The defense dove for Hunter, but he easily jumped over him before hauling ass down the last twenty yards for a touchdown.

I cupped my hands around my mouth and yelled. "Hell of a first play, guys!"

"Shit yeah!" Ari stood, clapping. Her grin was contagious, and I found myself smiling as well.

It was showtime now that Nelson had the ball. Whitmore's offense was stronger than their defense, and they would be the deciding factor of who would win, unless Kane, Jagger, Quinn and Hunter could consistently add points to the scoreboard.

Nelson came back with impressive plays of their own and also scored. We were only five minutes into the game, and we were already tied.

"How's your dad?" Ari asked while she kept her attention glued to the field.

"Good. We chatted last night. I think he's doing a little better. With Mom in treatment, he's had some time to sleep and clear his head. Catch his breath, so to speak." I glanced at her from the corner of my eye. "How are you doing with Theo? He was a huge help to me when my parents were missing."

"He'd better have been! You're like his second daughter." Her eyes narrowed briefly, then she relaxed again.

It hadn't been that long since shit had blown up with Ari and Theo, so I decided I should keep my mouth shut until she was ready to talk it through. I just understood that secrets could destroy a person from the inside out.

The game was well-matched, and the teams alternated the lead. The tension in the air was thick by the time we reached the end of the fourth quarter. At times the crowd fell silent, waiting to see who would win. It was by far the most intense match of the season, and both schools had everything at stake.

The clock ticked down while Hunter found an opening and closed the gap. Kane made a short toss right into Hunter's arms, and

Hunter sprinted his ass off toward the goal line. Unfortunately, a lineman clipped Hunter in the shoulder and sent him backward, slamming him into the unforgiving ground. The crowd gasped as the lineman flew through the air, throwing himself on top of Hunter even after he was down. A shrill whistle sounded, and the referee tossed the penalty flag in the air.

I covered my mouth, hoping like hell Hunter wasn't hurt.

"Unnecessary roughness, number twelve," said the ref, pointing toward the Nelson defensive line. "Automatic first down, Whitmore," he continued. And then, "Number twelve is expelled from the game."

Shouts and boos filled the stadium. I grabbed Ari's arm as the coaches and paramedics surrounded Hunter, still lying on the ground.

Wild cheers and supportive chants echoed through the stadium as Hunter stood, then jogged to the sidelines. Coach called a timeout and attended to Hunter.

"Holy shit, that was insane," Ari said, her hand on her forehead. "I hope he's okay. That dude was fucking huge. I'm glad he's kicked off the field because that shit was completely unnecessary. Hunter was clearly down, and number twelve just had his dick in a twist."

I couldn't help but laugh at her comment. "I'm happy that you love football, finally. We only have a minute and a half left in the game. I wonder if Hunter can finish." My pulse pounded in my ears as I waited to see if he was able to continue.

"I want to find that lineman and kick him for playing dirty." Ari harumphed.

I would let her take care of the defense. Even though I wasn't Hunter's biggest fan off the field, I was a big fan when he was on.

The Whitmore offense lined up several minutes later, but Hunter hadn't joined them. I held my breath, waiting to hear the update when Hunter jogged back onto the field before the announcer could speak. The crowd went fucking wild for him. I closed my eyes briefly, grateful that he was all right.

The game's last play sealed the deal, and Whitmore was officially in the playoffs. Kane and Hunter had performed their magic once again while Quinn and Jagger had done an impeccable job of guarding Kane, which helped tremendously.

When the final score flashed on the game board, everyone began stomping on the metal stands, filling the arena with an overwhelming thunder. Our boys hugged, yelled, patted each other on the ass, and were all smiles.

"Guess the party will be hella good tonight." Ari winked at me.

Since Gabby, Everlee, and Leighton were on the cheer team, they agreed to meet us at the party. Even though Ari had insisted I ride with them, I had a feeling I might duck out early and would need my car, so I politely declined.

As I pulled up to the elaborate mansion, the celebratory bash was already in full play. I grew up in one, and the girls were also wealthy, but this house was off the charts gorgeous from the outside. The circular drive was loaded with vehicles on both sides, and some had even parked on the lawn where the water fountain was located. Lights shone on the cherub as the water flowed from its bowl. It was stunning and oddly comforting.

I had no idea who the home belonged to, but they'd done a fantastic job with the landscaping.

I left my R8 at least a block away, where I hoped I would be able to escape easily. After pocketing my cell and key fob, I hid my purse in the glove compartment, then climbed out and locked the doors. I quickly found a group of people to walk with, so I wasn't on my own.

For some reason, I wasn't really in the mood to get drunk. With Mom in treatment, it felt strange. What if Dad called with an emergency, and I needed to drive to the airport? I couldn't let him down, so I'd promised myself a three-drink maximum over the course of the evening.

The thump of the music greeted me as I walked toward the entrance. Kids laughed and cut up near the front door, drinks already overflowing in their hands. I reached into the back pocket of my jeans and removed my cell. I messaged the girls on our group chat to see where I could find them.

Ari's reply came through first. She was already inside, and she would meet me at the entrance. Thank God for best friends. From the line of cars, it looked like the place was packed, and it would have been hard as hell to find everyone.

Everlee chimed in next that they were on the way and would see us in about twenty minutes.

Eager to locate Ari, I walked into the mansion and scanned the crowd. "Born For This" by Foxxi and Natalie Major reverberated through the house. I tapped my toe against the marble floors as I assessed my surroundings.

Massive white columns were on each side of the foyer, marking an entrance into additional rooms. The large, sparkling chandelier was centered over the open space. Students were dancing anywhere they could, while some had already claimed a corner to make out.

"Teagan!" Ari yelled as she hurried to me, then grabbed my arm. "You have to see this house. It's off-the-fucking-charts gorgeous!"

"Whose place is this?" I frowned, trying to figure out where we were.

"I have no clue, but I'm going to give you a tour," Ari giggled.

Loud, male laughter floated through the air, and I smiled. "Sounds like the football team is here."

"Yes, and they're getting smashed. It's going to be crazy tonight." Her eyes twinkled with mischief. My bestie had always loved a good party. I was happy that Jagger also enjoyed them. It would have been a complete drag if he stood on the sidelines like an old grump.

"Let's get something to drink. We can call an Uber if we need to." She slipped her arm through mine and led us through the sea of people.

"Sounds great." As much as I wanted to blow off some steam and celebrate the team's win, I still wanted to be able to drive myself home. I could sip my drink while Ari and I snuck through the mansion, peeking at the rooms.

Jagger joined us in line and threw his arm around my shoulder, grinning down at me. "Anyone you have your eye on tonight?"

I huffed out a laugh. "The night is young. Who knows what magical events could transpire?" I dramatically placed the back of my hand against my forehead.

Jagger chuckled. "I don't want to stop you from having fun, but I want to make sure you're not taken advantage of."

I leaned into his side and smiled at Ari. "I love your boyfriend for being good to me."

"Be careful, Teagan. He'll be asking for a threesome." She gave Jagger a *"Hell no"* look, and we all broke into laughter.

Glancing at the beginning of the line as we waited to reach the kitchen, I caught a pair of stormy green eyes that were fixated on me. Chills skated down my spine as I returned Hunter's stare.

Chapter Twenty

Hunter

My entire body hurt like a son of a bitch, but I would never admit it to anyone. After that fat fuck had played dirty and smashed me into the ground, stars danced before my eyes. Then, I saw Teagan's beautiful smile as my consciousness teetered on the edge of oblivion. It had taken me several minutes to regain my senses, and by that time, I'd managed to hobble off the field and to the sidelines.

I'd slammed a few shots as soon as I came home, welcoming the pain relief. Kane, Quinn, Jagger, Vance, Remington, Anderson and a few other guys had also come over as soon as the game was over. We had the house party-ready within an hour, which worked out since people had already started showing up.

I poured a few more shots of whiskey into my red Solo cup and leaned against the kitchen door frame, my attention sweeping over the crowd. The mansion was packed, and the music was thumping. I was fucking elated that we'd won the game and had ranked first place in the Pac-12. It was definitely a night to celebrate.

The euphoria of our win had me flying high until I spotted Teagan. I was aware that she would show up at the party, but she'd ignored my texts all damn week. Irritated didn't even begin to explain what I felt for her. At the same time, my cock had instantly hardened. I wanted her. I wanted her badly, and the more I fucked her, the more I craved her. She was beginning to consume my thoughts, and I hated her even more for it. Ever since that day, I'd promised never to allow anyone to get too close to me, but she was cheating and slowly getting under my skin.

Her brown doe eyes returned my stare and warmed my chest. The second Jagger had thrown his arm around her shoulders, I'd bristled. If he were smart, he would stop touching her. But I also wasn't stupid enough to approach him about it. I had too much on the line to get into a fight.

I took a drink and popped my neck before approaching Jagger, Ariana, and Teagan. Instead of speaking to Teagan, I addressed Jagger as though he were my best friend.

"Hey, man. Good to see you. Glad you could make it." I patted him on the back, making eye contact with him, then Ari. I could almost feel Teagan bristle as I blatantly ignored her.

"I'm never one to turn down a party," Jagger replied. "Awesome fucking game today," Jagger said. "How are you feeling after getting jumped? We thought you were down, man. The lineman was a big fucker."

"I don't think I've ever held my breath for that long," Ariana interjected. "I was so relieved when you picked yourself up off the field."

"Me, too," Teagan added softly.

My heart hammered against my chest. Why would she give a fuck what happened to me? She despised me as much as I did her. *Liar!* I shut down the annoying inner voice that reminded me that there was a minuscule line between love and hate.

I turned to Teagan, quirking my brow at her. "You have a funny way of showing it," I muttered only loud enough for her to hear.

Her cheeks heated with my underhanded comment. Realizing

that Jagger and Ariana were looking at us with quizzical expressions, I turned my back on Teagan. I would deal with her later. Before the evening was over, she would never consider disobeying me again.

After a few more minutes of chatting football with Jagger, I excused myself. There were a lot of people here I wanted to say hi to. Plus, I needed a spot to keep an eye on Teagan easily. I returned to the kitchen, where the guys were playing a game of beer pong, and a group of hot girls surrounded them.

A brunette jumped and cheered for Quinn as he sank the white ball into a cup. Her big tits bounced in her low-cut blue top, and her skirt barely covered her ass. She was definitely here to get fucked. Her friend wasn't wearing much more than the brunette, and I guessed they would end up in one of the bedrooms or the party room soon.

The girls trickled into the kitchen for drinks, assessing the guys as if they had their pick. Little did they know that some of the team were already fucking them. The society was a great way to hide our identities and get laid. Some of these chicks hadn't given us the time of day until they learned we played football. Then, the whores came out of the woodwork.

Quinn walked away from the beer pong, slipped an arm around the girls, winked at me, and led them out of the room. He was on his way downstairs to the party room. Only select people were allowed downstairs, so I had the door guarded by a few big-ass dudes. It was one big orgy once enough people arrived. Hell, girls on girls, three guys fucking one chick, others watching and jerking off. One time we tied up a girl on the table, blindfolded her, and took turns fucking every hole possible. Remington ate her out while I straddled her and fucked her mouth. We weren't denied anything we wanted after we were behind those doors.

The guys were on their own, though. I had another pussy I wanted.

I paid close attention to Teagan as the evening progressed. She, Ariana, and a few of their other friends danced together for a while, then the girls began to pair up with some guys I hadn't ever seen. Teagan stayed near her best friend and didn't seem to be drinking much. I shoved my fingers through my blonde hair as Jagger approached me. I tipped my chin at him before I polished off the last of my whiskey.

Jagger's mouth kicked up into a smile. "You've got a pretty good view from here." He leaned against the wall. His attention trained on his girlfriend, who was on her way to being shitfaced.

"Yeah, I'm not much of a dancer, but I love watching everyone. Eventually, someone will do something stupid, and make a video." I glanced away, patting myself on the back for the jab. I'd actually felt bad for Shae and the incident at Harrison's party a few summers ago. Usually, I would have kept my mouth closed, but it was clear that the alcohol was impeding my common sense.

"Videos can be a dangerous game for sure." Jagger folded his arms over his chest, his attention following mine. "I'll cut to the chase. You had a hell of a football win and you're celebrating, which you should."

My hackles raised. This asshole was full of himself. Jagger Whit-lock was giving me permission to do what the fuck I wanted to in my own goddamned house? I pinned him with a furious gaze. "Get to the point."

"Are you into Teagan?"

His words were a sharp clip to my jaw, rattling me to the depths of my being. "Why? I mean, what if I were?" I sure as fuck wasn't admitting shit to him, but I was curious to see what his reaction would be. Would I have the king's blessing to date her? I nearly smirked at him but caught myself.

"She's special, man. I think you're a decent guy, but I've got a few questions." He rocked back on his heels and squared his shoulders.

I chuckled. "You're her gatekeeper?" I bet he would be pissed to know I'd already fucked her and come all over her face multiple times.

"Guess I am. I know her well enough to know that she's dealing with some major shit and hiding it from everyone."

Jagger had no fucking clue that I'd heard all of Teagan's conversations and seen her texts to Ariana about her parents disappearing. I knew what she was going through, and it made her suffering and humiliation all the more fun. I'd found her weakness. Teagan Mercer, the popular, rich girl that everyone loved, had serious mommy issues.

"She and Ari have been friends for years, and she's like a sister to me."

I managed to hold back my comment about him fucking his sister. The best way to deal with Jagger was to let him think he was winning at this game.

"All I'm saying, man, is that I make sure my girls are safe. If your intentions are to fuck her and toss her to the side, that's between the two of you."

My forehead creased in confusion. "Then, what's the problem?"

Jagger leaned against the wall, still watching the girls dance. He turned his attention to me and held my stare. "The issue is that I can't find shit on you and your family, which does not work well with me. The only people to do that are the ones trying to bury secrets—most of the time some real fucked up shit."

Dammit! I rubbed my chin, my alcohol-coated brain scrambling for a response. No one had dug into my fucking past in the last three years. Leave it to Jagger Whitlock to break my lucky streak. If he continued, the results would be catastrophic.

"I'm an open book, man. I respect that you're watching out for the people you love." Maybe buttering this guy up would not only save my ass but my mom and dad too. "What do you want to know?"

"Why aren't you on social media? There aren't any images of your parents, and your dad is a tech mogul. Ari's father is in the press all the time for inventions and shit."

Those words sat in my gut like sour milk. I gave him a halfhearted chuckle, then patted him on the back. "If that's what's fucking with you, let me give you the rundown." I swallowed, hoping like hell I could remember all of the details I'd rehearsed over and over three years ago. "Mom was seriously bullied online when I was younger. It took a huge toll on my family, and in order to protect the one woman I love, I stood by her and deleted all of my social media accounts. I got used to not being on TikTok and Instagram, and I'm not interested in jumping back into the drama."

Part of what had just spewed from my mouth was true. The lack of social media was entirely different, but Mom had been bullied, and she was the one woman in my life I loved with all my heart. She'd dived into a deep depression when her best friend turned on her, but it wasn't nearly as bad as when our entire world was flipped inside out. I clenched my jaw so hard that pain shot through my face and head.

Jagger nodded, appearing to assess my words and body language. The dude was fucking brilliant, and if I didn't play it cool, he would keep digging.

Jagger visibly relaxed, but I wasn't sure if he was playing me or had accepted my lie as truth.

He stilled as his dark-eyed gaze focused on me. "Promise me if you are into Teagan that you'll treat her right."

I smirked. This guy was off the fucking charts. "That's rich, man."

Anger rippled over his expression. "I learned the hard way, and it hurt the girl I love the most. Don't fuck up like I did." He smacked my chest with the back of his hand, then tipped his chin up before he left and joined his girlfriend.

"Consider yourself warned, Hunter," Kane said from behind me.

I massaged the back of my neck, suddenly tense. "You heard all of that?"

Kane gave me a slow nod. "I wasn't sure if there was an issue, so I made myself available in case Jagger was looking for a fight."

I wasn't sure if I should be pissed that Kane had eavesdropped or grateful. One thing about the society was that we had each other's backs when shit hit the fan. "So, you heard him? Dude's got the wrong idea all the way around."

Kane stood in front of me, a silly grin on his face. Ironically, "That's Rich" by Brooke started to play. My attention swept the room as sweaty bodies gyrated to the beat, and I wondered who had put the playlist together. Chuckling, I hoped Jagger was listening to the lyrics.

"What are you smiling at?" I peered into my cup, mentally swearing that it was empty.

"Dude, are you sure Jagger has the wrong idea? Because from where the guys and I are standing, you've got it bad for Teagan. My only advice is to tread carefully, man. You've already marked her, now Jagger is sniffing you out. I would hate to see how this could blow up if you made a bad move."

Sweat broke out over my skin as fresh anger coursed through my body. Everyone was pissing me the fuck off. Kane was probably my best friend, but he seriously needed to mind his own damned business. What I did to Teagan was no one else's concern. "Fuck you, man. You and the other assholes need to remember who you're dealing with."

"I'm on your side, Hunter. I've dealt with Jagger, and you don't want to be on his shit list. If you like Teagan, then go for it. As long as you're good to her, then you've got nothing to worry about. If Jagger digs too far and learns about the society, we're all fucked. You have to remember that it's not just about you."

"I know, man. I'm fucking on edge. I need some air." I glanced to the staircase that led upstairs to my room, my vision blurry from the alcohol.

"I've got your back, dude. We all do." Kane slapped my shoulder, then disappeared into the crowd.

Stumbling to the foot of the stairs, I realized I'd drank more than I thought I had. I definitely wanted to step outside, but first I needed a few minutes alone. I patted my pockets, realizing I had my car keys and wallet on me but not my phone. I must have left it in my room. Clutching the banister, I slowly made my way upstairs, then unlocked my bedroom door from the outside. No one was ever allowed in when I had a party. Ever.

A whiff of my favorite cologne, Creed Aventus, lingered in the ensuite bathroom. I'd become an instant fan of the musk scent. I waved my hand in front of the motion-detecting light, then searched the top of my dresser and nightstand for my phone. After what seemed like an eternity, I located it in the adjoining sitting area that resembled a small library.

An ache spread through my chest as my attention landed on the group of photos that lined my bookshelf. I scooped up the framed image, staring at the smiling and happy faces. What good was winning the game, landing the number one spot in the Pac-12, or being a star player, if you knew deep down in your heart that you shouldn't even be alive? I replaced the picture, turning it down as tears pooled in my eyes.

As my head bowed, loneliness and agony ripped through me. It was fucked up how one minute I was fine, and the next, I struggled to keep my shit together. I made a beeline for my dresser, opened the drawer, and removed the whiskey still hidden in the brown bag. Ripping off the plastic that sealed the bottle, I took a hefty drink and shuddered as the alcohol hit the back of my throat and warmed its way down to my stomach. I shoved the pain into a dark corner, then made my way downstairs. The only thing I could focus on ... I had to get the hell out of here.

I nearly face-planted twice on my way downstairs. When I hit the bottom floor, I straightened myself, squinting as I attempted to clear my hazy vision. At least I hadn't dropped the bottle. I peered into the crowd, then my breath stuttered in my throat as my gaze locked with Teagan's. Her big brown eyes widened, then I turned my back to her and headed out the front door.

Chapter Twenty-One

Teagan

"What did you say to him, Jagger?" I placed my fists on my hips, furious with him for clearly interfering. Hunter had been all smiles and laughter until Jagger had slipped away. Jagger needed to work on his stealth skills because I saw him talking with Hunter a few minutes ago.

Ari grabbed my arm, confusion flickering through her gaze as her attention bounced from me to her boyfriend. "What's happening right now?"

"Your man had a chat with Hunter, and now he's in a pissy mood." I glanced over at the stairs and spotted Hunter glowering at me. He swayed on his feet before he staggered to the front door.

"I told him if he had a thing for you, he needed to treat you right. That was all." Jagger tossed his hands up in surrender.

Although I loved that Jagger was always looking out for me, it wasn't Hunter that he needed to be concerned about. Well, maybe he did, but it wasn't any of his business.

I focused on Hunter as he elbowed his way through the crowd and headed to the front door. Hadn't anyone taken keys from people when they first showed up? No one had asked for mine, so I doubted they'd asked for Hunter's. Fuck, if he tried to drive, it could end badly. I shuddered with the thought.

"Thank you for watching out for me, but I think you have the wrong idea. I'll be back." I followed Hunter outside. If he wasn't shit-faced, I wouldn't have ever traipsed after him like a little puppy.

The cold air sent a chill over my sweat slickened skin. Ari and I had danced our asses off until we were drenched. Thank God I had stashed a toothbrush, toothpaste, deodorant, a pair of clean panties, and a fresh set of clothes in my car. After my parents had disappeared, I wanted to make sure I was always prepared for an emergency.

I slowed and searched the driveway and lawn for Hunter, but I didn't see any signs of him. The sound of an engine starting caught my ears. Hunter was clearly in the driver's seat of his Porsche.

"Hunter!" I yelled, breaking into a sprint. I'd kept my promise to myself and had paced my alcohol intake. I was completely sober as I hauled ass toward him. "Hunter!"

He looked at me through his window. A malicious grin slipped over his face, then he peeled out of the driveway.

"What the actual fuck?" I groaned in frustration and whirled on my heel, nearly slamming into a few football players who had decided some fresh air would be beneficial. They looked a bit green, and if I weren't in a big hurry, I would have laughed my ass off. "Hey, who the hell is responsible for taking keys from the people at the party?"

"No one. Man, Hunter doesn't roll like that." The guy stumbled forward, leering at me.

I grabbed him and dug my fingernails into his shoulders. "Listen, jerkoff, Hunter just left and he's driving. Why hasn't anyone taken *his* keys? You guys are supposed to be friends."

"Why would we do that? It's his fucking house." The dumbass looked at me as if it had been the stupidest thing he'd ever heard.

I stumbled backward, shocked by the revelation. Glancing at the end of the long driveway, I spotted Hunter's taillights winking through the darkness. "Fuck!"

I kicked it into gear and sprinted to my car, cursing myself for parking a block away. If I hurried, I might catch him before he wrapped his Porsche around a tree, killing himself. Whatever had happened at the party had tanked his good mood. I climbed into the driver's seat, started my R8, then peeled out after him.

One thing my dad had done when I'd turned eighteen was take me to the racetrack. He'd paid for us to drive the race cars while speeding and learning to handle the curves. It had been a blast, but I had learned some safety tips when driving at high speeds. Hopefully, they would help me while following Hunter.

Once I was in my R8, I spotted him ahead. At least he wasn't flooring the accelerator, but he was weaving. I gunned the engine, hoping to catch up to him. Even though my Audi was fast, Hunter's Porsche could easily whip my ass. I couldn't afford for that to happen.

White-knuckling my steering wheel, I began to close some distance. I wasn't sure how, but he kept it between the yellow lines, thank God. Still, I had to get him to pull over. I just wasn't sure how. My pulse pounded in my ears, and I peered in front of us. At least we were on a back road, and there wasn't a lot of traffic. Maybe it would save us both.

After a few more miles, Hunter took a right. Frowning, I followed him.

"What the hell?" I muttered to myself. "Where are you going, Hunter?" I slowed my car since I was getting closer but kept my focus trained on him. Confusion clouded my thoughts as I realized he'd entered a graveyard.

He continued to wind through the cemetery, then slowed and parked his car. The door flew open, and he climbed out, then stumbled along a dirt path. I switched my headlights off, then drove quietly until I reached his Porsche.

Turning off the engine, I hopped out of my R8 and shut the door. I would have to lock it later. I didn't want him to know I was following him, and the beep-beep of the alarm would alert him that I was there. As far as I was concerned, my job was to make sure he got home safely, but I had to figure out what the hell he was doing first. Then, I would text Jagger to have someone pick up Hunter and take him home. *Home.* I'd had no fucking clue I'd walked through the doors of Hunter Calloway's mansion. This asshole was rich. So was I but holy shit, not that rich.

I crept closer to him, then crouched behind a tombstone in order to stay out of sight. Hunter nearly collapsed next to a grave, facing my direction as he took a healthy swig from what I suspected was a bottle of alcohol.

"I can't fucking do it." Hunter's shoulders slumped forward in defeat, slurring his words slightly. "Every goddamned thing that I want, I shouldn't have. *You* should."

The thump of my pulse tickled my ears as I strained to hear him better.

"Then ..." Hunter shook his head. "Then she showed up right in front of me. I had the perfect opportunity to make her pay for what she did, and I can't even do that right." His anguished cry reached me.

The sound of his strangled sobs stabbed me in the heart. I wanted to rush over and hold him, but if he knew I was eavesdropping, he would be hot-pissed. *But who was he talking to?* I wasn't sure how to help him since he'd been furious with me earlier in the week. I gripped the tombstone, then leaned forward as he began to speak again.

Hunter turned slightly, the glow of the moon illuminating his tear-streaked face. "I was supposed to destroy her, get revenge for both of us, but Teagan ..."

Holy shit! He was talking about me. My breathing came so hard, I struggled to hear Hunter. I still didn't understand why, though.

"I don't know what the hell she did to me. As soon as I learned we were both at Whitmore, I planned it all out. The Society, how I would humiliate and break her ..." Hunter threw his head back, a maniacal laugh escaping him. "Then fucking Jagger cornered me tonight. He's digging into my past. *Our* past! That shit can't happen. It *cannot* happen. I'm so fucking tired of hiding, looking over my shoulder, and waiting for more fucked up shit to happen. It's draining me, and I can't keep living a lie."

His words squeezed my heart and crushed my lungs. He blamed me for something horrific that had happened to him. But I didn't understand, and it was too dark to see the name on the tombstone.

The world blurred, and my stomach churned as Hunter removed a knife from his jeans pocket. The blade clicked into place, and his expression twisted with agony.

His pain hit my chest, hard. I exhaled an audible gasp, and I slapped my palms over my mouth. It was too late, though. Hunter had spotted me.

With precise, clean movements, Hunter jumped up and stomped toward me, his gaze fueled with anger.

The air ignited with his simmering rage, sucking the oxygen from my lungs as he glowered down at me. All the tiny hairs on my arms lifted. This wasn't good. Not by a long shot.

I stood, our stares locking. "You're drunk, and I was worried about you driving."

He leered at me, then shoved me to the ground and dropped to his knees beside me. His fingers wrapped around my neck, and he pinned me to the cold, unforgiving earth as his eyes narrowed, filling with hate.

"You," he hissed, spittle flying from his mouth. "You killed him!"

My gaze tangled with his, searching desperately and trying to understand where we went wrong. I kicked at him, but he'd quickly moved out of the way and laid on top of me. Clawing at the back of his hands, I mentally begged him to stop choking the life out of me. I was floundering, and a silent scream began to build. He had to let me explain. I hadn't ever killed anyone.

Darkness crowded the corners of my vision, and the harsh reality bitch-slapped me in the face. I'd left Hunter's house to ensure that he was safe, and I was about to say goodbye to my life instead.

Chapter Twenty-Two

Hunter

The color drained from Teagan's face as her eyelids fluttered closed. A stabbing pain shot through my head as if my skull would splinter at any second, and my past would devour me alive. The memories swirled faster, pulling me into the darkness. A nagging voice whispered that I wasn't a killer. If I didn't let her go, she would die, and I would have to hide the goddamned evidence.

I released her and hurled the reminders back into the blackness where they belonged. They should never have escaped.

Stumbling backward, I allowed her to roll over, and she broke into a coughing fit. When she wasn't gasping for air anymore, I stood, then jerked her up, practically dragging her over to where I'd been sitting moments earlier.

Tears streamed down her beautiful cheeks, and my cock stiffened at the sight of her fear.

"I didn't kill anyone," she whimpered, her eyes pleading with me. She stared at the gravestone. "I don't know anybody by the name of

Levi. The last name isn't engraved, so I'm at a loss. Please, you have to believe me, Hunter."

Furious, I shoved her to the ground, her shin smacking the corner of the tombstone. She cried out and grabbed her leg, then I spotted blood seeping through her jeans. Maybe I should have felt bad that I hurt her, but I didn't. It wasn't anything in comparison to what she'd done to me.

"Texas, three years ago, you were at cheerleading camp." I rubbed my chin, my mind beginning to clear a little from all the alcohol. Apparently, anger-driven adrenaline could shake you out of a whiskey-induced brain fog. Teagan froze with my words, her body trembling as she huddled on the muddy ground.

"You and a few other bitches were partying at the bleachers of the football field, giggling and talking shit about people. It was early evening, and no one else was around."

She gulped, her expression giving away that she remembered the time I was referring to.

"I didn't kill anyone, Hunter."

"Shut up!" My hands clenched into fists. "Shut your fucking mouth unless I tell you to speak."

She nodded and fell silent. I glanced in the opposite direction, resisting the urge to tear her clothes off and fuck her until she begged for mercy.

"There were two kids who approached you and another girl, begging for help." I stared at the ground, the memories slamming into me like a fucking tidal wave. I looked at her again, my anger and compassion jumping all over the place. I'd snapped. The pain and fear had finally pushed me over the edge, and I was terrified I wouldn't return to sanity.

"The guys told you that some dangerous men were chasing them, and that they needed to hide. When they asked for help, the two of you laughed and teased them for looking like scrawny nerds, then you told them to get lost." I rubbed my jaw, ready to deliver the final blow. "Do you know what happened to them?"

Teagan shook her head while mascara-darkened tears streamed down her face.

"They ran into the surrounding woods, but the men caught up to them from the opposite direction." I knelt in front of her, ensuring she understood what I was about to say. "The oldest was beaten within an inch of his life, then forced to watch his brother get stabbed to death only a few feet away from him." I paused, allowing what I'd said to sink in. "They let me live to warn my parents."

Teagan's eyes widened, and she hid her muffled cries behind her hands, understanding dawning on her.

"*I* was that older brother, Teagan. *I* was forced to watch my little brother die and bleed to death on the ground because you and your cheerleading friend thought you were too goddamn good for us. *You* killed Levi. If you had helped us, he wouldn't be dead. My mother held the box with his ashes, crying the entire flight to Oregon. We buried some of his remains and gave him a tombstone." My body trembled with my fury as I jabbed a finger in her face. "After I recovered physically, my family relocated, and I swore that I would hunt you down and make you pay." I choked on my misery, feeling a bit of relief that I'd finally spoken my truth for the first time in three years. Someone else could choke on my pain. God knows I had. I stood. Then, to my surprise, so did she.

Teagan squared her shoulders and tipped her chin up as she limped over to me. One thing was for sure, this girl had fucking balls. She placed her freezing palms against my cheeks and forced me to look at her. My stomach clenched. She was breathtaking when she was all fucked up. To my surprise, the next words that fell from her beautiful lips changed me forever.

Chapter Twenty-Three

Teagan

My skin was buzzing, and my mind was racing full speed ahead. It felt like a nuclear bomb was about to blow inside my skull. Swallowing painfully over the anguished lump in my throat, I looked Hunter straight in his eyes.

"Nothing I can ever say to you will make that day right, Hunter. I'm so fucking sorry for making fun of you and your brother. After you and Levi left, I knew in the pit of my stomach I'd fucked up. Please, please let me explain what happened." I shifted my weight, flinching as the pain shot through my shin. Disbelief and confusion clouded his features, and I forced myself to focus and continue.

"Honestly, I assumed it was a joke, two nerdy teens trying to get our attention. It only took me a few minutes to replay the scenario and realize I might have been wrong. If I hadn't helped someone in trouble, I wouldn't have ever forgiven myself. A few minutes later, I excused myself from the girl I actually couldn't stand and began to search for you and Levi. The woods were thick, and it was growing darker. I wandered around for an hour, but I had to return to camp. I searched everywhere. I thought maybe you guys had been playing with me when I wasn't able to find either of you. Even then, I couldn't seem to shake the nagging feeling that something awful had happened. I called the cops, reported the incident, and watched the news for several days, but nothing was ever discussed." I paused, my gaze searching his expression as his features softened.

"I wish I'd understood what was happening, Hunter. I did search for you. I did believe you. I realize it's not good enough, but I needed to tell you what happened after you and Levi had left." I dropped my hands from his cheeks. Uncontrollable tears streamed down my face, and I folded my arms across my chest, trying to hold myself together as his pain became mine. "No wonder you hate me," I whispered, daring a look at him.

"You looked for us?" Hunter's tone was laced with shock.

"Yeah. I just didn't know the woods well enough to follow you and Levi. I think I walked in the opposite direction ... maybe. I'm a city girl and was terrified I would get lost, but I had to keep searching. Plus, I hadn't ever stepped foot in Texas in my life until that week. I should have done better, though. I should have had my cell phone on me and called 911 immediately." I swiped at my tears.

"You came for us," Hunter whispered a few times as he stared at me. The muscle in his jaw tensed, regret creasing his forehead. "That's how the cops finally found us."

I nodded, allowing him a minute to wrap his alcohol-induced brain around what I'd just shared with him.

"All this time, I blamed you for something that ..." Hunter lowered his head and rubbed the back of his neck. "If you'd searched in the right direction, you probably would have found us but ... there's a good possibility you would have been killed too. Now that I know the truth ..." His lips pursed as he stared a hole in me. "In a way I'm glad you didn't find us." His tone was gentler than what I was used to.

Our dread and fear dissolved into thin air. I resisted the urge to take him in my arms and soothe his pain. At least it made sense why he hated me so much.

"Hunter? Who was after you?"

He threaded his fingers through his hair, worry and regret rolling off him in waves. I hadn't ever seen Hunter so vulnerable before, but I suspected the alcohol had something to do with it.

"I can't tell you." He looked away, then he focused on me again, his bloodshot green eyes locking on mine.

"Okay. I understand." I didn't understand, but I felt as though we'd gained some footing, and I didn't want to push the issue.

Hunter touched the front of my neck. "Are you all right?"

I placed my hand over his. "I will be. This is a lot to take in." Silence pulsed around us as we stood rooted in place. "A part of me is angry with you for being a fucking asshole, but if I were in your shoes, I'm not sure I wouldn't have done the same."

Guilt flickered in his eyes. "Teagan ..."

As shook up as I was, the truth was in the open, which was a huge relief, but I had to give myself permission to process after he was safely at home.

Hunter gently touched my shoulder, an extreme contrast to his actions a few minutes ago. "I'm sorry." His voice was soft and low.

I nearly stumbled backward and gasped. An apology rolling off his tongue was something I never thought I would hear. Not only was he capable of being awful, but apparently, he could admit when he was wrong.

My breath snagged in my throat as a flicker of electricity flashed between us, mixing with a surge of desire and longing. Suddenly, I saw the man hidden behind the rage and pain, and I needed to be what made him smile, breathe, and wake up in the mornings. I remained still, trapped in the twisted knots of his gaze, breathing in the intoxicating scent of him.

Hunter closed the gap between us and slid his arm around my waist. "I'm fucked up, Teagan. You should run as fast as you can."

I swallowed over the lump in my throat, my heart slamming against my chest. "I can't," I whispered. *Shit. I just admitted I had a thing for him even with how he's treated me.*

Hunter tucked my hair behind my ear and chuckled. "I like kinky sex—handcuffs, blindfolds, toys, butt plugs. Obviously, I enjoyed spanking you."

I couldn't stop my smile, my panties soaked in seconds as I recalled the memories of him inside me. "I didn't run from you as the King Cobra, and I don't plan on it now. I might be willing to explore your kinky side some more." I hesitated, weighing my words before I spoke. "But I would also like to know the man behind the mask."

"Even though I've treated you like shit? Don't get me wrong, I'm an asshole, Teagan, but I thought you were responsible for Levi ..." Hunter looked away, then focused on my lips. "I believe you when you say you searched for us. If I didn't, I wouldn't be standing here."

"I'm relieved that we talked." My voice cracked, my legs trembling against his. It was fucking cold, and I was in pain, but the heat from his body was helping.

He lightly traced the curve of my neck, then he tipped my chin up. Hunter pressed his lips to mine with a soft, gentle kiss. Goosebumps peppered my skin as desire licked through me.

His lips parted, his tongue sweeping over mine in slow, delicious strokes. Hunter slid his hand up my back and threaded his fingers through my hair while dominating my mouth.

"Jesus, you taste good," he whispered before kissing me again.

He broke our kiss, then slid my sweater up over my belly. He lowered the lace cups of my bra down and rolled my nipple. I shuddered as the cold air brushed across my skin. He dipped lower until his mouth latched onto the nub of my breast, and he tugged the sensitive bead. Grabbing the back of his head, I fisted his hair as he worshiped each nipple, leaving me breathless.

Hunter stood, then he unbuttoned and lowered the zipper on my jeans. He glanced around, then gingerly backed me up until a few tombstones were between us and Levi's grave. He took my hand and sank to the ground, taking me with him. Hunter eyed my shin, then carefully parted my legs and settled between them. He hovered over me, his blonde hair flopping into his eyes. He smiled, then sat on his knees and pulled my jeans and G-string down. The wet dirt chilled me to the bone, but I doubted I would notice shortly.

He shrugged out of his North Face jacket. "Lift your ass." I rolled to my side and grinned like a fool when he spread it out on the ground. "That way you won't be as cold." He gently patted my thigh. "I'm going to check out your shin. I didn't mean for you to hit the gravestone." He peeled the material away from my leg, and I muffled a cry as it stuck to the wound. I was afraid to peek, but it hurt like hell.

He studied my shin, using the light of the moon to inspect it. "I'll clean it up when we go back to my house. It's not bad, but it probably doesn't feel too good."

"It hurts, but I'll live. And I'm driving." Hunter was definitely sobering up, but not enough to get behind the wheel.

He focused on my bare pussy, and his tongue darted over his lip. He lowered himself between my legs again, his nose skimming across my core.

"I would willingly starve myself as long as I was able to eat you out anytime I wanted." His breath tickled my thigh, then he spread me apart and licked me slowly.

My back arched as he continued, licking and feasting. He nipped at my bundle of nerves, then slid his tongue inside me while he massaged my clit with his thumb.

"Oh, God." I wondered if he would get me off tonight, or if he was still playing games.

I gasped as he moved his hands beneath my butt and pulled me closer. Digging my nails into the soft material of his jacket, I lifted my hips, moaning as the pleasure swirled inside my belly.

"Hunter. Please don't stop. Not this time." I wasn't much for begging, but he felt amazing, and I wanted to ride the wave of ecstasy as long as possible.

He peered up at me, then sucked my sensitive nub. Hard. My body trembled beneath him as he continued until I was writhing on the ground like a girl possessed.

"I'm ... I'm ..." I threw my head back as stars exploded behind my eyes, shaking with my orgasm. He lapped at my pussy until I collapsed, grinning like an idiot.

He stood slowly, then pulled his wallet from his pocket and removed a rubber. Hunter quickly freed his cock from his jeans and stood over my face. He stroked himself as he stared down at me.

I licked my lips, wanting to suck him dry.

His mouth parted and he focused on me again. He stopped and rolled the condom on. Hunter repositioned himself, then pressed his dick against my slick entrance.

With a quick move, he pushed inside me, his heated gaze trained on me. "You're mine Teagan Mercer. I own you. Don't ever forget it." He pumped inside me, and I dug my fingernails into his ass cheeks.

Hunter filled me with every wonderful inch of himself, and I clung to our special moment. I had no idea what tomorrow would bring, but I wanted to be with him, to embrace all of his good and all of his darkness.

Hunter pushed my good leg to my chest, and he shifted, rubbing my clit with every thrust.

My core clenched around his shaft as his pace quickened, and he thoroughly fucked me, hitting every pleasure spot. I moaned, my hands wandering over his back as his corded muscles flexed with his movements. We fell into sync, finding our perfect rhythm. I never wanted it to end.

"Come for me, Teagan." Hunter pinned me with his heated gaze, rocking against me.

I sucked in a breath, my pussy pulsing around him as I danced on the edge of sheer, earth-shattering pleasure. My orgasm uncurled in the pit of my stomach, warm and sweet. It slithered down my legs and up to my chest and arms.

Hunter's moans filled the air while he slammed into me, his body shaking with his release. Once he stilled, he kissed me gently and brushed the hair out of my face. "Do you understand that you're mine now?" His eyes flickered with determination.

"What exactly are you saying? Do you want to be exclusive? That means no sex with other women ... just me." I sank my teeth into my lip, realizing what I'd just asked while he was still inside me. I didn't care if he dated anyone else, but fucking me and other chicks ... I deserved to be treated better.

He grabbed his shaft and eased out of me, then removed the used condom. I scrambled off the ground and quickly dressed, the silence nearly unbearable while I waited for him to answer.

Chapter Twenty-Four

Hunter

I grabbed my jacket off the ground and shook it out. Realizing it would need to be washed, I shoved the used condom into the pocket.

After losing Levi, my heart had split open, and I swore I would never allow anyone to get too close. But here I was staring at the most amazing girl I'd ever spent time with. If I'd been honest with myself, I'd fallen for Teagan's strength and determination when she still had no clue who was beneath the mask.

I approached her, then stroked her cheek with the pad of my thumb. "I haven't been with anyone else since the beginning of the school year." My chest tightened with my confession. Teagan had been a constant riptide—a tumultuous and emotional push and pull. "Normally, I am with other girls, but the first night with you as the King Cobra … you were all I wanted."

"Even as much as you hated me?" Concern flickered through Teagan's features. What she hadn't realized was that I knew how strong she was. I'd been aware of every text and conversation she'd had with Ariana concerning her parents since I'd bugged her phone. She'd been through a lot of shit lately, and I was guessing it had left her fragile, or she would have jutted her chin in the air and told me to go to hell after I'd fucked her on top of the grave. Eventually, I would need access to her cell to remove the device, but I wasn't sure I was willing to give up the control and insight into her life.

"Yeah. It totally messed with me. I felt like I was betraying Levi." If he were here, I wondered what he would say about Teagan and my twisted feelings for her. At first, it was easy to hold onto the hate, but the more I was with her, my heart gave my brain a big screw you. Suddenly, I wanted to protect her and make sure no one ever touched her again. The thought of some guy licking her pussy or fucking her nearly catapulted me over the edge.

I took her hand, her tiny fingers threading through mine. "You're covered in mud, and we need to take care of your shin. Let's go back to my place."

"I'm still driving. I can bring someone to get your car later." Determination settled over her pretty face.

"No one is getting behind the wheel of my Porsche, sorry." No two ways about it. I had friends, but it was too tempting to see how fast they could go.

"Fine. As soon as you're sober, I'll bring you back. Just make sure it's locked."

I smirked at her. "Damn, you're bossy."

"Yup, when it comes to taking care of the people I ... well, guess you'll have to get used to it."

"You care about me?" I gawked at her as I placed my palm over my heart, my tone thick with exaggeration and humor.

"Seriously? Me risking my neck to save yours isn't proof enough?" She shot me a pointed look before she rolled her eyes.

I cringed, realizing she'd just given me a sharp dig for nearly killing her. Hell, I deserved it. "I'll make it up to you. I promise." I removed the key fob from my front pocket and locked my car.

"Yes, you will." Her gaze narrowed. "Why don't you have keys taken away at your parties?"

I led her to the car, the wet leaves sticking to the soles of my shoes as we meandered through the cemetery. "Honestly, I was so pumped after the game I completely forgot. But no one takes my keys when the party is at my house."

That did it. Her brow quirked up. "I will. You could have been killed tonight. I doubt your parents need to lose their other son."

She might as well have punched me in the face. Not once had it crossed my mind. We climbed into her R8, then she started the car and blasted the heat. "I'll have to clean the leather. I'm pretty sure I have mud all over my ass and legs."

"I'll help. It was my fault. But I have to admit I've never fucked anyone on top of a grave before. I liked it ... a lot." I chuckled.

"At least it wasn't on top of your brother. Although I would be down for a threesome ..." She shot me a look, the corners of her mouth kicking up slightly.

I threw my head back and laughed. "If Levi had been a little older, he would have totally been good with the idea."

"And you?"

How had the conversation turned from being exclusive to a threesome? I was cool with me and two chicks, but Teagan would never go for that idea. I sure as hell wouldn't allow another guy to touch her. Anger and jealousy reared up like a monster jumping out of the closet.

Teagan focused on driving, and we fell into a comfortable silence. My brain drifted back to Levi. A huge weight had lifted off my shoulders when I'd confronted her, but more so with her response. Teagan had done everything she knew to do. It was more than I'd done. Doubled over after those men had beaten me within an inch of my life, I laid in a pool of blood, watching those bastards stab Levi to death. What was worse, he didn't die instantly. After the men had left, Levi crawled across the forest floor to me and took my hand.

This isn't your fault, Hunter. If I could do it all again, I would still want you as my big brother. I love you, man. Take care of Mom and Dad.

Tears welled in my eyes, reliving the pain of his last words. I stared out the window, clenching my jaw in order to rein in the regret and self-hatred for not protecting my brother. He'd trusted me, depended on me, and I'd failed him.

Teagan didn't know that I blamed myself as much as I had her concerning Levi's murder, but there were others involved as well. I just couldn't provide her with any more details than I already had. It would place her in danger.

"Looks like more cars are here if that's possible." Teagan eased up the driveway toward the house.

"Go around the back." I pointed to the left. "I can't guarantee it, but we might be able to slip in undetected."

"I won't hold my breath. I'm not sure I've seen a party this big."

She maneuvered through the vehicles and parked behind the manor. We climbed out, and she locked her R8.

I slipped my arm around her protectively. Taking a peek at her backside, I could see she was caked in mud. "I realize this is most likely not the case, but do you have a change of clothes with you?"

"Oh, shit. I do!" She hurried back to her car and popped open the trunk. Within seconds, she returned with a small Whitmore duffle thrown over her shoulder.

"I might be impressed." I rubbed my jaw, wondering why she would keep a packed bag with her. Maybe she'd had plans with Ariana after the party. If so, that had changed. She just hadn't realized it yet.

"Yeah, well, life recently kicked my ass, so I started making sure that I was prepared." She looked away from me.

Placing my hands on her shoulders, I gently kissed her, savoring the taste. "I have questions."

"Yeah? Are you sure I can't occupy your evening in a different way?" She smiled against my lips.

Seconds later, heavy footfalls sounded against the concrete. I turned just in time to meet a fist face first.

Chapter Twenty-Five

Teagan

A scream tore from my throat as Jagger threw Hunter to the ground and pounded him with his fists. Ari flew out of the house after him, and we both pulled on Jagger's arms, forcing him off Hunter.

Hunter sat up slowly, anger radiating off him as he glowered at Jagger. "What the fuck, man?" He spat blood onto the concrete and wiped his mouth with the back of his hand.

"Jagger, you better explain what the hell this is about." I knelt by Hunter, assessing his cuts. His eye was already swelling up, and his split lip was bleeding.

Jagger's fury ignited the air around us.

"Are you all right?" Ari asked Hunter, clearly concerned and embarrassed about her boyfriend's uncalled-for beating.

"You promised you wouldn't hurt her, man." Jagger stood slowly, his lethal gaze trained on Hunter.

"He hasn't hurt me, Jagger. I'm fine. I just have some dirt on my pants. I fell." I was lying, but I wouldn't throw Hunter under the bus for shoving me either. Hopefully, we were past all of that.

Hunter seethed as he scrambled to his feet, clearing Jagger by a few inches. "I hope you have a better reason, you son of a bitch. No one comes into my home and tries to beat my ass."

Jagger closed the gap, and the guys stood toe to toe. Ariana grabbed his arm. "Jagger, I think this has been a misunderstanding. Teagan is fine."

Jagger's ice-blue eyes remained on Hunter, his fists clenching. "Yeah? Does WITSEC mean anything to you?"

Hunter flinched and backed away, his attention bouncing to me, then back to Jagger. "Keep your goddamn mouth shut, or you'll screw up everything."

"Only on one condition." Jagger glanced at me, and my heart sank to my toes.

"What is he talking about, Hunter? I don't understand." My legs trembled as my brain put the acronym together. Hunter and his family were in the witness protection program? Bile climbed up my throat, nearly gagging me.

"What do you want?" Hunter asked. "What's your condition?"

"Leave Teagan alone. Don't call her, don't fuck her, you walk away now before any more damage happens." Jagger's hands clenched and unclenched.

"What? No." I asserted myself between the guys, glaring at Jagger. "That's not your decision to make. You're out of line."

Jagger's expression softened when he looked down at me. "You'll find a better guy, Teagan. He's not who you think he is. There's no way I could stand by and watch him use you. More than that, every second you're with him, you're in danger."

Fear wrapped her bony fingers around my heart, squeezing it until I couldn't breathe. I spun around and faced Hunter, the raw emotion in his eyes gutting me. "Is that true, Hunter?" I whispered. "Am I in danger?" I suspected I already knew the answer. Jagger could be a real dick, but he always ensured he had the facts before causing a huge scene. Even if that was the case, I had to hear it from Hunter's mouth.

Guilt danced across Hunter's features, and his shoulders slumped in defeat. "I can keep you safe, Teagan. I would never put you in harm's way."

"Are you sure about that? Doesn't seem like you've done a very good job so far," Jagger snapped, venom dripping from his words.

I spun on my heel so fast that I nearly gave myself whiplash. Before I realized it, I punched Jagger in the chest. "You're out of fucking line, asshole. Ariana, control your man for once, will you?"

Ari stared at me, her mouth gaping. "Teagan, I think you should find out what's going on. Be pissed at Jagger and even me, but the thought of you in some kind of danger ..." Tears welled in her eyes. "Please, just come home with us so we can talk. You've known me since we were in high school. I wouldn't ask if it weren't serious."

I stood rooted to the spot as I scrambled to make a decision. Angry wasn't even the right word for what I felt toward Jagger, but Ariana was right. She was my sister. I had only known Hunter for a few weeks. I'd seen beyond his hatred for me only hours ago.

I turned to Hunter. "I should go." I hated to leave him, but my friends were relentless when it was important.

"Teagan, please." Hunter reached for my hand. "Please, let me explain."

As much as I wanted to hear what he had to say, I needed to have some time to process that he and his family had been in WITSEC. If Jagger had found out about his secret through his MC connections, anyone could, which meant whoever was after him and his family could be nearby, and I would have never realized it.

"I'll talk to you tomorrow." Regardless of what I learned from Jagger, I would give Hunter the chance to explain later. It was only fair. Plus, Ari and Jagger had no way of knowing that I'd already given Hunter my heart. I was in too deep, and I wasn't sure I could walk away from him, even if it meant jeopardizing my own life. I pushed up on my tiptoes and kissed his cheek, then walked away to my car.

Ariana was right behind me, and before I could object, she slid into the passenger's seat, her blue eyes pleading with me. Jagger approached her, and she frowned at him.

"I'm so pissed at you right now. We'll meet you at the house, but I'm riding with Teagan."

Damn! Ari had just chosen my side. To my surprise, Jagger's face fell, resembling a wounded puppy. *Tough shit.* He would have to deal with the consequences of trying to solve a problem with his fists.

I hopped into the driver's seat and closed the door, then tossed my duffle bag in the back. My attention landed on Hunter, and I groaned, arguing with common sense. Every fiber in my being wanted to stay with him, but he'd left out a key piece of information. He'd been in the witness protection plan, and even if Jagger was behaving like a child, he rarely went after someone without cause. The only reason I'd realized that WITSEC was in the past was because I'd researched the program for a paper my senior year of high school. If he and his family were still a part of it, he wouldn't be having parties and they would be guarded twenty-four seven. Maybe Hunter would have told me eventually, but I didn't think he would be able to. Not if it meant keeping his family safe. My heart played tug of war with logic. The first thing I needed to do was see what Jagger had learned.

Shifting into reverse, Ari closed her door, and I began to back away.

"That was so fucked up, Teagan. I'm sorry." Sadness flashed across Ari's expression.

I rolled my eyes, angry with myself, frustrated at my predicament, and short-tempered because I was tired.

"Your boyfriend is a hot-headed twat waffle." My nostrils flared. "What the hell? Does he not understand that Hunter could press charges against him?"

Ari sighed. "I had no idea he was planning to attack Hunter. He was on the phone with Gunner for a little while, then he started looking for you." She leaned her forehead against the window, sighing.

"I need to know what he learned, but Ari, mark my words, I will talk to Hunter as well. This isn't Jagger's decision. It's not his life."

Ari gawked, then she pinned me with an intense gaze. "You've been sleeping with him haven't you?" Her voice was nearly a whisper.

This wasn't how I'd wanted to talk to Ariana about Hunter ... at all. Maybe it was time to tell her everything. If I was upset with Hunter for not telling me about WITSEC when he literally couldn't, then I wasn't much better for keeping secrets from my best friend. *But mine didn't put everyone around me in danger.* Internally, I groaned. At the moment, I had to keep an open mind until I knew what the fuck was going on. Hopefully, it wasn't too late.

Chapter Twenty-Six

Teagan

"Remember the secret I said I wanted to tell you, but I couldn't yet?" I glanced at Ariana to see her attention glued to me.

"Yeah. It's Hunter?" A frown of confusion marred her features. "Why would you need to keep him a secret from me?"

"If I fill you in, Ari, you can't tell a soul. Not even Jagger. If you can promise me that, I'll sing like a canary and share everything with you."

"Bitch, I swear I won't tell Jagger. That man doesn't need to know what we talk about. He's my boyfriend, but you're my bestie." She gave me a half-shrug and grinned. "It's how I roll."

I couldn't help but laugh, relief flooding my system. "I've wanted to tell you ever since it happened, but ..." I shook my head. "Ari, promise you won't judge Hunter. There's a lot to the situation, and you're going to pop your fucking top, but you have to trust me."

She shifted in her seat, chewing on her thumbnail. "Shit, this sounds intense, but you have my word on all accounts."

"Text Jagger that we're grabbing something to eat. I can't talk to you openly with him around. Plus, what I'm about to share with you ... I can't afford for it to get out. Jagger already lost his shit once tonight."

Ari removed her phone from her pocket and texted Jagger. Her laughter filled the car. "He's not happy about it, but he agreed. He's asking if you're coming to our place later, so he can talk to you."

Turning into the little diner that was open after midnight, I nodded. "Yeah. I need to know what he learned from Gunner. At least I'm assuming that's how it played out." I turned off the car, then we climbed out. Locking the R8, we hurried to the front door. The heat of the restaurant greeted us, and I slipped off my coat and peered down. "Shit. I have to go to the ladies' room to see if I can knock some of this dirt off me."

"I'll help. Your ass is pretty dirty." Ari smacked my butt, grinning. "I have to ask how you got so muddy, though."

I pushed open the heavy bathroom door, then checked for feet in the stalls. Once I'd cleared it for our conversation, I grabbed some paper towels and handed her some as well. I held up my jacket and shook it out. Little sticks and leaves tumbled off the fabric and fluttered to the white tile floor.

Ari went to work on my ass and legs while I began to remove as much dirt as possible from my hair and coat.

"I'm waiting." Ari scratched at a spot on my thigh, tickling me.

My giggles echoed through the room. "Stop! You know how ticklish I am!" I squirmed, but she grabbed my hip to steady me.

"As soon as you start talking, I'll stop. It's that simple," she laughed.

"He fucked me on a grave tonight." I sucked in a breath when Ari stopped the tickle fest. I peeked at her in the mirror. A combination of horror and intrigue twisted her features.

"Come again?"

"I did, thanks for asking." I pursed my lips together, holding my laughter inside.

Disgust flashed across my best friend's face. "So, the dirt I'm helping clean off you is ... graveyard dirt?" She gulped as her hand suspended in the air. "How much have you had to drink tonight?"

I turned around, leaning against the sink. "I had a few drinks over the first several hours of the party. I was completely sober when Hunter left the party in his Porsche. He was sloppy drunk, so I took off after him."

"And he went to the cemetery?"

I twisted around, attempting to gauge how much dirt was still on my jeans. "Yup." I grinned at her. "Am I clean enough to sit down at a booth? It would be better to grab a bite while I fill you in."

"Yeah, the rest will come out in the wash. It will work for now. But ..." she held up a finger. "Does your duffle bag have a change of clothes in it?" Her brow rose with her question.

"Oh, shit! With Jagger beating the hell out of Hunter on his own property ..." My nostrils flared, anger coursing through my veins again. "Yeah, I have clean jeans and a top in it."

"Excellent. I'll be right back." She walked to the door.

"Hey, bitch?"

Ari placed her hand on the handle and glanced over her shoulder at me. "You rang?"

I laughed as I tossed her my key fob. "That will help."

She caught it, then disappeared into the hall.

Nibbling on my thumbnail, I removed my phone from my back pocket. I stared at Hunter's text that had come through.

I'm sorry for lying to you. Hopefully, you'll let me explain. I swear I'll keep you safe, Teagan.

My chest ached with his words. I believed him, or at least I wanted to. My fingers flew across the keyboard with my reply.

Is your face okay? I'm sorry Jagger pulled that shit.

It's not that bad. I'm more worried about you.

I lowered the phone, closing my eyes briefly.

I'm not with Jagger atm. I need to hear what he has to say. You have my word that I'll ask for your side afterward.

The door opened, and Ari held up my duffle.

Gotta go. TTYL

Hunter didn't reply, and I took my bag from Ari, then walked to a stall.

A few minutes later, I had cleaned the blood off my shin, and changed into some fresh jeans and a burgundy cashmere sweater. My leg still throbbed, but the gash wasn't deep enough for stitches. "I'm much better." I washed my hands, then we entered the restaurant and selected a booth. The diner wasn't busy, so it was easy enough to find some privacy.

"Spill." Ari said, sipping the water the server placed on the table.

"Honestly, I'm not sure where to begin." Confusion, regret, and a hint of embarrassment overwhelmed me. "The day before I learned my parents had disappeared, I received an invitation to the society ... to meet the King Cobra."

Ari's mouth hit the floor. When she finally scooped it up, she stared at me like I had three heads. "No. Fucking. Way. I don't know anyone who has been invited. Hell, I'm not even sure how long the society has been around."

"Me either, so needless to say, I had no idea what to expect. I debated back and forth on going, until I realized my parents were gone and my credit card was canceled. When I returned home, I had another letter stating that I would earn a grand for showing up that night instead of the original date. I was a little desperate for money, so I went."

"Teagan! You can always come to me if you need money. You took me out all the time when Theo had cut my funds off." She reached across the table and squeezed my fingers, sincerity in her expression.

"I love you, but I needed food, rent, car insurance, and my gym membership. I was humiliated that my parents had ditched me, and the last thing I could do was ask you for help." I leaned back, realizing that I'd hurt Ari's feelings by not asking her. "I'm sorry I didn't loop you in. I was doing the best I could at the time. Honestly, Mom had told me for so long that I was a burden, I couldn't bear the thought of becoming yours."

"Teagan," Ari's tone was full of love and compassion. "You will never become a burden. I love you. We're family, and I will stick by you. I don't always agree with your decisions, but you don't always agree with mine either. Just remember, I will always have your back just like you do mine." She raised my hand to her mouth and placed a noisy kiss on my knuckles. Ari had the unique ability to lighten an intense conversation with a bit of humor, and I was grateful.

Over the next few hours, I filled her in on the King Cobra, why Hunter hated me so much, and how we'd barely cleared the air when Jagger had flown out of Hunter's house and beaten the shit out of him.

A wad of napkins littered the table from our tears. Ari had taken the story about Levi hard, and so had I. At one point, I nearly lost the food I'd eaten. As I was talking to her, I remembered that Hunter said he couldn't share who the men were and that it would put me in danger. I had a strong suspicion that Levi's murder had been the segue to his family landing in the protection program.

"I have a question." Ari popped the last French fry into her mouth.

"Yeah?"

"How did Hunter find out about your mom and dad leaving, and the fact that you needed money? *I* didn't even know about your credit card dilemma."

My eyes narrowed as I stared out the window into the dark, damp parking lot. "I have no idea, but believe me, I'm going to find out." Without a second thought, I texted Hunter.

How did you know that my parents had disappeared, and I didn't have any money?

Chapter Twenty-Seven

Hunter

My phone vibrated with a message, and I grabbed it off my nightstand. After Teagan had left, I no longer wanted to party. I'd planned on keeping her next to me all night, her legs wrapped around my waist or over my shoulders with my face buried in her pussy. My cock strained against my jeans, recalling fucking her on the grave, and how wet she was while I slid my dick in and out of her.

I blew out a sigh when I saw her message. Fuck. How would I explain that I had a chick bring me her phone when she was working out at the gym? The last thing I'd expected to fly out of my mouth was the truth about Levi. Even less expected was her response. I had no idea she'd searched for us in the woods.

Massaging the back of my neck, I realized what had to be done. As much as I wanted to ignore her, I tapped the icon and called her. She answered on the first ring.

"I figure if we're getting things out in the open, I need to tell you something," I said, my gut twisting into painful knots. There was no way she would take this well. I sure as hell wouldn't if I were in her shoes.

"I'm listening."

I imagined her shoulders were rigid with tension while she was waiting to see if my explanation was good enough.

"At the beginning of the school year, you were in the gym, and I paid some chick to get your phone from your locker and bring it to me. I planted a device that allowed me to listen to your calls and record your texts. I knew about your parents, and that's when I offered to pay you."

"What? You fucking knew? That was personal, Hunter!" She paused, clearly seething. "Is it still in my phone?" She sounded pissed, and I couldn't blame her.

"Yeah. You'll need to ..." I stared at the screen. "Teagan?"

The line was silent. She'd hung up on me. "Fuck! Fuck! Fuck!" I yelled, nearly throwing my cell against my bedroom wall.

"Yo, dude, you all right in there?" Remington called through the door.

Before I could answer, he cracked it open. "Oh, you're alone. At first, I thought you were having a really good time." He grinned at me, clearly still drunk. "Holy shit, what happened to your face?" He squinted at me as he crossed the room.

"A disagreement," I muttered.

"With who?"

I glared at him, his presence annoying the shit out of me. Hopping off my bed, I clutched my cell, wondering if Teagan would call me back. The little voice in my head said no, and that I'd fucked this situation in every hole possible.

"Some drunk asshole at the party, man. I took care of it." I slapped him on the shoulder, then redirected him out of my room. "I'll catch you later. Go make sure my house isn't getting trashed." With that, I shut the door on him. I doubted he would even remember our conversation in the morning.

I'd already decided what to say when everyone was sober, and I was sporting a black eye. My lip throbbed like a son of a bitch, but nothing compared to the stabbing headache I had thanks to Jagger.

The second WITSEC left Jagger's mouth, I'd realized I was in deep shit. I hadn't ever planned on telling Teagan because it was against the program's rules. I would have jeopardized Mom and Dad's safety as well as my own. Even though we'd left the program, we stayed out of the press, changed our names, and weren't on social media. I could be a dick, but I wasn't stupid. I loved Mom and Dad, and I would do everything in my power to keep my family safe. I'd already failed once. I couldn't afford to do it again. If I weren't able to do some damage control with Jagger, I would have to tell my parents what happened. I had no idea what those consequences might look like, and the idea of leaving the university ... of losing Teagan ...

Reality punched me in the chest, stealing my breath. I ignored the argument in my mind. As much as my stupid heart liked the idea of keeping Teagan in my world, I couldn't risk it. I'd been stupid and selfish for falling for her.

I wanted to slam my fist into the wall, but I couldn't fuck up my fingers. My career depended on them. It was why I hadn't slugged Jagger in his fucking mug. I was trying to protect my hands and arms when he'd jumped me.

I paced my room, scrambling to come up with a solution. However, it was difficult when I didn't know what I was up against.

A crushing silence filled the space as I sank onto the edge of my bed. Jagger was right. I had to let Teagan go. I'd allowed her to work her way into my heart, and it was up to me to keep her safe. I inhaled deeply, realizing what I would have to do. With the decision made, I reached into the deepest part of myself and did what I did best. Within seconds, I flipped the switch on my emotions, resolving to no longer give a fuck about Teagan or anyone else. My world was only big enough for my parents. I stood, squared my shoulders, and mentally sifted through some names of chicks the guys had shared with me. It was time to return to the King Cobra.

Chapter Twenty-Eight

Teagan

It was late when we arrived at Ari's house, and Jagger was waiting for us on the couch. He anxiously jumped up as soon as we strolled in. His dark hair was messy, and worry was etched in his face. Jagger smoothed his basic black T-shirt, then stuffed a hand into his jeans pocket.

It was probably wrong, but I was enjoying seeing him tormented. I also realized that his concern had more to do with his girlfriend than me.

"Ari?" Jagger asked softly.

Holy shit, this badass was totally pussy-whipped. Good for Ari. She just needed to learn how to put him on a leash occasionally. Left to his own devices, Jagger was lethal, and eventually, it would catch up to him. I would hate to see how that might play out. For my best friend's sake and his.

She walked over to him, her hands on her hips. I stifled my giggle, hoping I was about to witness Ari bring out her inner queen. It was always fun to watch, and this had the potential to be incredibly entertaining.

"I'll deal with you later. For now, you need to help Teagan." She massaged her temples, frowning.

Her frown faltered, and I groaned as she caved and kissed him on the cheek, then made her way to the kitchen.

I pursed my lips, attempting not to go off on Jagger again. The second I'd laid eyes on him, all of my anger had bubbled up like a geyser. I needed somewhere to direct it before I drowned.

"In case you're interested, I'm still pissed at you too. But ... I want to understand what's happening, then I can make my own decision about Hunter. And when I do, Jagger ... you and Ari have to respect it. No more fights and attacking people. It will only draw attention to Hunter, and from what I learned earlier, his life depends on this information not escaping. Not only did you dig up his secrets, but we now have the knowledge to ruin him and his family. I don't think that's what you want, but maybe I'm wrong?" I folded my arms defensively across my chest.

Jagger's forehead creased. "You already knew about the witness protection?"

Ari returned with a beer for Jagger and screwdrivers for us. She settled in next to him, focusing on me. I took a sip, relaxing a little now that I didn't have to drive. "I had no idea until you mentioned it. Hunter had just told me a little about his past, and we'd barely arrived at his place when you jumped him." I glowered at him again. "You have no fucking clue what you've done."

"I was trying to protect you, Teagan." He crossed his legs, ankle resting on the opposite knee, his expression intense.

"Hunter has been giving me shit for weeks, and I learned why tonight. Right before you attacked him." I shot him another withering glare.

Jagger remained quiet but gave me his undivided attention.

"His brother was murdered in front of him," I said, my heart breaking all over again.

Jagger released a low whistle and shifted in his seat. I could almost see the wheels turning in his brain as he processed what I'd shared concerning Levi.

"That's horrible," Ari said softly. "I can't begin to imagine what he went through, huh, Jagger?" Ari cocked her head and quirked a brow at her boyfriend, sassy attitude rolling off her.

Mentally, I sifted through the details, choosing what I felt wasn't a threat to share with Jagger. There weren't many. "Hunter mentioned some dangerous men were after him and Levi. He wouldn't go into detail about who, but I understand why now. He *couldn't*. So, what did you learn and from who?"

Jagger cleared his throat and clasped his hands together in his lap. "When I couldn't find anything on Hunter and his family, I talked to Gunner. If anyone could snoop quietly, I figured he would be our man. If not, then he knew someone that could. Since you and Ari are best friends, and Gunner and the MC love Ari, he said he would see what he could find out."

"In all fairness that part makes sense." I tightened my hold around my glass, my nerves already frayed.

"It was difficult for Gunner to learn much, but he found out that at one time Hunter and his parents were in WITSEC."

Frowning, I scooted forward on the edge of my seat. "How? That's supposed to be nearly impossible information to dig up. It's a federal program."

"Gunner has a few federal agents in his pocket," Jagger mumbled so quietly I strained to hear him.

"Holy. Fucking. Shit." I glanced at Ari, who was as surprised as I was by the revelation. "Maybe I should kick Hunter to the curb and hook up with one of the guys in the MC. It sounds like their reach is far and wide. It's kind of fascinating."

Jagger barked out a laugh. "Umm, no. An *'old lady'* is treated like shit. They're not allowed to know what's happening with the club. They're fucked, then they get to cook and clean."

I wrinkled my nose. "I'll agree with you there. Not for me. I want my king to treat me like their queen."

"Damn straight, girl," Ari quipped. "Equal footing."

Jagger grinned, slipping his arm around Ari's shoulders. "Just don't forget, baby ... a queen *always* bows to her king."

I choked back my laugh. Then images of Hunter handcuffing me and coming all over my face sent delicious chills through me. I'd willingly bowed to him. My pussy throbbed, slightly sore from our earlier romp in the graveyard.

Ari gave him a quick peck on his lips, whispering something I didn't catch.

I waited for those two to settle down, then pinned Jagger with my impatient gaze. "Jagger, are you stalling?"

He gave me a sheepish grin. "Yeah. You're not going to like this next part, Teagan."

Ari slapped his thigh. "Out with it already."

"I don't know who murdered Levi, or what set that chain of circumstances into motion, but ... Hunter's Dad rolled over on the mafia."

Stunned, I gasped, my hand flying to my mouth.

"Wha-What?" Ari nearly gave herself whiplash looking at Jagger so quickly.

"Why?" I gulped, then took a long drink of my screwdriver. Holy shit. This was huge.

"I don't have the details, but as soon as Gunner said mafia, I was willing to have you and Ari be pissed at me for the rest of your life. I had to do what was necessary and keep you safe. Teagan, if they have any fucking clue where Hunter and his family are ... they might already know about you." Jagger massaged the back of his neck, his green eyes peering at me. "I'm sorry it played out like this. What really makes me angry is that Hunter knows this shit and chose to pull you into that world anyway."

A heavy silence cloaked us while my heart and brain duked it out for first place.

"Teagan, I'm with Jagger. I want you safe but ..." She stood, collected my nearly empty glass, and began to back out of the room. "But Jagger did the exact same thing to me."

I blinked rapidly, reeling from the events of the evening. Ari was right, Jagger had put her in danger, and she still chose him. As much as I loved Jagger for protecting me, I had to talk to Hunter.

Chapter Twenty-Nine

Hunter

I'd finally managed to drag my hungover ass out of bed around noon the following day. The house was fucking trashed, which wasn't a surprise since a ton of people had shown up at the party last night.

Once I'd located the guys scattered around the main floor, sleeping, we made drinks, then got busy cleaning shit up. I'd asked Molly, our housekeeper, to come in and help as well. I offered her double pay, and she jumped at the chance. Mom and Dad would be home late, but I had shit to do after I took care of the mansion.

I propped my elbows on the kitchen counter, finishing my second drink. Hair of the dog was a real thing, and I definitely needed a few. My cell vibrated in my back pocket, and I fished it out, grimacing as I saw the message from Teagan pop up. She'd texted four times already, but I hadn't answered. Jagger had jeopardized my family's safety, which in turn put Teagan in danger. It was time that she found someone else to play with.

"Nice shiner," Quinn said, laughing. "Who kicked your ass?"

I wondered if he was still drunk because he wasn't usually this much of a dick.

"It was a misunderstanding. It's settled now," I responded as Kane strolled into the kitchen with two full trash bags.

"I'm going to take a guess that the misunderstanding was Jagger Whitlock in your business." Kane dropped the bags on the floor and collected two new ones from the box on the counter.

"No shit?" Quinn barked out an obnoxious laugh. "You're a brave bastard if you're tangling with Jagger. He's a good guy, but if you land on his shit list ..." Quinn released a low whistle.

"It's over," I announced loud enough for the guys in the next room to hear as well. "Don't worry your pretty little heads about it." My lips curved into a sneer. "Besides, the society needs my attention."

"Hell yeah." Quinn fist-bumped me, grinning like the horny motherfucker he was. Sometimes I wondered if Quinn was capable of thinking about anything other than football and pussy. Not that those were terrible things, but there was more to life.

"You sure about this?" Kane asked quietly from behind me.

"Very. I need you to take me to pick up my car." I didn't bother looking at him. My choices were none of his business as long as they didn't jeopardize our identities. Teagan wouldn't breathe a word about it, or I would ruin her. I'd been a fucking idiot to think I could have something real with her.

Confusion clouded Kane's features. "Sure. Let's grab it this afternoon."

"Thanks, man." I tipped my chin at him as my thoughts returned to Teagan.

Pure, cold hatred whipped through me—anger at the situation, at Teagan, and my father. I redirected my wrath that was begging to be let off its leash. It snarled and clawed at my insides, and I retrieved my phone and typed out a message to one of the cheerleaders as ...

the King Cobra. It was time to step back into the game and remember that I would never have a normal life. Falling in love, having a family, starting a career, and feeling safe weren't a part of my world, and the faster I accepted it, the sooner I could move on from Teagan.

My phone vibrated again, and I glanced at the screen, reading the response to my message. The King Cobra had a bitch to fuck later. I smirked as my gaze landed on the name I'd chosen—Gabrielle McCallister. I was going to Hell because I was about to make one of Teagan's best friends my sex slave.

Girls wouldn't admit it, but their panties were soaked as soon as their fearful eyes identified the priest's collar I wore. The idea of the forbidden and the fact that it was an act that went against every religious teaching they'd learned in Sunday school ... not only did it turn them on, but it was almost guaranteed that they would keep their mouths shut.

I stood in front of the mirror and adjusted my black shirt and slacks. Gabrielle was due to arrive shortly, and I needed to make sure I was ready. Although she was pretty in her own right, in my opinion, her beauty didn't touch Teagan's. I tied my black dress shoes, and my attention landed on the crumpled mask that rested on the table. The same mask Teagan had ripped off me and the same table I'd fucked her on. The taste of Teagan's pussy lingered on my tongue, and I swallowed, shoving the thought to the side. Hopefully, Gabrielle would willingly become my new obsession.

Checking my watch, I removed it and hid it and my car keys beneath the chair cushion. I couldn't risk any jewelry or personal items exposing my identity. I took a deep, cleansing breath, then slipped the skull mask into place and quickly tested the disguised voice. Strolling across the small room, I dimmed the lights. It was time to say goodbye to the old and welcome the new. I returned to the corner and waited for Kane to open the door for Gabrielle.

The door softly creaked open, and a nervous Gabrielle stepped into the room.

"Hello?" She looked around, then took a few cautious steps farther into the dimly lit area.

"Hello, Gabrielle," I said from my hiding place. It was game time.

Chapter Thirty

Teagan

Hunter was blowing me off, and I didn't like it one bit. I folded my arms across my chest, pacing my living room. Gabby, Leighton, and Everlee weren't home for the evening, so I had the rare treat of being alone. Honestly, for some stupid fucking reason, I assumed Hunter and I would be sitting down together, talking. If I were honest with myself, I shouldn't have hung up on him in the first place. But I did, and I needed to see if we could set things straight.

I huffed, irritated at myself for hanging up on him after he'd told me that my phone was bugged. It still pissed me off, but if I thought someone was responsible for my little brother's death, I would stop at nothing to take them down ... including tapping their cell.

I sank to the edge of the couch, massaging my throbbing forehead. How had I ended up here? Hunter and I had made progress. He'd even asked me to stay the night with him until Jagger's intrusion had ruined everything. Granted, the mafia was a huge fucking deal, but I didn't know the entire story yet, so I was trying not to jump to conclusions. Unfortunately, I wasn't doing a very good job.

It was nine, so it was too late to call Dad to check in and see how he and Mom were doing. Dad had texted me daily, and we chatted on the phone or used FaceTime at least twice a week. If Mom's treatment went well, they would head back home soon, but it was still up in the air.

Grabbing the remote control, I turned on the television, hoping it would take my mind off Hunter. The idea that Hunter's father had tangled with the mafia should have sent me running in the opposite direction, but I couldn't turn my back on him after everything he'd shared with me. I'd done that once already.

After another hour of pacing and mindlessly flipping channels, I rushed up the stairs to my bedroom. I quickly touched up my makeup and ran a brush through my long, dark locks. If Hunter wouldn't talk to me, I would go to him. I just had to figure out where he was. The obvious first stop was his house. Maybe he was chilling out and recovering.

The temperature had dropped, so I traded my shirt for a sweater in case Hunter was at the graveyard. From what I'd gathered, he seemed comfortable in the cemetery, which made me think that he talked to Levi often.

I checked myself in the bathroom mirror one more time before I located my phone and purse, then made my way to the front door.

A gust of wind smacked me in the face as I stepped outside. With the house locked, I dug for my key fob in my handbag and unlocked the car. Pushing through the shitty weather, I reached my R8 and practically fell into the seat. I shivered against the cold leather and proceeded to turn on the engine and set the temperature on high. Thank God, my butt and legs began to warm quickly.

The Bluetooth from my phone connected with my stereo, and "Love is a Bitch" by Two Feet thumped through the speakers. I stared into the darkness ahead, wondering what in the hell I would say to

Hunter. Offer him my support? Ask questions? What was I looking for exactly? It was possible that my subconscious was searching for redemption even though I'd tried to fix the situation with Levi the best I could. Hunter had seemed content with my explanation about what had happened, but the guilt was eating me from the inside. Granted, I wasn't the one who'd stabbed Levi, but I hadn't helped fast enough. If I had, maybe I would have been able to stop his brother's murder.

I backed out of the drive, my pulse kicking up a notch. If anything, Hunter needed to understand that I was on his side. Anger swelled inside my chest. Anger at myself and the shit hand of cards Levi had been dealt. I shifted into drive and eased down the residential road. It was dark and rainy, not a soul would be outside this time of night, but I still wanted to be careful and not speed. "Sooner or Later" by Years & Years began to play, and my fingers tapped to the beat on the steering wheel.

I'd never been nervous to talk to a guy, but Hunter was different. A laugh slipped out. Hunter *was* different, and I'd unintentionally landed a leading role in his shit show.

It was almost 10:00 p.m. when I pulled into Hunter's driveway. Only a few lights shone in the manor's windows, and I hoped he was home. Collecting my courage, I parked my car. Locating my phone in my handbag, I slipped the purse strap over my shoulder before heading to the front door. I cleared my throat and straightened my shoulders, then rang the doorbell. The loud chimes resonated through the house, and I glanced over the lush lawn. I hadn't noticed at first, but the fountain was off.

The sound of the door opening grabbed my attention.

"Hello, can I help you?" A woman with the same green eyes and sandy blonde hair as Hunter greeted me. Even though it was late, she was well put-together, wearing an emerald-colored silk blouse and black slacks. Her manicured, red-painted toes peeked out from the bottom of her pants.

"Hi, are you Mrs. Calloway?" I offered her a warm smile.

She provided me with a tight-lipped grimace in return. "I am. And you are?"

"Teagan Mercer. I know it's late, but is Hunter home? I need to talk to him about a school project."

Her steely gaze raked over me, and I suddenly felt like a kid selling Girl Scout Cookies for the first time—nervous and unsure of myself.

"He's not here, but I would be happy to tell him you stopped by." Her tone was clipped, bordering on rude.

"That would be great, thank you. Sorry to bother you." I gave her a little wave, scolding myself for bothering his mom.

The door closed, and the lock clicked into place. A huge sigh escaped me, and I walked to my car. I'd been hoping I wouldn't have to check the cemetery, but I wasn't sure where else to search.

My legs felt heavy as I dragged my feet across the cement drive. The sound of an engine reached my ears, and I peeked at the headlights that were breaking through the darkness as they grew closer to the house. I immediately recognized Hunter behind the wheel. Even though it was cold, I waited for him. Maybe we could go somewhere else to talk since his mom was inside.

Hunter whipped his Porsche into a space near my R8. I remained in my spot, my teeth beginning to chatter, but he hadn't made a move to get out of his car.

I walked over to the driver's side, then my mouth dropped as his gaze connected with mine. Not only was he wearing the priest uniform, but his mask was lying on the passenger seat.

The realization of what he'd done hit me like an eighteen-wheeler on steroids. I stumbled backward, shaking my head. Instead of returning my messages, that piece of shit had fucked some other girl. He'd lied to me. Hunter had nearly killed me, shared his sob story, then slept with me. It had all been an easy way for me to fall for him, then he moved in and broke my goddamned heart. Why had I believed a word that had left his mouth? He didn't give a fuck about me or anyone else. It had all been about revenge to him, and it still was. I'd simply missed the memo.

"You win." I fisted my hands. "I hope you're happy because you just accomplished what you set out to do: ruin. Me." Tears slipped down my cheeks, and fresh anger peppered my skin. "Fuck you!" I stomped toward my car, sniffling and trying not to lose my shit. But it was too late.

Chapter Thirty-One

Hunter

"Son of a fucking bitch." I slammed my palm against the steering wheel, then climbed out of the car. The second I had laid eyes on Teagan and realized she was waiting for me, I could sense deep in my bones that the situation would end badly. Even if I removed the collar, there was no way to hide the black clothes. With one sideways glance, she would know exactly where I'd been. I'd made a huge mistake and thought I could fuck Teagan out of my system and walk away from her. I was so wrong.

"Teagan, wait!" In a few long strides, I caught up with her and grabbed her wrist.

She spun around, her purse flying straight for me. "You bastard."

The impact of her handbag had been harder than I'd anticipated, and my brain rattled in my skull. I blocked the second swing and reached for her, but it was difficult to see around the two-toned brown bag that she was beating the shit out of me with.

"Who is she?" Teagan's breaths came in short gasps, her fists clenching and unclenching.

I gulped, unease spiraling out of control in my stomach. It was horribly ironic that I was wearing a priest's collar, yet I was about to deliver *my* confession to Teagan.

"Can we go inside the guesthouse, so we don't alert my parents with the screaming and swearing?" I wouldn't admit to her how well built the manor was, and I highly doubted that Mom and Dad would hear us, but I needed her to calm down.

Teagan tilted her chin in the air, defiance written all over her face.

"Hear me out, then if you want to leave, I won't stop you." What the fuck was I saying? I didn't want her to leave. I'd just been a stupid cunt ... and a dry one at that. I walked around the mansion to the guesthouse, and Teagan followed silently. Unlocking and opening the door for her, I motioned her inside, then closed it behind us.

"Do you want something to drink?" I was stalling, but I had to. My heart galloped in my chest, and fear rippled through me. I couldn't lose her.

Her eyes narrowed. "Say what you need to. I have somewhere to be." Teagan folded her arms over her boobs, my attention landing on them as they pushed up.

If looks could kill, I would be bleeding out on the floor. I shoved my hands through my hair, then squared my shoulders. There was no way to know how this would play out if I didn't have the courage to admit my massive screw-up.

"Who. Is. She?" Teagan tapped her foot against the tan-tiled floor of the entryway.

"Fuck. Teagan ..." I looked away, then to her again. I had never been a coward before, but I don't think I'd ever messed up this badly either. Walking around to the other side of the kitchen island, I wiped my sweaty palms on my slacks.

"You have until the count of three or I'm out of here." She glanced at the door.

I held my hands up. "It's ..."

Chapter Thirty-Two

Teagan

I had never seen Hunter Calloway turn pale, and I quickly decided it wasn't a good look on him.

"It was Gabrielle, one of your best friends."

My mouth opened and closed like a fish out of water as I tried to assemble the right words to say. This motherfucker broke me in two, and I shattered into a million pieces all over his shiny, clean floors. Hunter's words flipped my world inside out, my emotions spinning out of control. For the first time in my life, red spots danced before my eyes. "My Gabby?" My voice cracked with fury, but I was mentally pleading with the universe that I'd misunderstood him.

Hunter nodded. "But ..."

Now I understood why that son of a bitch hid behind the goddamned counter. He assumed that I would lose my shit, and he needed somewhere to hide for his own protection.

I stomped over to him, clenched my fingers into a fist, and slammed it into his sternum. He staggered back, and I punched him in the gut. I might be small, but Dad had taught me to fight and cause some serious damage to someone three times my size. His training had undoubtedly come in handy. My fists flew at Hunter's hard body, pummeling him over and over while I yelled at the top of my lungs.

"You stupid, stupid bastard!" Screaming wasn't typically my thing, but I had never been so livid.

Hunter tried to protect himself with his arms, leaving him wide open for a solid kick to the shin. The toe of my boot slammed into his bone, and he doubled over, hopping around on one leg. "Dammit! Let me explain, Teagan!"

I barked out a maniacal laugh. Shit, I was losing it for real. The second he straightened, I punched him in the chin. His head snapped back, shock coasting over his expression in slow motion.

"Fuck! Stop! You and Jagger ... shit." He stepped away, putting some distance between us. "Teagan, please, listen to me. Please."

His green eyes pleaded with me, but I had zero sympathy for him. Funny how fate had flipped mine and Hunter's roles. When we'd first met, he was the predator, and I was his prey. How quickly he'd become the hunted.

"There's nothing that you can say that will make things right between us. I was so stupid falling for you. You were an asshole in the beginning and you're still a fucking asshole. Why had I thought our relationship might be different once we'd cleared the air?" I shook my head, my shoulders slumping forward. My chest felt hollow from where my heart used to be ... before Hunter carved it out and stomped all over it. "I hope you suffocate in your misery. It has to be horribly lonely in the world you live in." I smirked, grabbed my purse from where it had fallen on the floor, and slipped the strap onto my shoulder.

Chapter Thirty-Three

Hunter

Her breaths came in short bursts, and my cock hardened immediately. Before she had another opportunity to hit me—or worse, leave—I backed her up against the living room wall. Pressing my hips into her, I roughly grabbed her cheeks in my hands. "Stop. You're not leaving until I've explained everything. It's not what you think, Teagan."

Her eyes glistened with tears, and I resisted the urge to push her down on her knees and order her to suck me off. Jesus, I was twisted, but seeing her this fucked up ... no one had revealed such raw pain and emotion in front of me, and she was stunning.

"I can explain, but you have to promise that you won't clobber me anymore. Jagger was enough for one weekend." Teagan could pack a fucking punch, and I would die before I admitted to anyone outside of this room that I got my ass beat by a little girl. My gaze fell to her perfectly plump red lips. God, I wanted her.

She nodded, and I backed away.

"Sit down." I pointed to the brown leather recliner.

"I don't want to." She tilted her chin, once again defying me.

"Fine. After Jagger lost his shit with me last night, I realized he was right. I put you in danger. I've been selfish. There's no way I can guarantee your safety. Hell, I couldn't even protect my brother." My pulse kicked up a notch, and my throat tightened. The images of his broken and bloody body flashed across my mind, gutting me again. I stared at my shoes, trying to continue while every part of me was scrambling backward from the conversation. I was furious with myself for allowing Teagan to get too close. Scrubbing my face with my palms, I glanced at her.

"Hunter, you played me, reeled me in, then yanked my heart out and trampled all over it. I hope you're proud of yourself. I hope that playing with my emotions healed the pain and anger you have toward me about Levi."

Her body trembled against mine, but I didn't move.

"I feel like shit, Teagan. I had every intention of stepping back into the role of the King Cobra and fucking as many chicks as I had to in order to get you out of my system. But it didn't work."

Her hand flew up, nearly making contact with my nose before I caught her arm. "With one of my best friends! You're a piece of shit, and I can't believe I ever fell for you," she spat. "Now *move*, Hunter. You were screwing Gabby, who had no clue who you were while I was trying to figure out how ..." She jerked away from me, then tossed her hands up, her palms facing me as though she was protecting herself. "Just let me go."

"No. Nothing happened with Gabby or anyone else. If you don't believe me, then call her right now. Ask her if she knew who was beneath the mask and if I touched a hair on her body." My tone grew louder with each word, and she flinched, fear flickering in her eyes.

"If I do, then will you let me leave and never speak to me again?"

No. "If you'll call her, then yeah. I'll give you what you want." *Liar!*

I hoped like hell that Gabrielle would answer her phone. If not, I would lose the only girl I'd ever loved. Unwillingly, I backed away from Teagan, giving her some space.

Teagan reached inside her purse and produced her cell, tapped her screen, then placed the call on speaker.

"Hey, girl," Gabrielle answered.

"Hey, how's your evening gone?" Teagan pinned me with an angry gaze, her cheeks flushed.

"Weird, but it's fine. I'm fine."

Without any hesitation, Teagan dove into why she was calling.

"I know about your invitation to the society." Teagan slammed her eyes closed as if she could block out the world and make all the bad shit go away.

"What? How?" Gabby's shock lingered in her tone.

"I'll update you in a second, but I need to ask you something. And swear to me you'll tell me the truth."

"Teagan, I've never lied to you ... well, I take that back. When we were younger, I always lied about my bra size, but that was about it." She laughed, then fell silent. "What is it?"

"When you entered the room, did anything happen? Did you have sex or oral sex or anything close?"

"Babe, I love ya, but those are some strange questions. Besides, how did you know I was in a room?" Confusion weaved through Gabrielle's words.

Teagan blew out a sigh, and I suspected she was weighing the consequences of sharing a secret with her friend. I also realized she was about to out me.

I nodded at her. "Tell her ... tell her it was me if you need to."

"Who are you with?" Gabby asked.

"I'll explain it later, but can you tell me what happened?" Teagan stared at the floor, her shoulders tensing.

"It was strange. I showed up at a building in the industrial part of town, then walked into a room with a recliner and table. It was dimly lit, so it was hard to see everything. Then, a disguised voice said hello, then ... I waited, trying to see who was there with me, but the next thing I heard was a door closing. I never even saw anyone."

Teagan covered her mouth with her hand, tears spilling from her eyes as she looked at me. "You didn't see anyone?"

"Nope. The building was eerily quiet, and there wasn't a soul around that I was aware of. I figured it was someone's idea of a joke. And, between you and me, I was a little disappointed. I could use some naked fun."

I kept my gaze trained on Teagan as relief trickled through me. But it wasn't enough. I wasn't going to feel better until she had the entire truth. I had to tell her the rest.

"So, how did you know where I was?" Gabby asked, with a hint of eagerness.

Teagan bit her thumbnail as she looked at me. "I've been there. I was officially invited to the society a few weeks ago."

"Wait! What? And you didn't tell me?" Gabby asked.

"I was sworn to secrecy, so I need you to keep that secret for me, Gabby. Please." Teagan wiped a tear from her cheek and pursed her lips together.

"I've got your back, but I want deets in exchange for my silence," Gabby said.

"Okay. I'll tell you later. I need to go but thank you for telling me. You just saved someone's life." With a wistful expression, Teagan ended the call.

This mess was all my fault, and I had no idea if she was about to forgive me or walk away for good.

Chapter Thirty-Four

Hunter

My pulse thundered in my ears as I watched Teagan stand still in the middle of my living room. I realized she was processing what Gabrielle had said to her, but there was more to share.

"Nothing happened, Teagan. I had it all planned out, but the moment I saw Gabrielle ... all I could think of was ... *you*." I placed my hands on my hips, cursing myself for allowing Teagan to break down my walls and reach my heart.

She blinked at me as if I'd spoken in a foreign language that she didn't comprehend. "Why would you do something like that, Hunter?"

"Because I'm an asshole. Because I'm fucked up. But ..." I sucked in a breath. I couldn't believe I was about to say this, but she had to understand. "My dick wouldn't work. You fucking broke me, Teagan."

Teagan barked out a laugh, then eyed my crotch. She folded her arms across her chest and cocked her head with so much attitude I could taste it. "Good. It serves you right."

She still wasn't getting it. Not yet. I grabbed her waist and pulled her against me. "I can't walk away from you. I don't want anyone else, Teagan, but it's fucking killing me to think, if we're together, that something might happen to you. I can't lose someone else I love."

I searched her beautiful face, witnessing the impact of my words registering. Her forehead creased in confusion, then her mouth pursed before it relaxed. Her gaze filled with wonder as she stared at me, speechless for a moment.

"Love?" she whispered.

"Yeah. I love you, Teagan. When I couldn't touch another chick, there was no way I could deny it anymore. I don't want to be with any other girl, and if you don't believe me, then consider this: why else would a guy not take an opportunity to get laid? It's because they love someone else. I left before anything could even start. Gabrielle confirmed what I told you. Nothing happened."

"How do I know that you won't get upset with me three months from now and pull this shit again?" She glared at me, a flicker of anger flashing in her eyes.

"Because I learned from my mistake, and I was honest with you. I could have lied about everything, but I didn't. I admitted my fuckup because I love you. You're the only girl I want to be with."

I could imagine the wheels turning in her mind, weighing out the pros and cons of walking out the door or giving me another chance. *Someday you're going to be out of chances, asshole.*

Teagan flashed me a slightly evil smile. "Do you know who Lorena Bobbitt is?"

My mind scrambled for any recognition of the name, but I came up blank. Teagan ran her fingernail down my chest, then cupped my dick through my slacks.

"Her husband pissed her off, and when he was sleeping, she took a very sharp knife and cut off his cock. Like, sliced right through the shaft."

I could literally feel the color draining from my cheeks.

"Then, she threw it in the middle of a field and search dogs had to find it." Teagan smirked.

For the first time, I realized what this girl was made of, and it was fucking hot. "If you ever pull shit like that again, or cheat on me, you'll also become a dickless wonder." She smiled sweetly, "Do you understand what I'm saying?"

I nodded, my brain imagining every horrible second of what Lorena's husband had gone through. I would have to Google the story later to see how it ended, but one thing was for sure. No way would I ever hurt Teagan again. "Loud and clear." My gaze lowered to her lips, and I shifted my weight to the leg that wasn't throbbing. It had been a long-ass time since I'd been kicked in the shin, but it still hurt like a son of a bitch.

Her features softened as her cold fingertips trailed across my cheek. "I've wrestled with my feelings since last night. Jagger didn't have a lot of details, but the mafia came up in conversation. It scared the shit out of me, Hunter. The idea that I could lose you, or my own life, terrifies me." She swallowed, then pushed up on her tiptoes and kissed me softly. "But I'm in love with you, and as insane as it sounds, I'll take my chances. You're worth the risk."

A waterfall of emotions washed over me—love, fear, and a fierce protectiveness I hadn't experienced for anyone other than my family. I slipped her purse off her shoulder and placed it on the counter, my focus glued on her. I bent down and grabbed the back of Teagan's thighs, and she instantly wrapped her legs around my waist.

"Say it again," I whispered against her mouth.

"I love you, Hunter."

Those words were all I needed to hear. I walked us into the bedroom and turned on the light. Setting Teagan down, I removed her coat and tossed it on the tan-carpeted floor. Teagan fumbled for the button and zipper on my slacks while I pulled at her sweater and bra. Her taut nipples made me smile.

She dropped to her knees and glanced up, freeing my dick from my pants. Her dark eyelashes fluttered as her tongue darted out and traced the tip of my painfully hard cock.

I fisted the back of her hair and slid myself in and out of her mouth. Her lips wrapped around me, her saliva slickening my skin.

"That's it, baby." I smoothed her hair as she sucked and licked me while she grabbed my shaft, stroking me as her head bobbed up and down. "Swallow, Teagan. When my come hits the back of your throat, I want you to swallow every fucking drop." Anticipation built inside me, and my balls began to throb in the best way. They tightened as I thrust, pushing past her gag reflex. I kept my attention trained on her while threading my fingers through her hair. Every muscle in my body tensed, and warm spasms shot through me as I released in her hot little mouth. I jerked, my eyes briefly closing while reveling in her touch. Once she'd drained me, I smiled down at her as my cock deflated.

I stepped back, focusing on her tits. "Take the rest of your clothes off," I ordered, discarding mine and tossing them into a pile on the floor.

Teagan stood naked before me, and my attention roamed over every beautiful and delicious curve. "Bend over the bed."

Uncertainty flickered across her face. "If you ever spank me like you did as the King Cobra, you and your dick will find yourselves separated." She gave me a pointed look.

I couldn't hide my smile. "I *will* spank that sweet little ass again, but I won't ever smack you that hard. Promise. But ... I find extreme pleasure in your pain. I warned you that I'm twisted, Teagan. Are you sure that you want to be with me?"

She bent over the bed, her palms against the striped burgundy and white feather comforter. "Yes," she said breathlessly.

Maybe I'd met my match in the bedroom. I placed my bare foot between Teagan's feet and nudged her legs apart. Dropping to my knees, I nipped at the inside of her thigh, sucking on the tender skin. She gasped as I parted her wet folds, my tongue flicking across her bundle of nerves. Her scent captivated me, and I inhaled, committing her to memory. Teagan Mercer was mine. No one would ever touch her again without my permission. Her moans of pleasure filled the room, and she rocked against my face.

I feasted on her pussy, claiming every part of her. Gripping her hips, I thrust my tongue deep inside her, feeling her slick walls trembling as I touched her innermost places. Her legs shook, and I moved away, realizing she was about to come, but I had something else in mind for her.

I smacked her ass cheek, then wiped her juices off my mouth before I stood. She glanced over her shoulder at me, then her lust-filled gaze followed my movements as I climbed onto the bed and made myself comfortable. I flashed her a devilish grin, then indicated what I wanted her to do.

Chapter Thirty-Five

Teagan

I straddled Hunter's face, my butt in the air while I ran my tongue along the tip of his cock. Hunter grabbed my cheeks and spread them apart, moaning into my wet flesh. He moved his fingers over my slit, then inserted one into my asshole.

I stroked and sucked him as he divided his attention between my core and my ass.

"That's it, baby." He finger-fucked me as he devoured every inch of me.

I rubbed my pussy against his mouth while I jerked him off. His hips lifted off the mattress, the creak of the bed the only other sound beside our moans and whimpers.

"Hunter. Oh, God. Oh, God." I gasped, my body teetering on the edge of oblivion. I nearly cried as he eased out, then gripped my thighs so hard pain shot through me.

Pouting that he hadn't allowed me to finish, I managed to turn around without hurting either of us, and jutted my lower lip out. He nipped at it, then gave me a heart-melting smile.

"Do you have a condom?" I asked. "I'm on the pill, so we don't need one if you're not going to be with anyone else ..." I searched his handsome face, waiting for his response.

"You're it for me, and I'm not saying that because my dick is hard again." He smoothed my hair from my cheek, then leaned up and pressed his lips to mine. My mouth parted, our tongues tangling as I welcomed him.

He broke our kiss, and I positioned myself over him. He placed his cock at my entrance, and I slid down his length, taking in every delectable inch. My back arched as he stilled.

"You feel so amazing." He looked at me. "I love you, Teagan."

Tears clouded my vision, my emotions and body tingling with his words. "I love you too."

He cupped my breasts, rolling and tugging on my nipples as I rocked against him.

"You're so beautiful, baby. Your cheeks get flushed when I'm inside you, and the way your lips part when you're riding me ... it takes my breath away."

He lifted his hips, thrusting into me while he firmly held me in place. No guy had ever been this deep inside me before. My eyes fluttered closed, and my head tilted back as Hunter sat up, his hot mouth pulling on my nipple. He cupped my other breast, and shivers of euphoria pulsed through me. I dug my fingernails into his shoulders, scraping his sweat-slickened skin. I stared down at him as I fisted his hair.

Sweet ecstasy licked every inch of me, and my muscles tightened as my clit rubbed against him. "Hunter ..." I gasped while my release rocked my entire world, and waves of intense pleasure flooded me.

"That's my girl." His low, guttural growl filled the room as his cock twitched, and he came inside me. I clawed at his back, intentionally marking him. By the time I was finished, he would be covered in red welts with beads of blood dotting his skin. His confession about inflicting and seeing someone else's pain went two ways.

"Fuck, your nails …" He was still breathless from his orgasm when I grabbed his chin, forcing him to look at me.

"You're mine now. Make no mistake that not only do you belong to me, but you've been marked, Hunter Calloway." I smirked. "Understand?"

He nodded, flashing a silly smile in my direction. Hunter kissed me, his hands running along my sides. He wrapped his arms around me, holding my body against him and burying his face between my breasts. I hugged him, enjoying the moment after our orgasms—just us, safe in our little cocoon.

Seconds later, the floor creaked, and Hunter practically threw me off him and across the bed. With the same precision he had on the field, he jumped off the mattress, slammed the door closed, and locked it.

Fear danced over his features. "I think someone is in the house. Get dressed." He tossed my clothes at me, and I quickly stepped into my jeans and sweater while he did the same.

He hustled to the nightstand, opened the drawer, and removed a pistol. "Get down and stay." Hunter pulled the slide, then ensured a bullet had moved into the chamber. He stood by the door, listening.

As hard as I tried, I couldn't hear over the pounding in my ears.

"Hunter? Is that you?" A female voice called out.

"Mom?" Relief washed over his face, and he lowered his weapon.

"It's me, Hunter. I thought an intruder was here."

Hunter opened the door to reveal his pale and terrified mother.

"What are you doing in here?" She finally spotted me on the other side of the bed, her displeasure creasing her forehead. "I didn't realize you had company." She tightly gripped the baseball bat she was carrying.

Irritation, then relief flashed across Hunter's expression. "Mom, first of all, where's your pistol? Second, why are you checking out strange noises instead of Dad?"

I didn't miss the anger laced in Hunter's words.

"He's asleep." She folded her arms over her chest, her icy stare landing on me. "Teagan."

"Hi, Mrs. Calloway. Nice to see you again." I gave her a little wave, wishing that the ground would swallow me whole. Clearing my throat, I focused on my bare feet. Even though we were dressed, the scent of sex was heavy in the air.

"Mom, Teagan is my girlfriend."

Wait, what? Girlfriend? I definitely loved the sound of those words on his lips.

Mrs. Calloway's eyes narrowed, shooting venomous darts in my direction. "I'm sorry, Teagan. Apparently, you're quite good in the bedroom because my son has lost his mind. He's focused on his football career and studies. He doesn't have time for a girlfriend. There's been a mistake."

I swear to God that my mouth hit the floor in slow fucking motion. *What the actual hell had she just said to me?*

"Hunter, we've discussed this. Dating isn't an option. I'll see Teagan out." Mrs. Calloway stepped past Hunter and entered the room.

"Mom. Stop. This isn't up for discussion." Hunter growled protectively.

Mrs. Calloway spun around, clearly startled that he'd taken a tone with her. Not once did she lessen her grip on the bat, though.

"Hunter. Don't do this. You'll only hurt her. You know this can't happen." Hunter's mom arched a perfectly shaped brow at him.

Their anger crackled through the room like a thunderstorm as they stared at each other. I held my breath, waiting to see who would back down.

Finally, Mrs. Calloway smoothed her blouse and huffed. "I'll be speaking to your father first thing tomorrow morning about this."

"Excellent. I have a few things I want to say to him myself," Hunter said, his tone clipped.

His mom's cheeks heated, burning a bright red before she

stomped out of the room, then slammed the front door on her way out of the house.

I smacked my forehead, my heart hurling itself against my ribcage. Hunter blew out a big sigh, his green eyes filling with an apology. "I'm sorry you saw that. Mom is pretty high strung since we lost Levi. I'll talk to my parents tomorrow."

"Hunter, she's scared." I wanted to look around the room to see who the hell had said that, but apparently, my mouth had bested my brain. I did *not* like that woman.

Hunter ran his fingers through his messy hair. "I know. But I've made my decision. I'm choosing you."

"Even if it causes problems with your family?" The pain of my question lingered on my tongue. Suddenly, my throat grew dry, and I wished I had some water.

Hunter crossed the room and gently gripped my shoulders. "Teagan, do you trust me?"

"Yeah."

"Let me handle this. Being with you won't put them in danger. Stay with me tonight. We'll stay here, then in the morning I'll talk to Dad. Mom is just rattled because she never thought I would make a choice."

He planted his warm palms against my cheeks, and I placed my hands over his. "I don't want you to have to choose between me or your family, Hunter. I love you, and if I have to let you go ..."

Hunter's mouth crashed down on mine, desperate and hungry. "I'm not letting you go, so don't even fucking finish that sentence."

He took a step away. "Get naked and in my bed. I'm going to make sure the front door is locked, and the alarm is on. I should have set it when we came in, but I was too distracted."

Before I could answer, he disappeared from the room. It was nearly eleven-thirty, and exhaustion tugged at me. Conceding, I stripped out of my clothes and slipped beneath the blankets. There wasn't anything we could do until the following day, so I might as well enjoy my time with him.

Hunter returned, undressed, then climbed into the bed next to me. "Come here." He patted his bare chest, and I snuggled against him, the warmth of his skin soothing me. Hunter placed a kiss on my forehead. "Get some sleep, baby."

I snuggled into him, wondering if I would be able to relax. I suspected that life would look a lot different when the sun came up.

Chapter Thirty-Six

Hunter

Sunlight trickled through the curtains, casting an angelic glow around Teagan. I smiled, then sipped my coffee as I watched her sleep. That night was the first time I'd spent the evening with a girl, then looked forward to talking to her the following day.

Guilt nudged me in the gut, realizing I'd almost made the biggest mistake of my life by inviting Gabrielle to the society. The second I'd seen her, I'd realized that I had fucked up. Thank God she had no idea who I was and hadn't ever laid eyes on me. I'd been an asshole thinking I could do something like that to the beautiful girl in my bed.

Teagan stirred, and I leaned against the bedroom wall, wondering what she was dreaming about. Hopefully, it was me.

My stomach knotted when I realized that I would have to speak to my parents. Mom had been furious, but so was I. Even after we'd left WITSEC and started our lives over, Mom was constantly looking over her shoulder. I got it. I was too. But I deserved to move on. I wanted Teagan in my life, and we would keep a low profile like I always did. Mom would have to trust me.

The other conversation I needed to have was with Kane. I wanted to know if he would be willing to run the society. Once Teagan had shared that she was in love with me, I'd decided that the society was no longer what I wanted. I just didn't want to let the other guys down.

One brown eye peered at me, then a smile eased across Teagan's gorgeous face, and my heart swelled. Fuck me if I wasn't whipped in the best goddamned way. After losing Levi, I'd given up on the idea that I would be able to hold onto anything good. Teagan curled up in my bed was proof that I was wrong.

"Hi." Teagan sat up and smiled, the covers dropping to her waist, revealing her perfectly round, perky tits.

"How did you sleep?" I tore my gaze away from her body and willed my cock to chill. I had other things to take care of before focusing on my girlfriend. Pushing off the wall, I sat on the edge of the bed nearest her.

"Good." She glanced at me shyly. "I need a shower. I reek of sex." She sank her teeth into her lower lip.

"I happen to like my scent all over you, but not when you're around a bunch of horny fuckers at school." I kissed her, then stood. "If we hurry, we won't be late for our first class. Before we go, I need to chat with the parents, though. I'll be at the main house while you get cleaned up. I've already showered, so when we're both ready, I'll follow you to your place where you'll park your car. You can grab some clean clothes, then you'll ride with me."

Her eyes widened. "Everyone will know we're together."

I raised my coffee cup to her, eyeing her over the rim. "Exactly. Every asshole in the school will know you're mine. If anyone even considers touching you, I'll deal with them."

"Sounds a little possessive if you ask me." She slipped out of bed and stood, sauntering in my direction. Teagan cupped my dick through my jeans and flashed me a wicked grin. My cock woke the fuck up and fast.

I threaded my fingers through her hair and tilted her head back.

"Get used to it. In fact ... I have something for you when I return," I whispered against her ear.

With that, I released her, my gaze raking up and down her nakedness. I smirked, then turned on my heel and left.

Glancing at the clock on my phone, I realized I had a few minutes and located Teagan's cell on the kitchen counter. I popped off her case, then felt around the black surface for the little device that had shared all of her secrets with me. Once I'd finished, I replaced her cell next to her purse, then hustled to the main house. Dad typically left at eight-thirty sharp, and I needed to talk to him even though I suspected Mom already had. I let myself in the backdoor and into the kitchen. As expected, Dad was having a cup of coffee and reading the paper at the table in the breakfast nook.

He peered over the top when I entered. "Son." His brow arched as I sat down across from him. Unlike the dining room table, this one wasn't large, so it was easy to have a quiet conversation.

"Hey. I'm guessing from the look on your face that Mom talked to you about Teagan." I rubbed my clean-shaven jaw, reminding myself to let it grow for a few days so I could tear up Teagan's thighs and pussy with my coarse stubble. I would mark her every chance I had. Stifling a yawn, I straightened in my seat.

Dad lowered his paper, his blue eyes weary. "She did. And you realize that I have to ask: does she know about our past?"

I folded my hands in my lap, preparing myself for the backlash about to come my way. "She was in Texas at a cheerleading camp when Levi was murdered. Teagan was the girl I asked for help. Well, there were several there, but I talked to her." I wouldn't lie to him. Hell, all I did was live a lie, but I owed him the truth.

Dad's expression twisted with shock. "You're sleeping with the girl that refused to help you and your brother?" Dad folded his paper into quarters, then slammed it against the wood surface.

"She searched for over an hour for us, then called the cops to report that we were missing. I only learned those details a few nights ago. Teagan wasn't responsible for Levi's death, Dad. We all know who was, and it wasn't Teagan. I just needed someone to hate."

Dad shot up out of his chair, sending it scraping across the floor. "There's no excuse, Hunter. Get rid of her. *Today*."

"No. I've protected this family for the last three years, and I deserve to be happy. I deserve to live a normal life." My insides trembled with anger, but to my father, I appeared composed. I had a lot of practice wearing a smile when I wanted to fucking tear the world apart and burn it down.

"And you will continue to protect the people who pay for your schooling and put a roof over your head. Hunter, you know what will happen if you get attached. You'll make a mistake and lead them to us." Dad shoved a hand in the pocket of his brown slacks, jingling the loose change as he glowered at me.

I stood. "I'll be careful. You have my word. Teagan has no idea why we were in WITSEC, so just relax."

"Don't tell me to relax. You're being careless and sloppy, son. Stop thinking with your dick and get focused on your football career." He jabbed a finger in the air. The muscle in Dad's jaw ticked, a blush dusting his cheeks. He was pissed. "Get your shit together and dump the girl. I won't tell you again."

"What career?" I tossed my hands up, frustrated. "I can't play for the NFL, Dad. I have no future in football! You and Mom keep saying that, but my hopes were cut short the minute you got involved with the fucking mafia and ruined our life!"

"You were a part of it, too. Your choice cost us everything. I explicitly told you to stay home, yet you and Levi snuck out of the house against our wishes. Where did that get you?" Dad looked away from me, rubbing his jaw.

The tiny thread of sanity that I was attempting to hold onto snapped like a dry twig. "*I* cost you everything?" I stepped closer to him, getting in my father's face. "*I?*" I snorted. "Nice play, Dad," I snarled, "but we both know it wasn't my actions and decisions that destroyed this family. You can't pin that on me. I won't accept it any longer. And clean your ears out, old man! I will not break things off with Teagan, so get used to it." My hands clenched into fists, and I realized I'd better get the fuck out of there before I lost my shit and hit the man who had provided for me my entire life.

Storming off, I took the stairs two at a time and hauled ass to my bedroom, then located my duffle. I grabbed the pistol I had stashed in my dresser along with several changes of clothes. Tossing my toiletries into the bag, I remembered what I came up here for. Rifling through my boxer briefs, I located the small package I'd purchased when Teagan had first met the King Cobra. I shoved it in with the rest of my belongings, then collected my chargers and pillow. It looked like I would be sleeping at the same place the society operated from. At least the building was mine, and I didn't have to worry about being caught. It had been one of the first investments I'd made into my future when we'd moved to Oregon. Breaking free of my family had always danced around the edge of my consciousness, but after Dad and Mom's ridiculous reaction to Teagan, I was finished.

Zipping the duffle closed, I tossed it over my shoulder and hurried out of the mansion and back to the guest house. Since Levi had died, I'd carried the responsibility to take care of my family. Guilt had consumed every part of me, and I'd failed my brother, but I wouldn't make the same mistake. Talking to my father had made me realize Levi's death was not my burden to carry. Yeah, Levi and I had snuck out and ultimately, that decision contributed to his death, but we were kids and had no idea what had really been going on around us. My parents were grown-ass adults and should have been honest with us. And now, if they couldn't support my happiness, then it was time to take a step back.

The second I entered the guest house I heard the shower turn off. Excellent, she was almost ready for me. My mood suddenly brightened as I walked to the bedroom and tossed my bag on the bed, grinning. We were going to be late for school after all, and my parents would just have to deal with it.

Chapter Thirty-Seven

Teagan

Wrapping a towel around my partially dried body, I opened the bathroom door. The steam billowed into the hall, and my bare feet slapped against the hardwood floors as I walked. Even though I missed my shampoo and conditioner, I was grateful that I smelled better.

I stifled a yawn and groaned. Once Hunter's mom had scared the shit out of us, I'd had difficulty sleeping. Images of his mother's scowl and rude words had imprinted on my brain, tapping me on my skull every time I was about to drift off. But learning that Hunter carried a pistol also plagued my thoughts. Dad had guns, so I wasn't bothered by the fact that Hunter had one, but it made the danger element of our relationship more real. It was hard to stay in denial when faced with the truth, and the truth held bullets.

His mother's clear disapproval had also upset me, but I wasn't sure her reaction was about me at all. I think she was terrified to lose Hunter, whether it be to a career or a girl. She couldn't keep him safe forever.

Sounds filtered down the hall from the bedroom, and I realized Hunter was back. Grinning, I strolled to the room we'd shared. It was nice to have our own space away from my roomies and his parents. Before I reached him, I caught a hint of his spicy cologne. My pulse kicked up as soon as I laid eyes on him. His broad shoulders flexed beneath his white long-sleeved T-shirt as he moved. His jeans hung on his hips, clinging to his sculpted ass and muscular legs. He looked yummy enough to eat.

"How did it go?" I frowned as I spotted the overnight bag. That wasn't a good sign.

"Not great, but it will blow over. I'll crash somewhere else for a few days. I, uh ..." Hunter gave me a sheepish smile. "I own the building where the society meets the girls. I'll sleep there for now."

"The fuck you will." My nostrils flared with the realization that he would sleep on a cot while gorgeous girls were in and out all evening. I'd never been the jealous type, but apparently, that had changed. "You'll stay with me. I have a queen-sized bed and an ensuite bathroom." I dropped my towel. A chill skated across my bare skin as I scooped my jeans and sweater off the floor.

"Are you sure?" Hunter's voice cracked as desire flickered to life in his attentive green eyes.

"Very. Besides, I have questions about the WITSEC program. If I'm in your life, then there are things I should probably know. My first question, because I'm nosy, is how your family has money if you were relocated, and your dad had to start all over with a new career. I mean, I'm assuming that you had to change everything about your identity. Next, is Hunter Calloway your real name?" I slipped my arms through the straps of my bra and hooked the front clasp. "We don't need to talk about it yet. I know we have to get to school." Instead of classes today, I wanted him to spin me around and kiss me until I was breathless, then spend the day in bed together. However, I suspected he wanted some distance from his parents.

"No."

I pulled my sweater on, glancing at him. "Hunter isn't your real name?" A pang of sadness clenched my chest. "What is it? I don't need to know your last name ... I just want to know the real you. Hopefully, you can share parts of that with me." I closed the gap between us and captured his hand in mine. A conflicted look painted his face, and an array of different emotions stared into my soul. I pushed up on my tiptoes and pressed my lips to his. "I love you, Hunter. Take your time. We can talk later."

"I love you, baby. I'll answer as many questions as I can, but some I won't be able to." An apology filled his gaze, then he turned his attention to a brown bag on the bed.

"What's that?" I was happy to change the subject as I finished dressing.

Hunter grinned at me. "Something for later." He shoved it into his duffle, then zipped it. "Are you ready?"

"Yeah, I need to grab my purse and cell on the way out. I think they're on the counter."

"They are. I put them there last night before I carried you to my bed." Hunter winked at me.

"Well, I hate to tell you ... but I cannot carry you to mine." I giggled, grateful for the lighter mood. "When we get to my place, we'll toss your bag in my room." Nearly giddy with the idea of waking up with him again, I willed myself not to skip out of his house like a little kid who had just bought her favorite candy.

I'd changed into a pair of light-wash boyfriend jeans and a powder blue sweater, applied some makeup, and brushed the tangles out of my hair before we left my place for the university. I felt more presentable as Hunter and I strolled hand in hand across the campus to our calculus class. The mid-morning sun lighting up the crystal blue sky added to my good mood.

Hunter opened the building door for me, and I wondered if I could focus with him next to me. It had been difficult before we were together, but now I would be using all my willpower to keep my hands off him.

Kane, Remington, Quinn, Anderson, and Vance were chatting in the hallway near our class, so there was no way we would slip by them unnoticed. It didn't seem to bother Hunter, though. If he was ready to tell the world we were together, so was I. A swell of pride warmed me as I gazed at him. Hunter Calloway was mine, and my stomach flip-flopped with a happy dance.

"Dude!" Quinn pointed at Hunter, grinning widely. "Teagan's off the market?" He snickered.

Rolling my eyes, I decided that Hunter could handle his team.

"Damn straight." Hunter slid his arm around my shoulder and pulled me closer. I placed my palm against his chest, feeling his heart beating beneath my touch.

"Kane, you're going to have to find someone else, man. Hunter stole your girl." Quinn slapped Kane on the back, and Kane lightly punched him in the side.

"Nice try, douchebag. Hunter knows I wasn't ever into Teagan." He quickly turned to me, his cheeks flushing. "Not that you're not gorgeous and sweet. I didn't mean it the way it came out."

Hunter chuckled. "It's all good. Quinn's just itching to see a fight. He's been jonesing for a few weeks."

After years of cheering, I was used to the football guys giving each other shit. I laughed, then decided I would duck out of their fun. "I'm going to grab us some seats. Stay and chat with your friends." I kissed his cheek, then strolled into the class.

The hair on the back of my neck bristled, and I glanced around as I rubbed my arms. Students were filing into the room and settling in, but no one looked suspicious or out of place. Nothing appeared to be wrong, and I scolded myself for allowing my head to play tricks on me. Hunter had been safe since he and his family had moved here. There was no reason for me to think anything was off. As much as I tried to talk myself out of my eerie feeling, I couldn't shake it. Instead of my usual spot in the middle, I chose seats near the back. At least from there, I could keep a lookout ... just in case.

Hunter and his friends trickled in and took up the empty chairs around me. I wouldn't admit it, but I felt safer surrounded by a bunch of big, strong guys.

The rest of the day passed without any more weirdness. Maybe it was worth mentioning to Hunter later, but my Spidey-sense had seemed to settle down. I suspected it was the lingering effects of the train-wreck meeting with his mom and the reason that Hunter owned a pistol.

I had agreed to meet Hunter at his building after football practice. Since we had my room for privacy, I wasn't sure why, but seeing the space that housed the society in the daylight would be interesting.

Driving to meet him, the sunset painted the sky with brilliant pink, orange, and blue hues. It would be nice to have a few minutes alone with Hunter after sharing him with his friends all day. I understood how close teammates could be. Gabby, Everlee, Leighton, and I had grown super tight when we started cheering together in middle school. A level of trust was necessary when thrown in the air. I was a flyer, so we relied heavily on the others to keep us safe.

Safe. I wondered how Hunter had felt, constantly looking over his shoulder over the last few years. A chill skated down my spine as I pulled into the parking lot of his building. Maybe the fact he needed a gun had spooked me more than I'd admitted. I chided myself as I spotted his red Porsche and parked next to it, wondering what he had in store for us. I shot him a quick text that I was here, then made my way to the front entrance.

Chapter Thirty-Eight

Hunter

Football practice had been precisely what I needed to help me blow off some steam and clear my head. At one point, I'd hoped to play for the NFL, but that dream had been crushed the moment we'd been placed into the witness protection program. So, when the coach mentioned that two recruiters were visiting and interested in Kane and me, I'd pretended to be thrilled while my heart had plummeted to my toes. It would never happen, and it had been sheer torture, but things had changed in the last few days, and Teagan had become my main priority.

My phone vibrated with Teagan's message that she'd arrived, and a huge grin eased across my face. I'd waited for her in the same room where I'd first fucked her, but I wasn't wearing the priest collar this time. I walked down the hall and met her at the door.

"Hey."

She smiled at me, then pressed a kiss to my lips. "Hey."

I captured her small hand in mine and led her to the conference area where the guys and I would meet and chat about the society. A large table sat in the middle of the grey-carpeted room.

"This is where we all get together and share chicks' names and our concerns. Sometimes the rooms are scheduled in advance, but it's easy to overbook, so scheduling is key." I glanced at her, trying to assess where she was as I showed her the space.

Teagan slowly walked around the table, her fingertips trailing across the smooth wooden surface. "Why are you telling me this?" She looked at me skeptically.

"Because my world is full of secrets, and the more I can tell you, the less I have to hide. I want you next to me, Teagan. And I'm finished with the society. I've asked Kane to step in and run it for me."

Her doe eyes widened. "Kane? He's a part of this?"

"Yeah, he and some other teammates. Can I count on you to not share any of that?"

She nodded her head. "Of course. Honestly, you're the only one that I want to know about. You said you were finished with that part of your life, and I believe you. You haven't given me any reason to doubt you."

I shoved my hands in my pockets, my thoughts shifting to throwing her on the table and fucking her until she trembled beneath me, my name rolling off her cherry-red lips.

"I want to keep it that way. I'm not your average situation where you date and fall in love with some guy. I come with difficult strings attached." I held out my hand for her. "I'll show you the other rooms."

She slipped her palm into mine and peered up at me. "For the record, I think you're worth the risk."

I couldn't stop my grin even if I wanted to. "I want to make sure you continue to feel that way." We stepped into the hall, and I closed the door behind us.

We walked hand-in-hand, then she poked her head into the

different rooms. "This almost looks like a school building with classrooms."

"It was at one time, which worked great for me. When the market is right, and I'm ready to sell, it will go fast since it's versatile." I slipped my arm around her waist and led her to another door.

"How did you get into real estate, or is this the only investment you have?" She snuggled up to my side, and I loved the feel of her body pressing against me.

"I have a few others, but I don't share that with anyone." I looked down at her.

Her big brown eyes latched onto mine. My heart skipped a beat, and right then and there I fell even harder for her.

Her tongue darted over her lower lip. "I understand. I won't say anything."

We reached the next door, and I stopped before I opened it. "My real name is Caleb." I tucked a strand of her soft hair behind her ear.

Surprise registered on her face. "I wouldn't have ever guessed. Would you be upset if I told you that I liked Hunter better?"

I laughed. "No, hell, I even like Hunter better." I cleared my throat. "For your own protection, I'm not going to tell you our last name. It's better that you know us as the Calloway's."

"Even if you did decide to share, you're Hunter Calloway to me, so I don't think learning your last name would change anything."

I turned the doorknob and opened the next door. A gasp slipped from her as I turned on the light and led her inside.

"Holy shit." She glanced around, her hand flying to her mouth.

"Take a look." I leaned against the wall and folded my arms across my chest, ready to enjoy her expressions as she studied the whips, chains, torture rack, and an abundance of sex toys. "A few of the rooms were set up for specific kinks. As you can tell, this one is bondage."

A flicker of curiosity filled her gaze. "What are the others?"

"One room has a cage, and another is designed to be a prison cell."

"Ohhh, for role play?" Teagan removed a whip off the wall and wiggled her brows. "This might be fun, but I'm curious about the cell." She replaced the whip and walked over to me. "What are your kinks, Hunter?" She sucked on her lower lip, and my cock hardened.

I leaned down, my nose brushing against her jaw, then her ear. "I'm about to show you."

Her eyes twinkled with eagerness. I led her out and down the hall to the prison room.

She looked over the tiny space, frowning. "It's small."

"It's supposed to be." I sat in the chair and rubbed my jaw, spotting the locked cabinet on the wall. I wondered how she would feel about my kink once I was finished with her. "Take your clothes off," I ordered.

Teagan responded to my tone and slipped out of her sweater and jeans without a word. I sucked in a breath as she lowered her black G-string down her thighs, revealing her bare pussy. As badly as I wanted to stroke my dick, it would have to wait.

Once Teagan stood in front of me naked, I rose from the creaky chair. Walking over to the cabinet, I reached in my pocket and produced a small key. Unlocking the door, I removed the items I would need. In a few steps, I towered over her, then slipped a blindfold over her eyes. I gently turned her, grabbed her hands, and pinned her arms behind her back, securely tying the ropes.

"Is that tight?" I asked.

"Yeah."

"Good." I led her to the cot and pushed her down. "Enjoy your stay." With that, I left the room and locked her in.

Chapter Thirty-Nine

Hunter

When I had purchased the building, the first place I set up was my office. Cameras were located on each corner, and I could turn them on in each room from an app on my phone. Once it was established, I shared it with the other guys, so they could record their fun. But, if someone was caught breaking the rules and recording someone else's session without permission, the guy was kicked out.

Some of the guys loved a threesome or foursome, especially Quinn. It was one of his kinks, even though he wasn't into men. That's why he had no problem the evening we hooked up with Teagan.

I never allowed the other dudes to watch me with Teagan. Since it was personal and revenge driven, I'd changed the camera code on the room where we always met. I was the only one who had access to start the recording or view the sessions.

Now, I was on the other side, watching Teagan shiver on the sheetless cot. I'd left her nearly an hour ago, and she probably wondered if I was coming back for her. But that was part of the game. She was mine to do whatever I wanted with—*when* I wanted.

After another thirty minutes passed, I decided it was time. I collected the fun little trinket that would disguise my voice, then left the office and slowly walked down the hall. Pausing before I entered the room, I removed my shoes, so she wouldn't hear me walking. I turned the doorknob so slowly it didn't make a noise. My gaze landed on her naked body, curled into a fetal position, trembling. The room was cold, and apparently so was she. My heart skipped a beat as anticipation coursed through my veins. In a few minutes, I would taste her fear, and I almost came just thinking about it.

I didn't bother to shut the door since I knew no one else would be in the building for the rest of the evening.

Before I reached her, I popped open the button on my jeans, then removed them along with my boxer briefs. My cock sprung free, and I slowly stroked it, watching her.

"Is someone there?" Teagan asked, her voice shaking.

I refused to answer her. She would know it was me soon enough, but her mind would question who was touching her.

I collected the lube and the butt plug I'd purchased. Grabbing her by the arm, I yanked her off the bed and bent her over the side of the mattress, her knees pressing into the cold, tile floor.

"Hunter? Is that you?" Anxiety dripped off her words.

Silence was my only response. I'd warned her I was twisted and that I fed on her fear and pain, but she was about to experience it firsthand.

I opened the lube and stared at her perky little ass in the air, calling to me. Digging my fingers into the flesh of her butt, she cried out and attempted to move away.

"Hunter? Is that you? Please say something."

Her pleas fell on deaf ears. I wanted her scared, wondering who was about to fuck her.

My palm smacked her ass cheek. "Silence."

Teagan froze when she heard the disguised voice, her body

tensed, and my cock throbbed like a son of a bitch. I suspected her mind was scrambling to piece together who was here. *Good.*

I separated her legs, realizing that her pussy was slick with her juices. She was turned on, ready for me. The fear of the unknown was a powerful aphrodisiac. I sat down on the cot's edge and squeezed the lube out. Rubbing it on the tip of my cock, I tensed with excitement. Next, I lubed the butt plug, parted her cheeks, and pressed it to her puckered hole.

She sucked in a breath, then I worked it inside her until it was securely in place. I picked her up off the floor and placed her face-first on the mattress. She turned her head, sucking in air. I gripped her hips and shoved my cock into her pussy without any warning. Jesus, she was tight, especially with the plug.

Teagan whimpered as I fucked her fast and hard, her slick walls clenching around my shaft. I reached around her waist, pinched her clit, then massaged it. I repeated the pain and pleasure over and over. Her cries nearly made me lose my shit. I pulled out of her, then knelt. Spreading her apart, I sucked on her bundle of nerves, nipping at her sensitive flesh. She squirmed, breathing in short, heavy pants. Her sweet juices ran down her thighs as I continued to devour her. Unable to take anymore, I rose, removed the plug from her asshole, and tossed it on the cot. I re-lubed my cock, then slid into her tight little hole.

"Oh, God," she whimpered as I moved inside her.

I turned off the voice disguiser. "Are you my dirty little slut?"

Her body visibly relaxed when she heard it was me.

"Yes," she whispered.

"Even though you weren't sure it was me, your cunt was so wet. Would you let a stranger lick your pussy while I watched?'

A muffled yes reached my ears.

"You confessed that you had a threesome with your ex and his cousin. One fucking your cunt and the other your ass. Do you want it again? Huh? Are you my dirty little whore?" I pumped inside her, watching her asshole take every inch of my dick. Jesus, this was hot as hell.

She bucked against me, nearly sending me over the edge. "Did you suck both of their cocks?" I smacked her butt cheek. "Tell me your sin."

She grunted with my thrusts. "They took turns eating my pussy while the other watched, then my ex fucked me while I sucked his cousin's dick." Moans of pleasure escaped her while I rubbed her clit.

Her body trembled, her orgasm rippling through her as she screamed my name. I slammed into her, then emptied my seed inside her.

"If anyone touches you again without my permission, I'll kill them." My tone was almost cruel as I pulled out of her.

Teagan collapsed on the bed, panting.

I untied her wrists, and she struggled to move her arms as I tugged the blindfold off. "I'm guessing your arms are asleep?"

"Yeah. And Hunter?" She rolled over onto her back, her eyes searching my face. "That was fucked up on a lot of levels."

Chapter Forty

Teagan

My arms flopped to my sides, and I wiggled my fingers attempting to regain feeling in my limbs. Hunter sat on the edge of the mattress and pulled me into his lap. He possessively pressed his mouth to mine.

"I told you I was twisted." He smoothed the stray hairs from my cheek, his expression serious.

"At first, I was terrified one of the other guys had found me ..." I hung my head. Hunter's touch trailed up my spine, then he began to massage my aching neck. "That feels good." I closed my eyes, allowing him to soothe the ache he'd caused, the fear and pain that he'd enjoyed and gotten off on.

"I know. The scenario is set up for a rape. The girl has no idea who is touching her, hurting her." Hunter pressed a kiss to my temple. "*Owning* her. She's simply a vessel used for his pleasure any way he wants to take it."

"That's twisted ... but it was also hot as hell. I kept telling myself it was you, but when I heard the disguised voice, I had no way of knowing for sure. Then, I remembered you saying no one else would touch me unless you allowed it. I had to trust you and play along."

Hunter's wicked smile slipped into place. "You did well." He wrapped his fingers around my neck and tightened his hold. "Just remember, I will *always* take care of you."

The sharp bite in his tone should have scared the shit out of me. I'd met Hunter as the King Cobra, and I knew there was a dark and depraved side to him, so I shouldn't have been surprised. But I was, and he had definitely tested my limits.

Hunter released me, then he stretched out on the cot and motioned for me to join him. He slipped his arm around my shoulder, and I snuggled up to him, welcoming the warmth of his muscular body.

"Something broke inside me when I watched Levi die, Teagan. Granted, you're the first girl that made me feel anything real again, but a part of me will never be the gentleman you're hoping for. Not in the bedroom anyway."

I peered up at him. "People have many layers, Hunter. All I want is you. Treat me right and I'll be your dirty little slut in the bedroom any time you want."

Hunter's intense gaze met mine. "I will always protect and take care of you, Teagan. I meant it when I said that I love you. I'm willing to walk away from my parents for you. But before our relationship progressed, I needed to share this side of me. I had to know if you could accept it or not."

Relief and understanding melted my fear of him becoming a complete monster. Over the last few days, I'd seen his genuine kindness, and I didn't want to lose touch with that part of him. It was the piece I'd fallen in love with. I was a little afraid to admit it, but I was drawn to the other side of him. It was thrilling and wrong, but his darkness recognized mine and we fell into a beautifully twisted place together.

Hunter was also full of surprises. My mind was still reeling from the anxiety, but my body had surrendered to him and loved every second of it. At first, I thought I was being raped, and raw adrenaline pumped through my veins. There was no denying that the fear had heightened the sex, and I wanted more.

"What are you thinking?" He smoothed my hair, waiting for my reply.

"That you're a complex man. I have a feeling you don't allow many people to see these shades of you." I listened as his heart thumped against his chest.

"Only you."

My brows shot up. Was I really the only person with whom he felt safe enough to share this with? I kissed his jawline. "Thank you."

A comfortable silence filled the room, then Hunter shifted and rolled over on his side. He propped his head on his hand, staring at me. I turned as well, facing him.

"You asked about our money, and you're right. When a person or family enters WITSEC, everything is left behind—careers, friends, homes ... everything. Since I was under eighteen, I had no choice but to align myself with my parents and the changes. I'd seen what those men could do, and hiding was our only option after ..."

I stroked his cheek with my fingertips. "Take your time, baby. We've got all night."

Hunter kissed me gently, a complete contrast from the rough sex we'd just had.

"Right before Dad testified in court against some powerful men in the mafia, Levi was killed. They were trying to silence him. Dad had been working for them and slowly leaking information to the FBI. During that time, Dad made several investments and began moving his funds to offshore accounts, ensuring our financial future. He said he could see the writing on the wall."

"What did your dad do in his old life?"

Hunter swallowed. "He was a very successful surgeon. One evening when he was on his way to his car after a long day, he was taken hostage. Some guy had been shot, and they demanded that Dad help. It's how he was sucked into the mafia."

"Oh shit. That had to have been terrifying! Was this in Texas? I mean I'm assuming that's where you're from, since ... that's where we first met."

"Yup. And I don't miss it one bit. The heat was a bitch, but the pressure to perform on the football field was worse. Texas takes their football seriously." He offered me a sad smile. "At the same time, it made me who I am today. Those coaches shaped my life. Unfortunately, I won't ever have a future on the field."

I sat up, shaking my head. "Hunter, scouts will be here soon. What are you going to do when they want to plaster your face all over the local papers and internet?" Dread twisted my stomach in knots.

"I'll have to be sick that day, or something else that won't raise suspicion. It had always been the plan to play ball, but I'll never have a career." A wistful, faraway look twisted his expression.

"I'm so sorry. It's not fair that you can't have the one thing you want." Tears pricked my eyes, and I looked away.

Hunter sat up, gripped my chin, and forced me to look at him. "*You* are my future, Teagan. As long as you're next to me, I have everything I need. I love you."

"I love you too ... Caleb." Goosebumps danced across my arms with the use of his real name.

He placed his lips on mine, dominating my mouth. Hunter finally pulled away, leaving me breathless and my lips nearly bruised from his kisses. "We should clean up, then let's go to your place. I suspect if your roomies are there, they will want a few minutes alone to ask questions once they find out I'm with you." He stroked my cheek with the pad of his thumb, and I leaned into his touch.

"Yeah, but they'll like having you around." I took his hand and kissed his palm. "I'm guessing you have a shower here?"

Hunter grinned. "Several, but I have one in my office." Mischief sparkled in his green eyes. "Sounds like you've been rather naughty today and might need to visit the principal's office for your punishment."

I hopped off the bed, grabbed my clothes, and darted for the door.

"You have to catch me first." My giggles echoed through the hall as I ran, naked. Hunter's laugh drowned out mine as he closed in on me. With one quick move, he wrapped his arm around my waist and pulled me toward him. Grinning, he bent, then scooped me into his powerful arms. I leaned my head against his shoulder, still laughing as he carried me to his office, then closed and locked the door.

Chapter Forty-One

Teagan

By the time Hunter bent me over the desk in his office, then spanked me, I was deliciously sore and thoroughly fucked. It had been a long time since I'd had sex on a regular basis, and my pussy ached.

After we cleaned up, he followed me to my place, and I blasted my stereo on high, dancing in my seat as "I'm Not a Woman, I'm a God" by Halsey played. Fifteen minutes later, I pulled into my driveway, watching in my rearview mirror as Hunter parked behind me. I waited in my R8 as he climbed out and gathered his duffle and I grabbed my purse and phone. Fat raindrops fell from the dark sky, and I squealed as he opened my door and the rain smacked my skin. Hunter's chuckle rumbled through his chest and warmed my heart as he reached for me. I placed my palm in his, grinning like a lovesick puppy. I was, and I wasn't ashamed to admit that I was also dick whipped.

Hunter closed my car door, and we ran through the downpour to the covered entrance of the house. I kissed him, then pointed my key fob at my vehicle and locked it.

"Are you ready for a million questions from the girls?" I wiped the moisture off my face with my sleeve, removing the strands of hair that had plastered themselves against my damp skin.

"Yup. Let's do this." Hunter squeezed my fingers, then I opened the door, and we strode into the house.

Everlee, Leighton, and Gabby were planted on the couch, glued to a movie that I didn't recognize. Everlee was the first to realize that I wasn't alone.

Her mouth formed a round 'O' as she noted our linked hands and his bag. "Hunter, right?"

"Yeah, and you're, Everlee? Did I get it right?" Hunter flashed her a panty-dropping smile, and I stifled my giggle as she nearly melted into the couch cushion. At least leather was easy to clean up.

Leighton eyed me and set her bowl of popcorn on the table, facing us. "The star of Saturday's game is holding one of my best friend's hands. This is unexpected." She grinned, letting him know she was playing with him.

Gabby draped her bare legs over the arm of the recliner. She loved to run around in an oversized hoodie and shorts with wool socks on her feet. She popped a few kernels in her mouth, crunching loudly. "A hell of a game by the way." She nodded, offering her approval.

Although I'd talked to Gabrielle about the society and some of my experience, I never revealed any names. Since she hadn't seen Hunter, there was no way that she could identify him anyway. For whatever reason, I felt protective of the guys' identities even though Hunter had confided in me who some of them were.

"Well, I guess no introductions are necessary. Everyone knows who you are." I smiled.

"It's good to see everyone." Hunter gave them all a small wave.

I patted Hunter's shoulder. "Hunter will be staying with me for a while, so don't run around the house naked."

"Noted." Gabby grinned, looking him up and down. "Good job, Teagan."

I rolled my eyes, even though I thought their ogling was funny. "He's not a piece of meat, ladies."

Laughter filled the house, and my chest warmed with happiness. Almost everyone that I cared about was here. I wasn't sure how it would play out with Ari and Jagger, but hopefully that would fall into place once they realized that Hunter and I were together.

"I'll show you around."

Everlee winked at me as I led him to the kitchen, then upstairs. I pointed at the girl's rooms as we passed them, then opened my door. "I share a wall with Everlee, and as you can tell she's not timid and speaks her mind, so we'll have to be quiet." I grinned as I slipped my purse off my shoulder and placed it on my desk. Hunter set his bag down in a corner, then wrapped his arms around me. I pushed up on my tiptoes and kissed him.

"Are you sure the girls won't mind me crashing here for a bit?" he asked against my lips.

"Nah, it's not the first time we've had a guy stay here." Hunter shot me a quizzical look. "It was Gabby's cousin." I giggled.

My cell phone chirped in my handbag, and I released Hunter and removed it from my purse. I glanced at Hunter, my stomach dipping to my toes. "It's my dad."

I tapped the answer icon on the screen, then greeted my father.

"Hey, how's my favorite guy?" I asked, eyeing Hunter while he stretched out on my bed.

"Good. How's your week going so far?"

"Wet." I laughed, realizing I was referring to both my crotch and the weather.

"Nothing like a Portland area fall and winter, huh?"

I pulled the chair out at my desk and sat down. "How's Mom?"

"She's making some great progress, honey. We'll be starting the trip home tomorrow, and I've already set up her care in Spokane. I also wanted to let you know that her current medication makes her ...

flat. She's not quite herself, but the doctors will continue to adjust the dosage and change the medication if needed."

"Flat? Like, does she just stare into space?" I twirled a strand of hair around my finger, trying to imagine my mother as a dull person. Regardless of what she did or who she was around, she'd always had a zest for life. Every mood she had was full of passion. I focused on the floor, wondering if it had been the bipolar all this time.

"Her moods are level, there aren't the highs and lows, but she's expressed that she feels strange and uninterested in painting or traveling."

I pursed my lips together, realizing that just because Mom had a diagnosis and medication didn't mean this was over. It was just beginning, and my heart ached. "How are you handling it, Dad? I can't imagine how difficult it is for you."

"It's ... different. I'm not sure I like it, but we sure as hell can't return to the way things were. I have to trust the doctors." He released a soft sigh. "She did say that she hopes you'll be home for Thanksgiving."

I glanced at Hunter who appeared to be resting or pondering life. I couldn't tell which. "Can I bring someone with me?"

One green eye peered at me, and Hunter grinned.

"I understand if not. Mom's going through a lot of changes."

"Who is he?" Dad asked without missing a beat.

I couldn't stop the silly smile that spread across my face. "His name is Hunter Calloway and he's our running back." Inwardly, I groaned with how I had introduced Hunter. He was so much more than a label.

"I would love to meet him. Let me see how your mom is doing in a few weeks, then we can discuss it. It would be nice to have some company, and I think it would do her a world of good. Hunter and I can watch ball while the two of you reconnect."

"That sounds really good, Dad. I miss you both."

"We miss you too. I'll call you after we're home."

"Drive safe and give Mom a kiss for me."

"Will do."

I disconnected the call and placed my phone on my desk. "I guess that was my strange way of seeing if you're interested in meeting my family over Thanksgiving. There's no pressure, and you don't have to. Mom and Dad still need to talk about it but ..."

Hunter scooted to the edge of the bed and grabbed my wrist, pulling me on top of him. I laughed, making sure I didn't accidentally knee him in the nuts.

"If it works out, I would love to. I know your mom is dealing with a lot. Regardless if I'm able to be there, you need to go. I don't want you to stay here on my account." Hunter's expression turned serious.

My good mood fizzled out faster than a dud firecracker, and my smile melted away. "Hey, we still have three weeks, so don't look sad. I'm sure it will all work out." Hunter kissed the tip of my nose, then I snuggled against his chest, finding comfort in his arms.

A soft knock came through my door, and I hopped off my boyfriend and answered it.

"Hey, some man is here for Hunter. He says he's your father." Gabby nodded to the front door. "I let him in since it was pouring outside. I hope that was okay?"

"Thanks. Can you let him know Hunter will be down in a minute?"

"Yup." Gabby bounced off, smiling.

I poked my head into the hall, watching her. She seemed awfully happy. I would have to investigate soon.

Chapter Forty-Two

Hunter

I wasn't surprised that my father had tracked me down. All my friends knew that Teagan and I were together, so when Dad started asking around, it would have been easy enough to find me. But why? After the way he'd treated me, why did he want to talk unless he was going to try to make me come back to the manor. That wasn't going to happen. If they couldn't support my relationship with Teagan, then that was their choice, but me not living with them was mine.

I made my way downstairs behind Teagan, focusing on her gorgeous ass. My mind drifted to our earlier sexfest, and my cock strained against my jeans. I tore my attention away and stared at my father. He looked out of place in his black suit. He adjusted his tie when he spotted me.

"Hi, Mr. Calloway," Teagan said.

"You must be Teagan." Dad extended his hand, and she shook it.

"Yes, it's nice to meet you. If you and Hunter need to talk, you're welcome to use my room. It will offer you the most privacy."

"I appreciate it, but I was hoping to take my son out for dinner."

I hesitated, wondering what he was up to. Standing nearly toe to toe with him, I slipped my arm around my girlfriend, my actions speaking loud and clear.

"Son?" Dad asked.

I glanced at Teagan. "Do we have plans?"

"Nope. Go spend some time with your dad."

I nodded, then gave her a chaste kiss on the mouth. "I'll be back in a little while."

"Have a nice time." She gave me a concerned look after my father turned away from us.

I bent down, then whispered, "I love you. I'll see you soon. Once I know where he's taking me, I'll text to see if you want something to eat." I smiled, my way of reassuring her that however this played out, everything would be all right.

Once Dad and I were outside, I realized his car was running.

"Too damned cold to turn it off for only a few minutes." He quickly walked to the car, and I followed him. Even though he was acting normal, there was something off. I could feel it in my gut. The best thing for me to do, though ... wait it out. Watch his moves and stay alert. All of the same things he'd taught me when we'd entered the WITSEC program and moved.

I climbed into his navy Jaguar, appreciating the heated seats as soon as my ass touched the leather. Once we were buckled in and out of ear shot from Teagan and her friends, I turned toward him. "What do you want?" My tone wasn't hateful or accusatory, but I wanted to cut the unnecessary bullshit.

Dad shifted into reverse and backed out of the driveway. His attention landed on me, and he swallowed. "Your mother wants a divorce."

His words punched me in the gut. "What? Why?"

Dad eased down the road, shaking his head. "Your mother has grown increasingly unhappy over the last several years. I think after we lost Levi ..."

"I'm sure she's just pissed off at me. I ruffled her feathers when I stood up to her. But seriously, she had no right to treat Teagan like a whore. I had to shut it down. Teagan is ... I'm in love with her. And anyone that can't accept that ... I don't know what to say. I won't tolerate her being disrespected because Mom is terrified of losing me." Pride swelled inside my chest. Not only had I stood up to my parents, but I'd laid out the details of how it was with Teagan. I wasn't asking their permission, and my relationship wasn't up for negotiation.

We pulled into the parking lot of a Mexican restaurant and Dad eased into a vacant space. He turned off the engine and climbed out of the car.

"Let's talk once we're seated. By the looks of it, they're not busy, so we should be able to have some privacy."

Five minutes later, Dad settled into his chair and stretched his legs in front of him. He ordered a beer for each of us, then turned to me again. "It seems as though you've made your choice concerning Teagan."

"I have." I grabbed the water the server had placed in front of me and took a drink.

"I'll talk to your mother later. She's spending her time at the women's shelter this evening. I think it's good for her when she's helping others. I assume she feels less helpless herself. Losing a child ..."

"I know, Dad. We all lost Levi. I had a front row seat to that shit show in fact." Levi's bloodied face flickered through my mind's eye, and I inwardly cringed. "You don't have to continue reminding me."

Dad rubbed his thumb along his water glass, the condensation dripping onto the top of the table. "Son, there are some things that I need to tell you."

My heart stuttered, skipping a beat. "Okay?"

Dad glanced around the restaurant, then leaned forward and cleared his throat. "When we lived in Dallas, your mom had a job she loved."

"Yeah, she was an executive assistant for the vice-president of Halec Corp., right?" I'd been little when she had started that job, but she stayed there until we had to move.

"Yeah. It was good for her, but then her boss left, and she gained a new one. Things really took a turn."

I frowned. "What do you mean?"

"Her new boss was dirty, Hunter. She got tangled up in some ... money laundering."

My brows shot up. "Mom?" That woman volunteered at an abused women's shelter. How in the hell had she gotten mixed up in something illegal?

"Yeah. Once she realized what was happening and what her part was, she was in too deep. After a few years, she finally confided in me what was happening. She'd been terrified that the mafia would come for her if she tried to leave."

"Mafia. You mean *both* of you were involved with them? I don't understand." I massaged the back of my neck, trying to fit the pieces together.

"Your mother was in grave danger. We all were, son. She got sucked into a fucked-up situation." He released a soft sigh, then he continued. "I began to move our funds overseas and saving every-thing we could. I realized that at some point, we were going to have to run. More than anything, I wanted to keep my family safe." He cleared his throat, his gaze full of regret and pain. "I told your mom to set up a meeting with her boss and explain that I was a surgeon, and I would work for them in exchange for our safety. All I was doing was buying us time, but I had to try. If anything had happened to your mom ..." Dad's eyes glistened, and he wiped them. "Before I performed my first surgery for the mafia, I'd reached out to the FBI, and they promised to move us into the protection program, but they wanted information first. During the time I worked for them, the FBI planned everything. We would move, change our names, and start a new life free from the criminal world as soon as I gave them what they wanted."

"And we did." I wanted to reassure Dad that he had done everything he possibly could to take care of us.

"One of the guys that always picked me up for surgeries found out I was working with the FBI. We never realized what was happening, they just went after you and Levi."

"Shit." My hands fell to my lap as I looked out the window. "That's why we moved the next day?"

"Yeah. Their message was loud and clear. It was time that we went into hiding. I know the first year was rough and everyone was scared when we stepped out of the protection program and moved to Oregon, but it's worked out so far."

"Why are you telling me this now?" My fingers drummed against my thigh, an uneasy feeling coursing through me.

"Because your mom blames herself for what happened to you boys, and I don't think she can live with it anymore. Every time she sees us ... we're a constant reminder of what she's lost and why."

Propping my elbows on the table, I blew out a sigh. It made a lot more sense. Mom's constant fear of losing me, not wanting Teagan around, refusing to let me move on with my life. She lived in constant turmoil. If she were at a breaking point, then I could understand why she wanted to leave. Mom was running from the pain. I understood that all too well.

"What can I do to help?" Nothing in the world could have prepared me for the words that were about to come out of my father's mouth. Since Teagan had forgiven me for almost screwing up with the society, I thought the bad shit was behind me. I was so fucking wrong.

Chapter Forty-Three

Hunter

My father's next words sucker punched me in the face.

"I wanted to talk to you about it first, but if your mother will stay with me, then I think a move overseas would be best. She could use a fresh start, and so could I. Even though it's been almost four years, I'm constantly looking over my shoulder. It's no way for us to live. She deserves better. So do you."

I gawked at Dad, words escaping me. "Europe?" Normally, I could just fly over anytime I wanted to see them, but the more I traveled openly the greater the risk of being found. Plus …Teagan.

"I know it's a big surprise, son, and I'm sorry. If she agrees, I think it would be a good idea for you to join us."

I stared at him as though he had three heads. Why hadn't we done this sooner? Maybe there were rules in the protection program that I wasn't aware of, but Europe? I'd rebuilt my life here. How could he ask me to leave?

I tugged on my shirt collar, frowning. "If I stay, will I have access to my money, or will I need to get a job before I finish school?"

Dad shifted in his chair. "I'll continue to pay for your college and housing. If you stay, then you need to realize that your football career is on a college field. You'll never have your dream. If we're in Europe, you can play professionally without a lot of notoriety, unlike the NFL."

My spine went rigid, and my frown deepened. "Football has been my life focus, and it gave me something to hold onto after we lost Levi." I steepled my fingers together, trying to sort out my feelings about the situation. "We both know that one injury could end any professional career *if* I was good enough to get drafted in the first place."

"True, that's why I want you to finish your education. A backup plan is essential."

Dad was interrupted as our server took our order, dropped off our beers, then disappeared again. "Hunter, think about it. I'll be speaking to your mom this evening. Imagine what it would be like to have a future on the field and play professionally or to settle down, get married, and have a family if that's what you want. You can have it all. It's at your fingertips."

There was one possibility Dad hadn't mentioned. "And what if Mom says no?"

He cleared his throat. "Regardless, if she wants to stay or file for divorce I'll still be moving overseas. You should come with me."

Shit! Dad wasn't playing. He wanted a new life just as much as it sounded like Mom did. But was the future he was dangling in front of me worth losing the life I had here?

The server brought our plates, and my stomach churned. Realizing that my world was about to drastically change, my appetite disappeared.

Dad lightened the conversation and we chatted about ball, play-offs, and school. I'd been slow to pick a major, but I would complete my basic classes by next spring. I had to get my ass in gear and make up my mind. Unfortunately, it was difficult because I loved football. It had always been my first love, and the possibility that I might be able to play professionally, even if it wasn't for a team in the States, was appealing as hell.

Dad dropped me off a few hours later with a promise to call me after he and Mom talked. I texted Teagan that I was on my way. Since I didn't have a key, I would need someone to let me in.

Thoughts of Dad's offer were on repeat in my head, and I felt like a dog chasing its damn tail. I'd sifted through multiple scenarios, but each time, the outcome sucked. Plus, if I left the Society, or stepped away as its leader, well, there were rules in place to make sure I would give up full control. I wasn't sure that I wanted to say goodbye to all my hard work. What if Teagan and I didn't make it? Our relationship was so new ... I realized that I wasn't interested in participating in the society as long as we were together but giving up ownership was a completely different scenario.

A gust of wind brushed across the back of my neck as I hurried to the front door. Teagan was waiting for me with a big smile on her face. All I wanted to do was kiss her until she was breathless.

"Hey, how was your evening?" Teagan held out her hand for my coat.

"Interesting." I leaned down and kissed her. I wasn't ready to talk to her about the possible move yet. Not until Dad had an answer from Mom. Either way, I had to decide in a few weeks so Dad could make arrangements. I wished that Dad had been able to not have this conversation with me until after the playoffs, but he couldn't control Mom.

"Yeah? Is that good or bad?" Teagan took my hand and led me to the couch where we sat down.

"Where are the roomies?" I leaned my head back, stretching my neck. It popped several times, and I relaxed a bit.

Teagan gave me a quizzical look, and I assumed it was because I'd dodged her question concerning my evening. "Leighton is upstairs studying with Gabby. Everlee isn't home."

"Everlee is a bit on the chatty side, huh?" I grinned so Teagan would understand that I wasn't being an asshole about it.

"Oh, you should hear her when she's excited." Teagan's giggle floated through the living room.

"Speaking of ..." I grabbed Teagan around the waist and pulled her onto my lap. She straddled me and I lifted my hips up, pressing my erection into her. I desperately needed a distraction, and there was no one better than my girlfriend.

Teagan cupped my cheeks and kissed me, rubbing her pussy against me. I nibbled at her bottom lip, then thrust my tongue inside her mouth, tasting and taking from her. I broke the kiss, then tucked her hair behind her ear. "I have something upstairs for you."

Excitement flashed in her brown eyes, and she crawled off me. "Yeah? Is it fun?"

"Guess you'll just have to find out." I stood and held my hand out to her.

She giggled as I led her upstairs to her room. Teagan closed and locked the door behind us. I strolled over to my duffle, knelt, then unzipped it. Collecting the package, I walked over to her desk chair. Before I sat down, I flipped open the button on my jeans and lowered my zipper. I freed my hard cock, then sat down. I placed the box on the desk.

"Be a good girl and take off your clothes for me."

Teagan's gaze fell on my erection, and she licked her lips.

"We have to be quiet," she reminded me.

"Noted." I watched her remove her sweater and bra. She took it nice and slow, teasing me. Her fingertips ran between her breasts and down her stomach. Teagan shimmied out of her jeans, leaving her pink lace thong in place. If she didn't get rid of it soon, I would tear it off her with my teeth. Jesus, she was hot. I palmed my dick and stroked it.

"Come here." I practically growled at her.

Without hesitation, she moved closer. I lifted one leg and placed it on the chair next to me. She frowned, not clear on what I was doing yet. "Stand on the chair."

The corner of her mouth kicked up in an almost smile as she planted a foot on the outside of my thighs. Since the chair was sturdy and had no wheels, it would work perfectly.

I glanced up, my nose grazing the fabric of her thong, her scent causing me to moan. Her gasp filled the room as I moved the material to the side and nipped her clit. Sucking her bundle of nerves, I grabbed her hips, tilted my head back, and brought her pussy to my mouth. Her juices soaked my tongue and my cock throbbed.

Peering up at her, I watched her tits move up and down with her panted breaths. I could look at her this way forever. Licking and sucking her until her body trembled, I dug my fingers into her thighs. I suspected she would have bruises the following day, but it didn't slow her down any. She thrived on pain as much as I did.

Her mouth parted as she looked down at me, then she tensed and shook as she released. Her cheeks flushed with her orgasm and her legs wobbled as she came down from her high. I helped her off the seat, then pushed her to her knees and tipped up her chin.

"Who owns you?" I stroked my dick and fisted her hair with my free hand.

"You do."

I rubbed my cock against her lips, smearing my pre-cum on her. "And what if I want to share you?"

Chapter Forty-Four

Hunter

Her brows shot up. "Guess we would have to discuss it." We'd had a conversation about a threesome, but if I left, then I should entertain the idea ... or try. Threesomes and orgies were common in the society, but I couldn't wrap my brain around the idea of sharing the girl that I was in love with. Not even close.

"Suck my cock, my dirty little slut." I inhaled sharply as she slid my shaft into her hot, wet mouth and raked her teeth over me. Teagan's saliva slicked me up, and I shoved her head down, hitting the back of her throat. I thrust my hips, gagging her. Her eyes watered as she struggled to breathe. She was so beautiful, and I wondered if I could live without dominating my girl. Watching her struggle sent me over the edge, and I exploded inside her mouth. Dammit, I'd meant to last longer, but the evening wasn't over yet.

I pulled back and she grabbed her throat, coughing as she nearly collapsed to the floor. Kneeling next to her, I helped her up and wiped the tears from her face.

"Fuck, Hunter. I was about to pass out." She picked up the water bottle on her desk and gulped it greedily, her voice slightly hoarse.

"Eventually you will." I smoothed her hair. "At some point I will fuck and choke you until your world turns black."

She set her drink down while she focused on me. "And what's my reward?"

Ah, she was learning. I glanced at the package, then sat on the chair again. "Bend over." I patted my legs, and she eyed me warily. She didn't argue as she positioned herself over my thighs. I gave her ass a firm slap and chuckled. "You're going to get me hard again."

"Good."

I reached for the box, then opened it, removing a nice-sized butt plug. This time she would have to leave it in for as long as I told her to. A small tube of strawberry flavored lube was also in the box, and I prepared the plug for her. I spread her ass cheeks apart, and she peered up at me, anticipation in her lust-filled gaze.

She moaned as I worked the toy in her ass.

"You're hot as fuck right now. I almost wish some dude was eating your pussy while I put it in." I touched her soaked slit. "Oh yeah, you like that idea." I licked her juices off my fingers and my cock stirred. "Stand up."

She wiggled around, then stood. I assumed she was trying to adjust to the plug. I rose, then grabbed my phone.

"Bend over the desk and spread your ass cheeks."

She stared at me like I'd lost my mind.

"It's no different than you over my lap, Teagan."

"The phone is." She glared at the cell I was holding.

"Don't worry. We'll view the video together, but when you're not around, I want something to watch." I quirked my brow at her, daring her to argue.

"Then I need videos of you jerking off." She walked over to me, dropped to her knees, and pulled my jeans down a little more, allowing her better access.

She shoved my dick in her mouth again and sucked fast and hard.

My attention flew out the window as she ran her hand the length of me, her mouth working as she did. To my surprise, she stopped and rose. "Deal?"

I wasn't sure which side of Teagan I liked best ... her obedient one or the one that challenged me in return.

"I'll give you any videos you want." I flashed her a mischievous grin.

"With your face in them."

I chuckled. "Fine." She played the game well. There was no doubt that we were a great match in the bedroom.

Teagan did as I ordered, and I started the recording on my phone. My dick was begging to be in her pussy, but it would have to wait for a minute. I closed the gap between us and rubbed her clit, bringing the phone closer.

"This will go well with the collection I have of us as the King Cobra." I chuckled, recalling coming all over her face and ordering her not to wash it off. At the time, I wanted to humiliate her. Now, I was in deep. Maybe too deep.

I rubbed my dick over her, then shoved inside. She gasped and gripped the desk so she wouldn't hit her head against the wall. Moving in and out of her soaked pussy, I recorded her hungry little cunt taking every inch of me. With the butt plug in her ass, it made her slick walls tighter, and I groaned as I continued.

"Hunter," she gasped. "God, that feels good. Fuck me, baby."

Her core clenched my shaft, and I could feel that she was on the precipice of coming. Our bodies slapped together, the heavy scent of sex in the air.

"Come for me, Teagan." I slammed into her, nearly dropping my phone.

Her strangled moan escaped her as she grunted and stilled, her pussy so tight around me I couldn't hold on any longer. My balls tightened, and I slammed my eyes closed as I shot my come deep inside her.

She collapsed against the desk, and I eased out of her.

"Turn around, my dirty slut."

Teagan peeked over her shoulder and spotted the phone. I was still recording, and I needed one more thing. Curiosity flickered in her gaze as she looked at me.

"Get on your knees and lick me clean."

She knelt. Her tongue ran the length of me as she did what I asked. When she was finished, I stopped the video and tossed it on the bed. Pulling her up, I kissed her, tasting her juices on her mouth. Jesus, she was hot. Addictive.

"Did you enjoy that?" she asked.

"More than you'll ever know." I kissed the tip of her nose.

"Don't forget to take the butt plug out." She looked at me expectantly.

"Oh, I won't. It stays in until I decide to remove it. Probably tomorrow night." I smirked at her before I collected my phone, then headed to the bathroom.

"Um, excuse me?"

I laughed as I closed the door on her. My cell buzzed in my hand, and I glanced at my father's name as it lit up my screen. The fun was officially over.

Chapter Forty-Five

Teagan

Hunter thought he was getting one over on me with the butt plug, but I didn't have the heart to tell him that my ex-boyfriend made Hunter almost seem angelic in the bedroom. Maybe eventually I would share that with him, but I was enjoying creating new memories with Hunter. I just hoped he wouldn't hurt me like my ex had.

I would give Hunter major kudos for creativity, though. When he blindfolded me and left me naked for hours, then arrived in the room again, it had spooked me. Normally, Hunter wore cologne, but that day he hadn't, and I was terrified until I recognized his touch.

I searched my dresser and found my pajamas, waiting for Hunter to finish in the bathroom so I could clean up. His come was dripping down the inside of my thighs, and I had no intention of falling asleep that way.

His muffled voice escaped the bathroom, and it took me a minute to realize he was on the phone. I was a bit shocked that he would take a call there, but we were short on space and privacy.

A minute later, Hunter returned, but he no longer seemed as happy as he had a few minutes ago.

My heart took off in a sprint as his green eyes landed on me, regret and fear flashing in them.

"Hunter? What's wrong?" I walked across the room, still naked.

"Go get cleaned up, then I'll tell you. I need a minute." He kissed the top of my head, then I stared at him as he left the room. My stomach dropped to my toes as if I were on a wild roller coaster. Some days it felt as though I was. Between Mom and working things out with Hunter, I never knew when those dips and hills would appear.

I closed and locked the bathroom door. Turning on the shower, I waited for the hot water to reach the perfect temperature. Different scenarios played through my mind as I washed my hair and soaped up my body. It was difficult to ignore the plug, but I managed. Once I was clean, I turned off the water and toweled off. I dressed in my pajamas, then entered my room. Hunter was sitting on the edge of my bed, staring at the floor.

He looked up at me, and my chest tightened. Hunter patted the bed, and I joined him. He took my hand in his and blew out a big breath.

"I love you, Teagan. I love everything about you. Your heart, your mind ... it's almost like you were made for me."

"I love you too." I placed a kiss on his knuckles.

"There's no way to say this, so I'll just get it over with. Mom and Dad are moving."

My face fell, his words registering quickly. "Where?"

"Europe." His lips pursed and a pained expression flickered across his features. "They want me to move with them, so I can have a chance at playing professional ball. We won't have to look over our shoulders anymore, and it would be a fresh start."

As hard as I tried not to, my body betrayed me and began to tremble. "You're leaving?" I asked, my voice cracking. I released his hand and looked away. I knew what we had was too good to be true. Somewhere deep inside, I understood that his past would catch up and rip Hunter away.

"I don't know, Teagan. It would be amazing to not have to worry if the mafia had caught up with us. What if something happened again? What if they killed the rest of my family? I'm tired of hiding."

"I would be, too." I squeezed his leg, trying my hardest to support him. It would be unfair of me to ask him to stay. We'd only been together a few weeks, and there was no guarantee we would last, or that he wouldn't eventually relocate again.

"You should go, Hunter. You've already lost so much."

Hunter pinned me with an intense stare. "I'm so tired of looking over my shoulder."

Tears clouded my vision as my heart jumped to my throat. "When will you leave?"

"If I go, then after Thanksgiving, so December."

I wanted to beg him to stay, but in my heart I couldn't. If he was mine, then he would find a way to stay with me.

My phone trilled with an incoming call, and I was grateful for the distraction. It was Dad. I excused myself from the room, walked down the hall, then answered the call.

"Hey, Dad. How are you doing?" I leaned against the wall, tears streaming down my cheeks.

"We're doing well, honey. How are you? You sound a little sad."

Before Dad had to babysit Mom all the time, he could always tell when something was wrong with me.

"I think Hunter is moving. I'll be all right." I really wouldn't be, but I couldn't tell Dad that. He had enough to manage with Mom.

"Well, that's why I was calling actually. Your mom and I thought it would be a great idea to have him come home with you for Thanksgiving, but I guess that won't work." Disappointment clung to Dad's words.

"If he moves, it won't be until after the holiday. I'll ask him." I chewed on my thumbnail, trying to hold my shit together when I was shattering into a million pieces inside at the mere thought that he would leave.

"All right, honey. Just let me know. Your mom is looking forward to spending time with you either way."

"How is she?" I hoped like hell the meds were helping.

"Better. We're seeing some progress. She still isn't crazy about the meds and the side effects, but she's willing to work with the doctors. She's also in therapy … well, we both are. It's helping. There are days I don't know how to help her, and I get overwhelmed."

"I'm really proud of you, Dad. I'm not sure a lot of husbands would go to therapy. Don't tell Mom, but you've always been my favorite," I said, in a slightly amused tone, then sniffled. "I'm proud of her too. I can't wait to see you both in a few weeks."

"You, too. I'll talk to you in a couple of days. I'm sending a big hug from here."

The idea of my dad's big strong arms wrapped around me broke the dam loose, and I slid down the wall until my ass touched the floor. "Thanks," I managed to say. "I just need a few minutes, then I'll be fine."

"Call your old man if you need me. I'm guessing the girls will take care of you but know that I'm here."

"Okay. Bye." I tapped the screen and disconnected the call as the tears flowed hot and heavy down my cheeks. The floor creaked to my left, and I lifted my head in time to see Everlee. Her expression twisted with concern as she bolted over to me. Without a word, she held me as I fell apart while Hunter was on the other side of the wall.

After a few minutes, I sat up and wiped my eyes.

"I'll fucking kill him," Everlee practically yelled.

"Shhh!" I slapped my palm over her mouth. "He's in my bedroom, and it's not what you think."

She narrowed her gaze at me, and I dropped my hand. "I think he's moving … to Europe."

"What? Why? He has his entire football career in front of him. I don't understand." She placed her back against the wall and stretched out her legs, crossing them at the ankles.

"His parents said he has to move with them, or they'll stop paying for his college and housing." I totally lied to Everlee, but there was no way I could tell her about the mafia and the witness protection program.

"Wow, that's intense." She patted my leg. "You know we've got your back, babe. Whatever you need when this goes down ... vodka, tequila, hot strippers, ice-cream ... whatever helps your heart heal." Everlee kissed my cheek.

"Thank you." I suspected I would need every one of those.

"Hell yeah. What are best bitches for?" She slipped her arm through mine and leaned her head on my shoulder.

After another ten minutes passed, I felt composed enough to talk to Hunter.

"I should try to get some sleep. It's been a long day."

Everlee nodded, stood, then helped me up. My nose was stuffy from crying, and I wiped it on the back of my hand.

"If you need to talk, you know where to find me." She strolled down the hall, then threw me a kiss over her shoulder. "Love ya, babe."

"Love you too." I offered her a sincere smile. These girls were my family, and I loved them so much. If it weren't for their support, I wasn't sure I would be able to get through the heart break.

I slowly opened my door, peeking to make sure that Hunter wasn't standing in front of the door naked, but he'd stretched out on my bed fully clothed.

"Hey," I said, closing the door.

I joined him on the mattress, but before I could stretch out, he grabbed me and pulled me to him. "I'm so sorry, Teagan. If I'd known, I would have never ..."

I placed my finger over his mouth. "I know." And I did. "If you decide to go with your parents, you won't move until after Thanksgiving. What do you think about coming home with me to meet my parents? Ya know, our first and last holiday together."

Hunter smoothed my hair. "I would love to."

Chapter Forty-Six

Hunter

Kane stared at me, drumming his fingers on his jeaned thigh. We'd met in my office to discuss some changes in the society, but he clearly had something else on his mind.

"Dude, you've been in a funk for days. What gives?" Kane propped his feet on my desk, making himself comfortable.

"If I tell you, you can't breathe a fucking word of it to anyone." That got his attention. I would have laughed if the situation hadn't sucked so bad.

"Not a word, bro."

I hesitated. "My family is moving, and they want me to go with them ... to Europe. If I go, we will leave after finals in December."

Kane released a low whistle, his eyes widening. "No shit? What about your career here and Teagan? Do you have to go? I mean you're twenty, so if you can support yourself ..."

I shifted in my seat, uncomfortable. "I've thought about it, man." Even though I knew better, my mouth opened without permission.

"Kane, my family and I were in WITSEC for a few years. I'll never be able to play pro ball here."

Surprised, Kane jerked, sending his chair toppling backward. He landed with a thud and his feet in the air. I stood and peered over the desk at him.

"Dude, are you okay?" A chuckle bubbled up inside me when I didn't spot any blood. He hadn't hit his head, so I assumed he would live.

"Fuck, that didn't just happen." He scrambled to stand, clearly embarrassed. When he sat down, he kept his feet on the floor. "That's some heavy shit." Kane shoved his fingers through his dark hair. "It makes sense, though. No social media. You avoid showing your face in the newspaper or pictures online." He shook his head, bewildered. "I won't ask how it happened, but son of a bitch. It had to be bad to land your ass in federal protection."

"It was." I tugged on my hoodie, suddenly not able to breathe. "I don't want to leave. I have the society, Teagan, and your stupid ass." I smirked at him. "But I won't have to look over my shoulder anymore. I can play pro ball there. I could have a future. Plus, my parents really want me to go with them. I keep deciding to pack up, then changing my mind. I don't think I can leave Teagan." I swallowed over the scratchy lump in my throat.

"That sucks dicks. You have friends here, but you have to live your dreams. If not, you'll regret it for the rest of your life. Plus, you'll be able to move on." He hesitated. "Will you step down from the society?"

"I'll have to. I can always start a new chapter in Europe." I rubbed my forehead, anger and sadness twisting my stomach into knots. Teagan was the best thing that had ever happened to me, and I was about to leave her behind. "Fuck!" I shot out of my chair and punched my fist into the wall. The pain ricocheted through me, and I welcomed the relief from the emotional torture I was enduring.

"Dude, if you want to go, then why don't you ask Teagan to go with you?" Kane asked quietly. "You two are clearly in love with each other. Make this work, man. You don't have to end it with her if she means that much to you."

I inspected my hand and flexed my fingers. Thank God I hadn't broken anything. I was obviously fucked up in the head to have punched a wall. I stared out of the window across the dirt and gravel parking lot.

I frowned, suspecting I already knew the answer to his question. "She can't leave. Her family is here, and her mom was just diagnosed with bipolar disorder. Teagan has a lot on her plate."

"How do you know she can't go with you? Have you asked her yet? What if she finished the school year here, but visited you every six weeks? I could see where security and international cameras would alert your stalkers where you were, but she can travel all she wants. Her mom would have time to get settled in, and even then, she can fly back and forth a few times a year. More if her mom needs her." Kane looked at me as though I were stupid for not putting the idea together already.

I turned slowly, his words sinking into my heart. I'd thought about it, but I was afraid it was too soon. I rubbed my stubbled jawline, pondering what Kane had just said. Was he right? Was there a possibility that Teagan and I could make this work? I snatched my phone off the desk and called my girlfriend. I couldn't wait any longer. The last week had fucked me up in a million different ways, wondering how in the hell I would make it without her.

Her cell rang but went to voicemail. I swore under my breath and checked the clock on the wall. Teagan was still in class.

Irritated, I tossed the phone down on the stack of papers that the guys had submitted detailing possible society girls. Those would have to wait until I was clearer about my future.

"Go get your girl, Hunter. We'll deal with society shit later. I'll look through the suggestions, then give you my recommendations later."

"Thanks, man." I patted my pocket for my keys and wallet, snatched up my cell, and hauled ass out of the office. As soon as I burst through the exit door, the rain slapped me in the face, but I just laughed it off. As long as Teagan was next to me, I could make it through anything, including thirty-three-degree weather, high winds, and pouring rain. I slowed as I neared my Porsche, my inner voice nagging me as I unlocked the door and climbed in. What if Teagan said no? Could I really walk away from her, or was I lying to myself?

Chapter Forty-Seven

Teagan

As hard as I tried to listen to my English Lit professor, I couldn't. Every minute away from Hunter was a wasted moment that I would never be able to get back. He hadn't decided to leave yet, but I knew in my gut he would. I couldn't blame him at all, but my heart would never be the same.

Squirming in my chair, I peeked at the clock on my phone for the millionth time since class had started. Thank God there were only ten minutes left, but it felt like an eternity. I pulled my North Face jacket tighter around me and shivered. Even though I'd worn a lilac, wool sweater with my jeans, I was still cold.

I looked to my right, spotting a dark-haired guy staring at me. He tugged on the collar of his navy sweatshirt, and a sinister expression twisted his features. Little bells began to ring in my head as I finally placed him. He'd been watching me in calculus, but not as blatantly since I was always with Hunter and the other guys on the football team.

Returning my attention to the front of the room, I couldn't help but look at the creeper again, but he was gone. Frowning, I searched the area. The classroom door opened and closed quietly, and I spotted him slipping out. *Thank fuck.*

When class was dismissed, I shoved my book and notebook into my backpack, then filed out last. Rounding the corner, someone grabbed my wrist and whirled me around. My back slammed against the wall, knocking the wind out of my lungs.

"What the hell?" I stared at the creep from English Lit who was only a few inches away. "Don't touch me," I spat.

His sneer rattled my nerves. I had to figure out how to put this fucker on the ground and run.

"Who are you?" I asked as he pinned me in, his hands on either side of my head. Realizing he was the reason I'd felt strange that day in calculus, a shiver danced down my spine. *This dude is fucking stalking me?* Fuck, what if he was with the mafia and after Hunter and his family? My legs wobbled beneath me, and bile churned in my stomach. Hunter was right, he would never stop looking over his shoulder unless he moved to Europe. If this was anything close to how he felt all of the time, it fucking sucked.

"Your admirer. The moment you set foot on campus I wanted you for my own. I know everything about you. Or haven't you noticed because you're too busy spreading your legs for Hunter Calloway?"

The hair on the back of my neck bristled. "He's my boyfriend. Besides, what I do isn't any of your business." Since I didn't have any room to move and strike him, I pushed against his shoulder, but he was stronger than his skinny ass appeared.

I glanced around, searching for anyone to help, but it seemed that everyone had cleared out.

The guy's nose brushed against my hair as he shoved his hips into me.

"Stop. Get off me!" I raked my nails down his cheek. Fast footsteps echoed through the hall. *Please, someone, please find me.*

"Get off my girlfriend," Hunter growled and jerked the asshole away from me.

Shock twisted the guy's features as he flew backward, then toppled to the ground. Hunter stomped over to him, his hands clenching, then he repeatedly slammed his fist into the bastard's face. The sound of bones crunching echoed through the area. Hunter delivered a swift kick to the creep's gut, then grabbed the collar of his shirt and jerked him into a sitting position. Hunter's green eyes burned with rage.

"You fucking touch her again, and I'll end you. Don't even look at her sideways, you piece of shit. Do you understand?"

The son of a bitch grunted and nodded before Hunter released him, his head smacking the floor. He curled up, holding his stomach and moaning.

Hunter trained his attention at the heap on the floor and held his hand out to me. He glanced over his shoulder and his gaze raked over me. "Are you okay, baby?"

"Yeah." I approached the crumpled-up form, then landed a solid kick to his back. He yelped and squirmed in pain.

"Let's go before anyone sees us." Hunter led us out of the building and into the rain. We jogged across the lawn toward the parking lot, and a giggle broke free from my lips. *What the hell had just happened?*

Once we reached Hunter's Porsche, he opened the passenger door for me. Seconds later, he climbed into the driver's seat and started the car. The tan leather seats began to warm my butt and the back of my legs immediately. I stared at him, grinning. "Thank you. I couldn't get any space between me and ..." I shivered. "Do you think he was with the mafia?" My stomach flip flopped with my question.

"No, nothing about him screamed mafia. He wouldn't have been stupid enough to approach you in the middle of the hall for starters." Hunter cocked a brow. "Anyone could have seen the little shit. I think he just lost his goddamn mind for a minute. Did you realize that he's in our calculus class?"

"Yeah. I caught him staring at me, then realized where I'd seen him before."

Dismayed, Hunter shook his head. "I'm just glad I got there in time."

"Me too. I don't understand people, Hunter. Why would he think it was okay to scare me like that?" I wrung my hands in my lap, anxious and perplexed. "If I'd had my purse, then I could have beat the shit out of him with it." My shoulders slouched. "I hate how many girls are attacked on college campuses. It's fucking scary." I stared out the window. "I doubt he'll mess with me again thanks to you." I barked out a laugh. "I'm sorry, I get the giggles when I'm stressed."

Hunter forcefully cupped my chin and kissed me. "You're just laughing because that bastard got his ass whipped." Hunter smirked, releasing me. "Everyone knows that you're mine."

"I've never seen you fight." I sank my teeth into my lower lip. "It was kind of hot."

Hunter's blonde brow rose. "You liked it, huh?"

"Mmhmm." Silence filled the car, and I rummaged through my backpack for the workout towel I'd shoved inside that morning. Then, I mopped up the raindrops from my cheeks and hair and gave it to my boyfriend.

"You have blood on your hands, babe." I nodded toward them.

"He's lucky I don't have more on them." He wiped his face, then attempted to clean the spots off his skin.

A heavy sadness pushed against me, crushing my chest. He would be leaving soon, and I would be left behind and broken while he started his new life overseas. I fucking hated everything about that plan. I wanted him to be happy but with me, not anyone else.

Hunter offered the towel back to me. He wrapped his fingers around the steering wheel, gripping them so tightly they turned white.

"Teagan." His voice was deep and husky, and goosebumps dotted my skin.

"Yeah?" Suddenly nervous, I clutched the hand towel in my lap and waited for him to continue.

Anguish flickered in his intense gaze. "I'm not sure that I can leave you."

My heart skittered to a stop. What was he saying? I held my breath, mentally encouraging him to spit it out and put me out of my misery. I wanted him to stay more than anything in this world.

"You can say no, babe. But ..." He pinned me with his heated stare and took my hand. "Come with me, Teagan. We can finish school there, and you can FaceTime everyone. Plus, I'll make sure you have the money to visit your friends and family any time you want to. I can't take the risk of traveling, but there's no threat to you. Live with me ... let's build a future together." He gulped. "Please. I don't want to live my life without you." His expression filled with hope as he waited for me to give him an answer.

My pulse stuttered, and I stopped breathing for a moment. *Mom. Dad. Ari. The girls* ... Everything and everyone was here. Hunter's mother despised me, but his parents would be the only other humans I would be able to connect with until we were settled. Was Hunter worth leaving everyone I loved?

I focused on our linked fingers, then on his gorgeous face. Closing my eyes briefly, I dragged in deep gulps of air. "Hunter ... it's a huge decision." I turned in my seat. It was only fair to give him my undivided attention.

"I know. I know I'm asking a lot, Teagan."

My heart climbed into my throat. "I need to think about it. Mom and Dad need me. Everything I know is here, but ... I'm not sure I could tell you goodbye."

Hunter leaned in and crushed his lips against mine. "I love you. Take your time, babe."

I nodded, tears welling in my eyes. "Thank you for understanding."

The hours ticked by as I paced my bedroom, weighing the pros and cons of leaving with Hunter. I loved him. That wasn't the problem.

Dad wouldn't allow me to drop out of school to help take care of Mom, so I wasn't sure moving mattered. If Dad needed help, he would move to Canada first and allow Grandpa and Grandma to help.

I plopped onto my bed, my knee bouncing with anxiety. Hunter was right. I could FaceTime every day with the girls and my parents. It would be a long day of travel, but I could easily hop on a flight and come home. Hell, I'd probably go home more than I did while living in Oregon.

I blew out a sigh, swallowing my fear. The moment Hunter asked me to move with him, I had my answer, but I wanted to think it through before talking to him. I needed to make sure it wasn't a spontaneous choice that I would regret later. Although those could be fun, this one was big and affected too many people. I had to be sure.

After most of the day looking at the pros and cons, I was finally crystal clear about a decision.

Grabbing my phone off my desk, I texted Hunter to meet me at his building around ten that evening. I stuffed my cell in my back pocket, then collected my keys and purse before heading to my car. I would share the news with him in less than half an hour, and I was terrified.

My heart pounded against my chest as I strolled through the hallway with purpose. I wiped my sweaty palms on my jeans while I made my way to Hunter's office. I swallowed over the tightness in my throat when I spotted his door open, the light spilling into the otherwise dark hall.

"Hi," I said, entering the room.

Hunter jumped out of his chair, worry flickering through his gaze. "Hey." He gave me a gentle kiss and pulled me into a hug. "I'm afraid to hear your answer," he said in a low, gruff voice as he sat in the chair behind his desk.

I laid my head against his chest, listening to the *thump-thump* of his heart racing. I stepped away and peered up at him. "I'll go, baby. I'll go with you to Europe."

A slow smile slipped into place. "You'll move with me?"

Tears welled in my eyes. "Yes! I've always wanted to study abroad. If I'd gone through a program, I would be gone for a year without returning to the states, anyway. This sounds way better. Plus, if I see Mom and Dad every few months, it's more than I see them now and I'm only one state away. I can hop on Zoom with Mom and Dad and the girls. I'll miss them the most." I grinned, unable to hide my excitement any longer. Hunter reached for me and pulled me into his lap. I straddled him and placed my hands on his shoulders, beaming. As thrilled as I was that he asked, I was also surprised. It was a giant leap for both of us.

He gently cupped my cheeks. "I love you, Teagan. There's no one else I rather have by my side. If I make it pro, I want you with me every step of the way. I want to chase you around our apartment and fuck you on every surface. The first thing I want to see every morning is your beautiful face. You've just made me the happiest I've ever been."

"I love you too." A tear escaped, and Hunter brushed it away with the pad of his thumb before he gently pressed his lips to mine. He deepened our kiss, his tongue seeking mine. I moaned as he shifted his hips, and my core throbbed with longing.

"Babe?" I moved away from him.

"Hmm?" He smoothed my hair.

"You're going to have to do something about your mother. If we're going to live together, she needs to understand that I'm not a whore trying to trap you into a horrible life." I kissed the tip of his nose.

"I've already talked to Dad. He gets it, but I'll sit them down and explain that you're moving with me." He palmed my ass.

"We can talk to my family at Thanksgiving. It's only a few weeks away."

"It will give us some time to plan and look online for a place to live. Dad has connections over there, so we should be able to find a nice flat in London, Madrid, or Paris. We have options."

I smiled at him, my heart overflowing that he loved me enough to ask me to go. I placed my forehead against his. "I hate to leave, but there's something that I need to take care of."

Hunter feigned surprise. "What? Now? I was hoping we could celebrate." He nipped on my lower lip.

I laughed and kissed him before crawling off his lap. "Even though I want this moment to last forever, I need to go."

Chapter Forty-Eight

Teagan

I rang the doorbell, waiting for Ariana to answer. Surprisingly, she'd been at home when I'd called her. Although I would wait until tomorrow to talk to the other girls, Ari was my best friend, and I would be lost without her. It was only right to tell her first.

The door swung open, and Ari flashed her million-watt smile at me. "Hey, bitch. Get your sexy ass in here."

My chest tightened as I entered. "Is Jagger here?"

"Nope. It's just us for a few hours." She walked over to the couch and plopped down. Her black yoga pants and hoodie looked more comfortable than my sweater and jeans. She tugged on the scrunchie, releasing her long blonde hair. It cascaded over her shoulders, and she fluffed it out.

"Well, I'm not sure how to say this, so I'll just ..." I sat on the sofa's edge.

"Babe, what's wrong? Did something happen with you and Hunter?" She scooted over and took my hand.

The stupid tears returned. "I don't know why I'm crying, I'm actually happy." I sucked in a breath. "I love you. You've been there for me like no one else has."

"Ditto." Her blue eyes searched mine.

"Hunter and his parents are moving to Europe ... and I'm going with him."

Ari gawked at me, her shocked expression an understatement. "What?"

"Since Hunter had been in the witness protection program, and is still laying low ... Ari, he will never play pro ball here. He and his family are constantly looking over their shoulders, and they need a fresh start. Hunter needs the opportunity to play professionally. It's what he loves."

"And he asked you to go with him?"

I nodded. "Yeah, like an hour and a half ago." I smiled through my tears. "In one way, it was an easy decision but leaving my family ... my girls. That's what will suck."

"Shit. Like, you'll be gone. No more sharing ice cream and talking while we snuggle up on the couch." A cry escaped my best friend as her shoulders slumped. "Is he what you want? Are you in love with him?"

"Yeah. I'm stupid in love with Hunter." I sniffled. "I want to be with him. I'll fly back and forth, and you and I will Skype or Face-Time, or whatever works. We'll talk every day and still share ice-cream. Once we're settled, you can visit as often as you want. Maybe the guys can even become friends. That way Jagger can come with you."

"Okay. Well, fuck. That isn't why I thought you wanted to come over." She offered me a sad smile. "If you're happy, then I'm happy for you. I know it's been a bumpy road with Hunter, but sometimes the rough rides turn out to be the best." She leaned over and plucked a few tissues from the box on the coffee table. "When do you guys leave?"

"After finals, so three and a half weeks. We'll be spending Thanksgiving with Mom and Dad."

"I'm guessing since you just made your decision, they don't know yet." She blew her nose, then flopped back against the couch.

"No. We'll talk to them while we're there. I want them to meet Hunter. Hopefully, they'll like him."

Ari patted my knee. "They will. I'll talk to Jagger and reel him in, so don't worry about it. Honestly, I'm not sure Jagger dislikes Hunter, he was just worried about you when he learned about WITSEC. So was I."

"I love you both for looking out for me, but we'll be safer overseas." I hesitated before I spoke. "Ari, I know you and Theo haven't patched things up ... but you should. With my parents missing for a week, mom receiving a bipolar diagnosis, and Hunter losing his brother ... life is too short, babe. Talk to him. Theo was in a bad place when he made that decision. He's always loved and taken care of you. You've had a good life with him. I realize I'm sharing my opinion, and I promised that I would give you time to think it through and heal, but please consider it. Go home for Thanksgiving, Ari."

Ariana gave me a wistful smile. "I'm trying to work through it. Honestly, I just needed some space. Jagger and I were ready to have our own place to live and start our life together. With everyone looking over our shoulders, it was hard to sift through what Theo ... Dad did."

"Yeah, I've thought about that too. Jagger is a good guy. I used to think he was a little over the top possessive of you, but have you met Hunter?" I giggled. "He just beat the shit out of this creeper who had been following me."

Ari shot up, sitting ramrod straight. "What? Girl, you're in serious trouble. You've been holding out on me!"

"No! It just happened this afternoon." I rolled my eyes. "Oh, my God, the drama, huh? Anyway, the guy is in my calculus and English Lit classes. I've seen him around a lot but ignored it. I mean, you see people you have classes with." I gave her a half-shrug. "Apparently, he decided pinning me against the wall was a good idea ... it wasn't.

Hunter showed up and beat the living hell out of him. I doubt he'll mess with another girl like that again."

"That's fucked up, Teagan. What if he's straight up obsessed with you? That shit happens. Thank God for Hunter." She narrowed her gaze at me. "I don't understand. Your dad taught you to fight, so why didn't you take care of the asshole?"

I blew out a sigh. "I want to ask Dad about that actually. I've never been pinned like that, and I couldn't move enough to lift my leg or take a swing at him. I need to know how to protect myself better."

Ari nodded her agreement. "Same. Jagger and Hunter can't be with us all the time."

"Nope." I stretched my legs in front of me and propped them on the coffee table. "Got any popcorn?"

Ari grinned, then hopped up. "No, but I have drinks and dinner. If you get tipsy, then Jagger can take you home. Well, I guess Hunter would pick you up."

I watched Ari disappear into the kitchen, my heart breaking with the realization that I would leave her in a few short weeks. If there was one thing I was sure of, though, ... we were best friends, and not even distance could pull us apart.

Chapter Forty-Nine

Hunter

The chat with my parents had gone better than I'd anticipated. Maybe Mom would settle down now that we would be able to move and stop looking over our shoulders all of the time. I knew I was ready.

The following weeks flew by as Teagan and I made plans and searched online for an apartment in Spain. Dad and Mom were also searching for a home in Madrid. Mom's mood had perked up, and she'd been fun again. I think Dad made the right decision. We all had.

I glanced over at the beautiful girl in my passenger's seat. She wore a form-fitting black dress, the skirt hitting her mid-thigh. I'd actually picked it out for her to wear. It was the same one she wore when she met the King Cobra the first time. She was busy tapping out a text while I drove. The trip to Spokane was six-and-a-half-hours, but I suspected we would make it faster since we were in my Porsche. However, I planned to have a little fun with my girl on the way.

Glancing in my rear-view mirror, I spotted an eighteen-wheeler gaining on us. I would move into the left lane soon, so it should work out well for everyone.

"Hunter?" Teagan leaned against the headrest. "It's freezing. Why did you ask me to wear a dress?"

I gave her a wicked smile. "Because this drive is boring as hell."

"No shit, and not even the tumbleweeds are out today." She gave me a sassy look. "Do you know why?"

The corner of my mouth kicked up in a grin. "Why?"

"Because it's cold." Exasperation flashed across her features.

"Pull your dress up," I demanded. "Show me your pussy."

She frowned but moved it up to the top of her thighs. The red material of her G-string peeked out.

"Ditch the G-string and spread your legs."

Her chest heaved, my attention on her instead of the road. Goddamn, I wanted to fuck and come all over her tits. It would have to wait, though.

Teagan slid the G-string off and kicked it onto the floorboard.

Rechecking the mirror, I spotted the truck moving a little closer. The timing was everything. My hand moved over the console, in-between Teagan's creamy thighs, touching her swollen lips.

She looked around nervously, spotting the few cars around us. "Someone is going to see us."

"Oh, I'm counting on it." I grinned at her.

She glanced behind us, then her mouth hung open. "A trucker?"

"It will make his day, babe. And mine. Sit back and relax." I slid my finger into her wet slit, and she sighed.

Her tongue darted across her lower lip as I watched her think it through. One thing about Teagan, she was always up for something different. A mischievous look graced her beautiful features, and I realized she was game. Plus, I was already playing with her.

She gasped as I pinched her clit. "This shouldn't be so hot, Hunter."

Soft moans escaped her while I massaged her flesh. I spread her apart, giving myself a full view of her bare cunt. Her juices glistened as I stroked her.

"Fuck." I shifted in my seat, trying to adjust my painfully hard dick without any luck. My discomfort was the downside of touching my girlfriend while driving. The upside was that she would be ready to take care of me once we were settled in her bedroom later. I shoved my finger inside her, then I removed it and licked it clean. I grinned and returned my attention to her.

Teagan arched her back, and her lips were parted. She gripped the seatbelt, bucking her hips.

"That's it, baby." I leaned a little closer, focusing on the road in front of us. Other than the truck, the rest of the vehicles had passed me.

The eighteen-wheeler eased up next to us, and I caught a glimpse of the driver. He appeared to be in his early thirties with brown hair. His eyes widened, then a huge grin slipped into place.

"Oh yeah, he sees us." I peeked at her as she writhed beneath my touch.

"Hunter. Oh, God."

I looked at the driver and chuckled as his arm moved up and down. He was jerking off while watching the show. Teagan was hot as hell, so if I'd been driving the truck, I would've been rubbing one out too.

"When we get to your Daddy's house, are you going to let me lick you while you suck my cock?"

"Yeah," she responded breathlessly.

I slapped her pussy, and she jumped. "Who does this belong to?"

She squirmed beneath my touch. "You."

"Damned straight. I'm going to tear you up tonight." I chuckled. I hadn't shaved for the last several days, and my stubble was rough as hell at this stage. She would beg me to stop even while my tongue was buried in her slick walls.

"Looks like our guy is about to get off. He's slowing down. You're about to make him come, Teagan."

Her hands balled into fists as she screamed my name, releasing all over me. When she drifted back down to earth, I stopped.

"There are wet wipes in the glove box." I smirked at her.

"Of course, you had this planned." She looked at the window, her cheeks burning red. "I can't believe I just did that, but it was amazing." She located the wipes, then removed a few.

I quirked a brow at her. "Clean yourself up, but don't pull your skirt down. We're not finished yet."

Road trips could be a hell of a lot of fun if you planned accordingly.

It was early evening when we arrived at Teagan's parents' place. When I was finished playing with her a few more times, she'd fallen asleep. When we reached the edge of Spokane, I woke her to freshen up before we saw her parents. The GPS said we were only ten minutes away.

My pulse kicked up a notch. I had never met a girlfriend's mom and dad, and honestly, I was super nervous. Not only would we spend the holiday with them, but we were going to tell them Teagan had decided to study overseas with me. Teagan and I had chatted about the possibility of her mom and dad saying no and cutting off her funds, but I had plenty of money to take care of her. We just didn't want the conversation to go south. It was important for her to have their blessing—for me too. Teagan and her father were close, and I was worried she might back out if they disapproved.

When she'd brushed her hair and freshened up her makeup, I allowed her to put her G-string on.

Once I'd parked, we climbed out of the car, and I collected our suitcase from the trunk. It was nearly four, and the last wisps of golden hues streaked the sky. According to Teagan, the sun set half an hour earlier in Spokane than it did in the Portland area.

"Are you ready?" She smoothed her dress. Her toned legs made my dick instantly hard. I couldn't wait to have them wrapped around me. After getting her off multiple times, I was ready to fuck her senseless.

I reined in my lust-filled thoughts and squared my shoulders. "Yeah." I leaned down and gave her a sweet kiss instead of what I wanted to give her. I was aware that her parents might be peeking at us through the window.

Teagan led the way as I checked out the quiet neighborhood. Her residence was huge, so I don't know why she thought mine was a big deal. She squeezed my hand, then fished out her keys from her purse.

"Are you ready?" She rang the doorbell, then unlocked the front door.

"There's no time like the present." I chuckled. "Why did you ring the doorbell to your own house?" I closed the door behind us, noting the white marble floors that flowed from the foyer and down the hall. Sounds came from our left, and I suspected it was the kitchen.

"I was taught that if I didn't live at home, I needed to respect my parents and knock or use the bell." She glanced around. "Oh, the place looks gorgeous. It's so nice to see the furniture again." Teagan pointed to the family room on the right. A tan and red Persian rug covered a large amount of the marble, and a fire was burning in the fireplace. "Dad likes to read and watch the game from his favorite recliner. Dad! Mom! We're here," Teagan called out as we headed toward the sounds.

A man in his late forties with dark hair hurried out of the kitchen. His attention landed on Teagan, and a smile lit up his face.

"Honey, it's good to see you." He wrapped her in a big hug.

"Hi, Dad. It's good to be here. The new floors look great by the way."

He patted her on the back. "Wait until you see the upstairs. There's no more carpet. It's all marble, which increased the value of the manor, of course."

Teagan kissed him on the cheek, then turned to me. "I can't wait to see it. Dad, this is Hunter. Hunter, this is Ron Mercer."

I stuck my hand out. "It's nice to meet you, Mr. Mercer. Thank you for having me for the holiday. I look forward to learning more about you and your wife."

Ron's eyes cut over to Teagan, then returned to me. Had Teagan not brought home guys with manners? If I wasn't on my best behavior and my parents ever found out about it, they would kick my ass no matter how old I was.

"It's nice to have you, Hunter. Teagan says that you're quite the running back. I've followed your games, and she's right."

Teagan's shoulders visibly relaxed while we chatted about the upcoming playoffs.

"Where's Mom?" Teagan asked, patting her dad on the arm.

"In the kitchen. Why don't you say hello, and I'll show Hunter around?"

"Okay. But be nice, Dad." She winked at me, then turned away from Ron. *"Good luck,"* she mouthed, then disappeared down the hall.

Fuck. This was it—the talk about treating his daughter right, what were my intentions, and plans for our future. Ron certainly wasn't wasting any time.

"I'll give you the grand tour, and we can take your suitcase upstairs." He offered a warm smile, but the corner of his mouth twitched, and my stomach clenched. This was the make it or break it moment.

Chapter Fifty

Teagan

I entered the kitchen, realizing Mom's back was to me. A punch of anxiety hit my chest while I approached her. I wondered if she would acknowledge me or if things really hadn't changed between us. Slipping my purse off my shoulder, I set it on the counter and watched her.

She opened the oven, removing a sheet of chocolate chip cookies —my favorite. I waited until she'd safely placed them on the stovetop.

"Hey, Mom."

She turned to me, but she didn't speak. Dark circles shadowed Mom's eyes, but the color in her cheeks had returned. Dad had kept me updated with her progress when he called a few times a week. Even though he'd tried to explain it to me, her usually vibrant brown eyes seemed flat. Her red sweater and dark-wash denim jeans flattered her curves. She hated her shoulder-length hair in her face when she cooked, so she swept it back into a low ponytail.

"Hi, Teagan." Finally, a sweet smile appeared, and she opened her arms to me. "How's my favorite girl?"

Skeptical but attempting to be hopeful, I embraced her. I detected a hint of her soft floral Oscar de la Renta perfume over the baked goods. I held my breath, feeling the warmth of her embrace. Memories seized my brain, her abusive words stabbing me repeatedly in the heart. I forced them into the background, reminding myself that she was getting help. She deserved the opportunity to change just like anyone else.

Mom released me and patted the side of my head. "It seems that you're more beautiful than the last time I saw you."

Catching myself, I stopped before pulling back in surprise. She'd never said anything like that to me, and I held my breath, waiting for her to tear me to pieces with her following statements. Mom had a keen ability for tearing open the unhealed wounds, gutting me, then leaving me to bleed out on the floor when she was finished. I swallowed the ball of emotions that was ripping through me. Reconnecting with Dad had helped, but I hadn't realized I resented her so much until she'd said something nice. *How fucked up is that?*

"How was the drive? It's boring as hell through Ritzville." She strolled to the refrigerator and removed a carton of milk.

"It was good. Having Hunter with me made a big difference." *Three orgasms kind of difference.* I smoothed my black form-fitted dress and hid my smile.

"I'm glad he's here. It will be nice to meet one of your friends. I mean, other than the girls." She removed a few glasses from the new contemporary silver cabinets. Even though I hated that mom had dismantled the previous cabinets, I loved the new ones.

"Me too. He's special."

She paused before she poured the milk. I collected a plate for the cookies, then busied myself and fanned them with the spatula. They were still too hot to scoop off the pan.

"I assumed that he meant something to you when you asked if he could join us for Thanksgiving. It seems crazy that the holiday is only a few days away, doesn't it?"

She had no idea. "Time has flown by this term."

Hunter and Dad's laughter echoed through this side of the house, and I smiled.

"Ron was thrilled when he found out *the* Hunter Calloway was joining us. Your father thinks he's an excellent athlete and has a bright future ahead of him." Mom replaced the carton of milk in the refrigerator.

I pursed my lips together, not trusting myself to blurt out that we were moving. If I wanted my parents to treat me like an adult and understand that I was serious about Hunter, I had to keep my mouth shut until the right opportunity arose. "He does. He and Kane Cooper have done a great job with the team this year."

Loud whoops escaped the family room.

"I suspect the men will be busy for a while. I'll have to meet Hunter, then give them some space to get to know each other." She rubbed her palms against her jeans. "Plus, I want to talk to you, Teagan. Let's take the cookies in, then we can chat."

The world spun in slow motion. Here it was. The shoe was not only dropping, but it was about to smack me right in the fucking head on its way down.

I refused to look at her, unwilling to reveal my fear and sadness.

After a snack and introduction between Mom and Hunter, we returned to the kitchen. I sat at the little table in the corner and stared out the window. Surprisingly, Mom had taken another cookie and refilled her milk before she joined me.

"I can't drink alcohol on the new meds, so I treat myself every once in a while." She picked at the edges of the chocolate chip goodness.

"Teagan, this is difficult, so please bear with me." Mom peeked in my direction, then focused on her food again. She had always loved Thanksgiving, and by the looks of the white paper plate with green trim and turkeys on the rim, I suspected she was trying to get into the holiday spirit.

"Okay." I dug my fingernails into my palms. Small scars were still visible, but no one paid attention. If they had noticed, I would have blamed it on the gymnastics. My nails cutting into my hands until I bled was better than the pain my mother inflicted. Her harsh words stung, but I'd found a good distraction when she was doling them out like they were candy. *You'll never amount to anything. You're pathetic. Why did God find it necessary to give me such a horrible child?* I blinked back the tears, again reminding myself to hear her out.

"I'm so sorry, Teagan. I'm so sorry." Mom's shoulders shook with her cries as she hid her face behind her hands. "I have treated you so poorly, and you'll never know how awful I feel."

I stared at this woman, speechless. From what I could tell, she wasn't putting on an act at all, but I was still leery.

Mom pulled it together and dabbed beneath her eyes, removing the smeared mascara with her fingertips. "I can't explain the crushing depression that would hit me after the mania. I was trying to tame an unknown beast. Unfortunately, I probably caused irreparable damage to my daughter, and I'm hoping for the chance to heal what I broke."

"Mom," I whispered. "I can't imagine how hard it's been on you and Dad. You're getting help, though. I have to think that with some work, we can move forward."

She nodded and sniffled. "I'm seeing a therapist twice a week, and I talk about you often. Especially how proud I am of the woman you've become despite how I treated you. Teagan, you're so talented and smart. I felt trapped behind a glass wall, trying to connect with you, and I couldn't. When the depression visited, all I could think of was how much I wanted to be you—free and young."

My forehead creased in confusion. "You were jealous of me?"

"I know it sounds awful, but yes. It wasn't that I didn't want you to succeed, I just couldn't figure out how to get out of the prison I was caged in. I lashed out at the people I loved the most. Someday, somehow, I hope you can forgive me. I'm working hard to find my new normal, and I desperately want my amazing daughter in my life again."

As much as I wanted to believe her, it would take a while to heal and rebuild the trust she'd broken over and over. For all I knew, she was just spewing pretty words, and in five minutes, she would cut me open again.

I reached over and took her hand. "I won't lie to you. It's going to take time. The more consistent your moods are, the nicer you are to Dad and me … I think that's the beginning. I want to forgive, move on, and have a good relationship with you, Mom. I'm sure it took a lot of courage to talk to me about the bipolar diagnosis and the past." I tucked my hair behind my ears. "One thing is for sure: I love you. I always have and I always will. Let's see if we can rebuild and make things even better than what we had when I was younger."

"Thank you, baby."

I reached behind me for the tissue box on the windowsill and offered her one. After she'd erased the moisture from her cheeks, she smiled. "Would you like to order your favorite pizza and watch movies tonight?"

My stomach growled, and I laughed. "That would be amazing. I'll check on the guys and see what kind they want."

We both stood, then I hurried to her and threw my arms around her neck. "I love you, Mom," I whispered.

She held me as my tears flowed. "I love you, sweet pea."

My heart squeezed tight. She hadn't called me sweet pea since I was ten. I released her and grabbed a tissue for myself.

"By the way, Hunter is gorgeous." She winked at me and laughed. It was music to my soul. A sliver of hope flickered to life inside me for the first time in years. Maybe … just maybe, everything would turn out okay.

Chapter Fifty-One

Teagan

When I'd finished eating and drinking a few beers, I curled up next to Hunter. He slipped his arm around me and kissed the top of my head. I wondered what family time was like after he lost Levi. My family was far from normal, but as I grew older, I realized that the real world was dark and twisted. It was the people that I surrounded myself with that made the difference. They were my light. Until I'd met Hunter, the girls had been my rocks. Even though I would move soon, I understood that nothing could break our bond.

After the first movie, Mom excused herself around eight-thirty. Dad said that the medication messed with her energy sometimes, but he was glad that she was sleeping better.

Wanting some time alone with Hunter, I faked a few yawns, then told Dad goodnight.

"I'll go check on Mom, then meet you upstairs," I said to Hunter.

"Okay." He smiled, but I didn't miss the sideways glance he gave my dad.

I wondered if it was awkward for him to sleep in the same bed with my parents here.

Grinning, I left them alone and walked to the part of the house where Mom and Dad's room was located. I gently knocked on the door, then cracked it open.

"Mom? I wanted to check on you and say goodnight." I peered into the dark space, then spotted the light from the bathroom spilling out beneath the door. "Mom?"

I strolled over to the door and knocked. "Mom? Goodnight. Thank you for the pizza and movie." I waited, but there was no answer. Jiggling the handle, I realized it wasn't locked and opened it slowly.

Bile churned in my stomach, my attention sweeping the area. I stilled and stopped breathing, my brain unwilling to digest the scene. Mom's wrists were slit open, and she was unconscious, lying in a pool of blood on the floor. A scream stuck in my throat, then my feet propelled me forward.

"Mom! Mom! No, no, no!" I ran to grab a towel, but my foot slipped in her blood, and I landed on my ass with a thud. I ignored the pain as I scrambled to her. "Mom!" I crawled as fast as possible, my knees and palms tracking the sticky red substance across the room.

"Dad! Daddy! Daddy!" My call for help came again, echoing with grief and terror. Crying so hard, I struggled to see through my tears. I wrapped the towel around her wrist and held it in place as tightly as I could.

"Teagan?" Dad called.

"Daddy! Call 911!" I sobbed, applying pressure to her wound and wondering how the hell I would be able to reach her other one.

Dad flew into the bathroom, shock twisting his features as his eyes darted around. The color drained from his cheeks as he fumbled for his phone. Hunter stopped behind him, fear written all over his face.

Hunter side-stepped Dad, then removed his hoodie, revealing a white T-shirt beneath it. He pulled it off next and began ripping it into pieces.

"Can you press against her wound any harder, Teagan?" His voice was calm and soothing as he began to walk me through how to help Mom. Dad's words broke through my cries, explaining that help was on the way.

"Okay." I focused on him as he wrapped her other wrist with his shirt, then pressed the wound tightly. "There's so much blood, Hunter."

"I know, baby." Tears and pain welled in his eyes as our gazes connected briefly, and I realized he was probably reliving his brother's death while helping my mom.

"Hang on, Mom. Please. Don't leave us yet." I kissed her knuckles, not caring that Hunter and I were sitting in her blood. All that mattered was that she lived.

"She asked me to forgive her tonight. For the first time, she said she was sorry for hurting me." I shook my head, my vision cloudy from my cries. "She ... Oh, God, Hunter, she was saying goodbye."

Loud voices carried through the house, then the bathroom was full of strangers. "Kids, the medics will tend to her. Hurry up and change clothes so we can follow her to the hospital," Dad ordered.

I nodded, barely registering what he was saying. Hunter took my arm and led me into the hall.

"Baby, look at me."

"Hunter? I ..." My chin trembled. "She can't die." I started to touch my cheeks, but Hunter grabbed my arms.

"Teagan, don't touch your face, baby. You have blood all over your hands. I'll help you clean up, but we need to hurry. Do you understand, babe? I'm right here with you."

"Okay." I glanced down at my blood-soaked dress and legs. "Okay."

I barely remembered Hunter taking me upstairs to my bedroom, then sticking us in the shower. After soaping our bodies, the red water circled the drain, and I shivered at the sight of it.

"Teagan, who do I need to call?" He opened the shower door, grabbed towels from the cabinet beneath the sink, and began to dry me off. "Go get dressed while I dry off. I'm right behind you. But baby, who do I need to call?"

In a daze, I walked to the dresser in my bedroom, then realized our clothes were in our suitcase. Dad would need to call my grandparents in Canada, but they were too far away to help at the moment.

"Ari. I need to call Ari. She and Jagger should be at their parents' house. She'll want to know." I quickly pulled on black yoga pants and a sweatshirt. "I don't know where my phone is, though."

"Your purse is probably in the kitchen. You had it with you when you went to talk to your mom." Hunter dressed faster than I had, then took my hand and led me downstairs. Locating my handbag, he snatched it off the counter, checked his pockets for his keys, then we waited for Dad by the door. When I was about to give up and look for him, he appeared.

"Let's go, kids. The ambulance is ahead of us by a few minutes. Hunter, why don't you follow me in case I end up staying the night?"

It was then that I spotted the gym bag that he was carrying. We hurried out of the house and to Hunter's Porsche. I glanced over my shoulder, my heart hammering against my chest. "Dad?"

He paused before he climbed into his black Jaguar. "Yeah?"

"I love you."

We stared at each other briefly. "I love you too, baby girl."

Minutes seemed like hours as we waited and paced the emergency room.

"Teagan!"

I turned to see Ari rushing toward me, Jagger hot on her heels.

"Oh, babe, I'm so sorry."

I grabbed my best friend, blubbering into her coat.

"I'm here, honey. Whatever you and Ron need." She kissed the top of my head.

"I'm so glad you're here," I said between my sobs.

"Bitch, please, where else would I be?" Ari released me and offered a sad smile. "Jagger is talking to Hunter." She nodded at the guys, then Dad joined us and hugged Ari.

"Hey, how are you holding up?"

Dad wiped his moist eyes. "As well as to be expected, I guess."

Ari slipped her arm through mine. "I'm glad that we're all here. Just let me know how we can help. Dad is on standby too. Coffee, food, whatever you need."

Dad patted Ari's back. "Thank you. It means the world to me that you're here. I'll say hello to Jagger." Dad excused himself, and Ari and I sat down.

"How's Hunter doing? I can't imagine that was easy to see. From what you said, there was a lot of blood."

I nodded. "So much blood, Ari. I don't know how she's still alive." Leaning back in my seat, I glanced in Hunter's direction. "It's shitty circumstances, but maybe the guys will patch things up."

Ari looked at them. "Stranger things have happened, right?"

"Maybe. I think tonight with Mom takes the cake." My knee bounced, the words forming on the tip of my tongue. "Ari, I should have known. Mom asked me to forgive her for all the shit she'd ever said to me." I shook my head, my chin trembling. "It was ..."

She pointed at me and narrowed her eyes. "No ma'am. You will not go there, Teagan Emery Mercer. You've been at college and haven't spent any time with her since her diagnosis and treatment started. How in the world would you have realized something was wrong? Hell, if I'd been a fly on the wall, listening to your conversation, I would have thought the meds were working."

"I should have sensed something was off. My instincts are usually spot on, so I should have picked up on it. When it mattered the most, my gut feelings were wrong." I stared at the drab white hospital wall in front of us.

"Babe, I will pull your hair if you don't stop. Instincts are easily clouded by emotions. You know that. We studied it in Psychology last year. You can't take this one because it wasn't your fault. At all. I'm sure Hunter will be able to weigh in on the situation as well." Ari wrapped me in a warm hug, and I laid my head on her shoulder, wondering how in the hell I would ever make it overseas without her. Then I realized that the move to Europe looked different from earlier that day.

Time seemed to stop as we waited for news about Mom. We weren't even sure she was going to live at this point. If she did, she would be under a psychiatric hold again. Thanksgiving wouldn't be the same this year, but I wouldn't have traded those last moments with Mom for anything.

Hunter and Jagger made a coffee run together and appeared to be getting along. Under the circumstances, I sure as fuck wouldn't put up with any of Jagger's meddling. He was lucky he was behaving himself.

Hunter had been attentive, and I couldn't have asked for more. The pain he must be living through while we waited for news was most likely tearing him to pieces. As hard as I tried to comfort him, I didn't have much to offer, and I was afraid it wouldn't be enough.

It was nearly one in the morning when the doctor joined us.

"Mr. Mercer? I'm Dr. Goldman."

"How's my wife?" Dad asked, folding his arms over his chest.

We gathered around to hear the update. My body trembled, and I leaned on Hunter for support.

"She's going to make it," Dr. Goldman announced.

I gasped, my hands flying over my mouth. "She's alive?" My legs collapsed beneath me, and Hunter caught me before I hit the floor.

Dad fell into the seat nearest him, his shoulders sagging with relief.

Hunter wrapped me in his arms and helped me to my feet while he planted a kiss against my temple.

"The cuts were deep, and if you had called 911 any later, I don't think she would have pulled through. The important thing was that she did. Whoever bandaged her wrists saved her life. That took quick thinking in a tough situation. We had to reconnect some tendons and muscles, but she should have full use of her hands again. At the moment, she's been admitted for a psych evaluation, but you and your daughter can see her before they begin the lockdown."

"Babe?" Hunter placed his warm palms against my cheeks. "She's going to be all right."

I nodded, absorbing everything the doctor had just shared with us. "She's alive because of you. You're my real-life hero." I stretched up and pressed my mouth to his.

"Why don't you and Ari go to the bathroom and rinse your face with cold water? It might help clear your head a little." He kissed the tip of my nose. "Regardless, you're beautiful, I just don't want it to upset your mom. When you're finished visiting with her, I'll be right here waiting for you. Just remember that I love you," he whispered.

"I love you too." I gave him a quick peck, then walked to the women's restroom. Ari joined me and slipped her arm through mine.

"I'm so relieved your mom is all right," Ari said softly.

She opened the door, then locked it behind us. "Babe, I had no idea that Hunter loved you like that. It makes me feel better about you leaving for Europe."

I froze, then slowly turned to her. "How am I going to tell my dad we're moving across the world when he needs me the most?"

"Hey, you can't worry about it right now. The only thing that you need to do is see your mom. That's it. One thing at a time." Ari turned me around, then walked me to the sink. "Wash up, babe. It will help a little."

I stared in the mirror, not recognizing myself. My hair was wild, and most of my makeup had run down my face. I cleaned up, then took a deep breath.

"Are you ready?" Ari squeezed my shoulder. "Keep your chin up."

"I will. Are you and Jagger leaving or will you be here?"

"We're staying at the hospital. Jagger loaded us up on snacks in case we got hungry." She took my hand, then we left.

A few minutes later, Dad and I walked into Mom's room. The soft beep of a machine broke through the quiet.

"Mom?" I asked, not sure if she was awake.

She rolled her head, one eye peering at me. "Hi, baby. I wasn't expecting to see you again."

My heart split open as I peeked at Dad. I suspected that Mom was out of it after the surgery and hadn't realized what she'd said.

"I'm a little more difficult to get rid of." Avoiding the bandages, I patted her arm.

"Hi, hon," Dad said.

"Hey. I'm sorry I put you both through this." Mom's voice was groggy and heavy.

"We don't need to discuss anything yet. Just get better," he said.

I squeezed his hand as mom's eyelids fluttered closed. Her soft snore filled the space, and I nearly collapsed to the floor with the sound of her breathing. She was alive, but I would never be able to unsee the images of her laying in a pool of blood with her wrists cut open. For the first time, I understood how Hunter felt about Levi, and it fucking sucked.

Chapter Fifty-Two

Hunter

I rubbed my dry and exhausted eyes. The hospital seats were hard as hell, and my ass began to throb. I stood and stretched, walking the perimeter of the waiting area again before I finally stood near the large window that provided a beautiful view of downtown Spokane and the Spokane River.

The second I'd seen Mrs. Mercer on the floor, it had sucked me into my dark memories. Images of Levi's lifeless body bombarded my mind. I rubbed the back of my neck, trying to remain calm and composed. Teagan needed me, and I wanted to be there for her. The road to recovery for her mom and family would be tough. I'd been there. Hell, I was still trying to reconnect with Mom and Dad. I would never say it aloud, but I was grateful Teagan and I hadn't moved overseas yet. *Fuck!* How in the hell would we break the news to Teagan's parents? Dread knotted in my stomach. If I were in Teagan's shoes, I would be reconsidering Europe.

A gentle hand landed on my back, and I spotted Ari next to me.

Her blue eyes were filled with compassion. "Thank you for taking care of Teagan."

"You don't need to thank me. I love Teagan, and I'll move heaven and earth for her." I swallowed, wondering if we had a future together. "Do you think Teagan will still move?" It was a bold question, but Ari knew her better than anyone else.

"Honestly, I don't know. I suspect she will, it just won't be in December. She might need to meet you there later." Ari crossed her arms over her chest, a heavy sigh escaping her. "I'm not even sure she'll be able to focus on another term of school if she does stay. Maybe online would work best. She'll probably move back home. I mean, I'm speculating, Hunter. I do know that Teagan is head over heels in love with you."

"She definitely is. If you do anything to hurt her, I'll fucking snap you in two," Jagger said as he joined us.

It had taken me a while, but I finally realized that Jagger and I were a lot alike. Instead of getting pissed, I turned to him. "I sure as hell hope so. If I were in your position, I would tell some guy the same damned thing."

He held up his fist, and we tapped our knuckles. Jagger slipped his arm around Ari's waist, then asked me an important question. "If Teagan wants to wait to move to Europe, will you stay here for a while or go ahead and leave?"

I'd asked myself the same and pondered my answer over the last several hours.

"What do you mean Teagan is moving to Europe?" a deep voice asked behind us.

My pulse stuttered as I realized that Ron had just overheard us. *Goddammit.* How had this evening continued to get worse?

I turned to him, man-to-man. "We were going to tell you and your wife while we were here, then talk to my parents. I don't know that Teagan will leave you now, though." I rubbed my forehead where a nagging pain was beginning to throb.

"Dad?" Teagan's presence broke through my panic. She walked over to me and threaded her fingers through mine. "I'm in love with Hunter. And I realize this is a shitty time to talk about it, but no one knew you were going to overhear a conversation. We'd planned on sitting down and talking to you and Mom. I'm sorry you found out this way." She looked up at me. "I'm not sure when I'll go, though. I can't leave you and Mom like this."

My heart swelled with pride. I was so proud of her for making a bitch of a decision, but she would have never been able to forgive herself if she'd left with me and something else had happened to her mother. I rubbed her back, supporting her. When she learned that her mom was alive, I suspected that she would stay at least for a little while. But I'd also made my choice.

My phone vibrated in my back pocket, and I removed it. Glancing at the screen, I frowned. It was five-thirty in the morning, and my dad was calling me. My pulse spiked. There was no reason to call this early unless …

"I need to take this. I'm so sorry, baby." I hurried to put some distance between myself and the group, then I answered.

"Dad? Is everyone all right?" After the events surrounding Teagan's mom, my nerves were fucking fried. I couldn't handle anything else, but apparently, fate had other ideas.

"Son? Are you sitting down?"

"No. I'm at the hospital with Teagan and her family." I leaned against the wall for support.

"What? What happened?" Dad's concern bled through the phone.

"Her mom attempted suicide. She's going to make it, though. It's just been a fucked-up evening."

"I'm so sorry to hear that. Please tell Teagan that if she needs anything at all, that we're only a call away." Dad's tone softened, compassion threading through his words.

Relief flooded my exhausted system. Maybe he and Mom were

beginning to accept that Teagan and I were together. It would have to be sooner rather than later because I needed to update him on the move after I'd had some sleep.

"Why are you calling so early? Is Mom okay?" I closed my eyes, steeling myself for the next blow. But the words that tumbled out of my father's mouth changed my life forever.

Chapter Fifty-Three

Hunter ~ Six Months Later

I smiled for the camera as the flashes continued to go off, nearly blinding me. Kane and Coach stood beside me, wearing a huge smile.

I waved and held up my first NFL offer, the crowd cheering. Even though I had two more years of college to finish, I'd been signed early. It was fucking unheard of, but we were thrilled. Contingencies were in place, but I had always embraced a challenge.

Teagan clapped like crazy, her beautiful smile brighter than the camera flashes. I blew her a kiss, and the reporters followed my attention. Teagan glowed in the limelight, and I couldn't wait to have her by my side through this insane journey called life.

Never in a million years had I expected Dad to call while we were at the hospital when Teagan's mom had attempted suicide. His news had changed everything. The FBI had made a big bust and arrested several mafia members. What was even sweeter, though? There had been a mass shooting between the mafia and cartel. The cartel had mopped the floors with them, including the three men who

Dad had rolled over on. Even their bosses had been gunned down and murdered. Although we realized the mafia had strong ties, it was over. They had more significant problems to address than coming after us.

Teagan's doe eyes connected with mine, and my heart hammered against my chest. I would never forget the relief and joy on her gorgeous face when I'd joined her in the hospital waiting room. It was an awkward but happy conversation with her dad, Ari, and Jagger. Poor Ron had no idea about my past, but with the news, he seemed to accept it as that—the past. I assured Teagan that we could find a place together in Oregon and that we would visit every weekend if needed while her mom continued treatment. The doctors had found a good combination of meds for her mom, and she was making some significant progress.

"Who is the young lady?" One of the male reporters asked.

I zeroed in on the guy, staring a hole through him. Hopefully, he understood that I would mess him up if he flirted with my girl.

Kane nudged me with his shoulder, grinning like the asshole he was. I snorted, then gave him the papers I was holding.

He patted me on the back and took them. My attention landed on my girlfriend, and I made my way through the crowd. She giggled as I reached her and laid a searing kiss on her lips, claiming her in front of the entire world. My cock stirred. He was ready to celebrate too.

I cleared my throat and stuck my hand in my jeans pocket, producing a black velvet ring box. I dropped to one knee and flipped it open.

The cameras went ballistic as Teagan's mouth hit the floor. The two-carat princess cut diamond ring glittered majestically against the light.

"Teagan Mercer. I wouldn't be here if it weren't for your love and support. I can't imagine a life without you. You saved me when I was at my darkest, loved me, and gave me a future. Now, I want you to be mine. Teagan, will you marry me?"

The room grew silent, and my pulse pounded so hard in my ears that I wasn't sure if I would be able to hear her answer. I realized I'd taken a huge risk when I decided to ask her in front of the world. But she was worth it. I wanted her to have the proposal she deserved.

Teagan sank to her knees, her eyes filling with tears. "Yes. Yes, I'll marry you, Hunter Calloway."

With clumsy hands, I managed to remove the ring from the box and slip it onto her finger. I stood, pulling her up with me, then kissed her until I couldn't see straight. The crowd roared as she wrapped her arms around my neck.

We released each other, and she snuggled up to my side. I glanced down at her. "I have one more surprise for you."

The beginning of a wicked little smile graced her lips, and I chuckled. Damn, it felt good to laugh and walk around a free man.

I secured the blindfold in place, then helped Teagan out of the Porsche. "No peeking. If you do, then I'll have to punish you."

"Promise?" She giggled.

I was definitely about to bend her over my knee and spank her sweet ass. Unfortunately, it would have to wait for a few minutes.

I led her up the sidewalk, then lifted the blindfold. "Welcome home, Teagan." Those words felt so fucking good as I stared at the two-story white bungalow-style house.

She blinked rapidly, then took my hand. "This is for us?"

"Yeah. No more campus living. The house has new wood floors, three bedrooms, and three and a half baths so we can have whoever crash when they've had too much to drink. You'll love the kitchen and—"

Teagan's mouth was on mine before I provided any more details. "How?" She looked up, beaming at me.

"I sold the society building." I grinned at her.

Surprised, she gave me a quizzical look. "The society is no longer in existence?"

"Oh, it's still around, just at a new location with new leadership." I chuckled. "You don't think the team would give up all that pussy, do you?"

Teagan slapped my arm and shook her head.

"Also, I was able to pay cash for the house. The mortgage and title are free and clear."

"Oh, my God, that's amazing!" She bounced up and down on her toes, and I made a mental note to fuck her while she was wearing her high school cheer uniform. "When I'm with the NFL, we can rent it out or whatever we want, but it's ours either way. I just wanted to have a place of our own because ... home is where you are, and you own my heart."

Teagan kissed me again, and I pulled her flush against my body.

"We better get started. I'm guessing there are a lot of surfaces that need to be broken in." She wiggled her brows, then hugged me. "Thank you, baby. I can't wait to see the inside."

My nose brushed against her dark hair, and I inhaled her cherry vanilla scent. I cupped the back of her head, cradling her and imprinting her smell, her supple body, and the way she fit against me into my mind. I would tuck this memory safely away because I understood how fragile life could be. When I was away from her playing professionally, this would be what I held onto. Because at that moment, nothing else mattered. It was Teagan and me against the world, and I had no doubt that we would take it by storm as long as we were together.

Chapter Fifty-Four

Epilogue ~ Teagan

"Holy crap." I grabbed my stomach and groaned. "I don't think I've ever been this sick before."

Hunter smoothed my hair and placed a kiss on the top of my head. "The doctor said you should be over the morning sickness soon, baby."

I snuggled against him, unwilling to get out of bed even though I had no choice. Life existed beyond the comfort of our master bedroom.

Hunter cupped my chin, and I looked into his eyes. "You're my hero, Teagan. You're a bodybuilder."

I scrunched my nose at him. "A what?"

"A bodybuilder. You're building a body. Everything our baby needs, you're making sure he or she is safe and sound."

Although the nausea was kicking my ass, I couldn't help but smile. "Well, our little munchkin should knock it off already. I miss real food like french fries and ice cream."

Hunter chuckled as he wrapped his arm around me and pulled

me closer. The warmth of his skin against my cheek calmed the tumultuous sea inside my belly.

The doorbell rang, and I sat up in our bed, holding the navy sheet over me. "Who in the world could that be?"

A mischievous expression flickered across my husband's face. "I'll check." He slipped out from beneath the covers, and I watched as he grabbed a T-shirt off the chair and tugged it over his head. If I had felt better, Hunter wouldn't be wearing a stitch of clothing right now. I sank my teeth into my lower lip as his arms and back muscles flexed while he pulled on a pair of black basketball shorts.

"It sounds like Anita is answering the door." He winked at me before he left.

I flopped onto my pillow and stared at the ceiling. Hunter would have to leave tomorrow for football practice, and the doctor had given me strict orders not to travel until I was farther along with the pregnancy. Tears welled in my eyes. Not only did I hate being apart from him, but I was still in the danger zone. I'd been pregnant twice already but lost both babies. Hopefully, the third would be different. I willed myself to let go of the pain, but it wasn't that easy.

A familiar female voice carried up the stairs, and my mouth flew open. Tossing the covers off, I climbed out of bed and slipped my feet into my bunny slippers with little ears that matched my pajamas— pink and white.

My heart grew hopeful as I hurried to the foyer.

A squeal escaped me as I spotted my best friends looking exhausted but happy. I rushed to Ari, Everlee, Gabby, and Leighton.

"Oh. My. God. What are you doing here?" I practically tripped over myself, running to them.

"Hunter called us. We're here for a week to take care of you." Ari beamed at me.

I threw my arms around her. "I've missed you so bad."

"Bitch, same."

After a round of tearful hugs, I led them to the living room as

Hunter helped our housekeeper, Anita, take the luggage to the guestrooms.

Everlee flashed us a huge grin. "I love that Hunter is this big, famous NFL player, but he still helps the housekeeper! Maybe I'll get as lucky as you and Ariana someday." Her smile slipped away, and sadness flickered across her expression.

"You and me both." Gabby sat on the cream leather sofa and yawned.

"Girl, I know. The red-eye was the only flight available last minute." Leighton tucked her hair behind her ear and settled in next to Gabby.

"You didn't sleep?" I squeezed Ari's hand before we got comfortable on the loveseat across from the other girls.

Everlee barked out a laugh. "How long has it been since we've seen each other in person?"

"Until this trip, a year," Gabby added.

"Too damn long," I said.

Everlee shook her head. "So you know we didn't rest at all. We were actually hushed a few times for laughing while other passengers were trying to snooze."

Leighton snorted. "Some people." She rolled her eyes, giggling.

I stared at my friends, overwhelmed. "I can't believe Hunter kept it a secret."

"He didn't have to for long. He called us yesterday morning to see if we could catch a flight. Since we were all attending the fashion show in New York, it was easy to coordinate the trip to Kansas City."

A tear rolled down my face. "I'm so glad you're here. Hunter has been spoiling me rotten, and I'm scared and sick all the fucking time." I hiccupped through my tears.

"We've got you, girl." Ari pulled me in for a hug.

"Once a bitch, forever a bitch," Everlee said, placing her hand over her heart.

The other girls chimed in as I tried to pull myself together.

I grabbed a tissue from the end table and dabbed my eyes.

A throat cleared before Hunter entered the room. "Ladies, I owe you one. Thanks for keeping Teagan company. I'm hoping that the doctor clears her to join me in a few weeks, but until then, it's best that she stays put."

"Living on the road can be rough," Ari said. "I have that life with Jagger, and as much as I love it, I miss our house and any normalcy we used to have."

I rolled my eyes and nibbled on my thumbnail.

Hunter strolled over to me, concerned. "Are you ready to try something to eat?"

"I think so. I'll grab some 7Up and crackers." I stood and wrapped my arms around my husband's waist. "Thank you for calling the girls."

He placed his forehead against mine and gently cupped the back of my neck. "You don't have to thank me, baby. I'll move heaven and earth for you."

"I swear I just melted," Everlee sighed.

Giggles filled the room. I hadn't realized how much I'd missed my besties until now.

Once Anita had made breakfast and the group had eaten pancakes and bacon while I nibbled on saltines, everyone except Ari crashed out.

An hour later, I was on my knees in the master bathroom. My best friend held my hair while I hurled what little food I'd eaten.

"I hate that you're so sick, Teagan." Ari turned on the faucet and wet a washcloth. "Here." She folded it into thirds and handed it to me before she sat next to me on the white marble floor.

"Thanks. I'm glad you're here." I wiped off my mouth and leaned my back against the bathtub.

"Me too." Ari flipped her long hair behind her shoulder. "Why didn't you tell me you were so sick?"

I blew out a sigh. "There's no reason for you to worry." I gave her a slight shrug. "Maybe it's a good sign. I wasn't nauseous at all the last two pregnancies, so there's that."

Ari pursed her lips. "I want this one to be okay. You and Hunter have been through so much trying for a baby."

"At least part of it's fun." I wiggled my brows at her and attempted to lighten the conversation. "I'm almost there, Ari. The doctor thinks if I can make it another week, then I should be able to carry to full term."

Understanding coasted over her pretty face. "No wonder Hunter didn't want to leave you alone."

"Yeah, he knew I was scared. So is he." I placed my hand on my flat belly. "I mean, Anita is always around, but it's not the same. Next Wednesday, Mom and Dad will fly in, though."

"That's great! I'm so glad you and your mom are doing better."

"Me too. Those years with her were tough, but I'm grateful she got the help she needed. Dad is the happiest I've seen him in a long time too."

"That makes my heart sing." Ari leaned back against the bathroom cabinet, fidgeting.

My gaze narrowed at her. "You're not telling me something. What is it?"

She laughed and rolled her eyes. "Nothing."

"Liar," I giggled. "Quit holding out on me because I've been sick." My smile faltered as I stared at her, my mind wondering what she might hide from me and why.

I crawled over to her and took her hands in mine. "Don't you dare not share your life with me, bitch." My voice cracked with emotion, suspecting what she was going to say.

"Teagan, I wasn't going to tell you yet." Guilt twisted her features.

"Don't you ever do that again. Don't you ever hold out on me because you think your happiness will hurt me. That's a bullshit lie." I gritted my teeth, fighting against a wave of nausea.

"I love you, but you're having a really hard time right now. The last thing I wanted to do was tell you how excited Jagger and I are that we're pregnant."

Before she could say another word, I threw my arms around her. "I love you and no matter what is happening in my life, I will always be there for you. You and Jag walked through hell and back, and you deserve to have everything you've ever dreamed of."

Ari hugged me tightly. "I love you, Tea. More than anything else in the world, I want us to raise our kids together."

I sniffled, fighting tears of joy this time. Pulling away, I wiped the moisture from my cheeks and smiled. "I'm going to be an aunt."

Ari's soft laugh filled the room. "Me too. Only one more week. You're surrounded by people who love you, and we will take good care of you while Hunter is gone."

I leaned my head on her shoulder. "I know. Let's just hope it works."

I stared at the overnight bag on my bed, racking my tired brain for anything else I might need to pack for the weekend. Even though Hunter's game was at home this week, we had planned to spend a few days with Ari and Jagger at the condo we all rented together in order not to sit in traffic for hours and hours. Plus, I would much rather have the extra time with Hunter and my friends.

"You know that you can buy anything you forget. Don't over think it," Ari said over the phone. "From what I see on the map, there's a Target up the street from where we're staying. While the guys are practicing, we can take a walk ... and reward ourselves for exercising with some Bon Bons."

Laughing, I adjusted my AirPod in my ear.

"I'm just relieved that you and the baby are doing well. Poor Jagger came running as fast as he could when he heard me screaming." She laughed. "When I told him you were pregnant, his face lit up. I swear he's already planning our holidays together with the kids."

I hurried to the bathroom and grabbed my prenatal vitamins and the last toiletries I needed to pack. "He can congratulate me in person in a few hours."

"I have a confession," Ari said.

"Oh?" I closed my suitcase and zipped it.

"I love it when Hunter and Jagger play against each other. It's usually such a good game."

"Hell, it's just hot. Sexy." I barked out a laugh.

"Yeah, it really is. And I'm totally ignoring the fact that you just called my husband hot and sexy."

"Bitch please, if you hadn't snatched him up, I would have been first in line." A silly grin eased across my face. "I'm excited to see you both. For the record, I plan to eat ... a lot."

"I don't think I've ever been so relieved to hear you say that."

"Hunter too. I think he's ready to ravish *me*." I scooped up my handbag and slipped the leather strap over my shoulder. "I've been so sick that sex has been a no go."

Footsteps caught my attention before Hunter entered the room. "Teagan? Are you ready?"

"Hunter's here. I'll see you soon, Ari."

"Hurry your ass up. I'll need details," Ari said before ending the call.

"You look stunning." Hunter gently kissed me as he placed his palm against my stomach.

"Thank you. I'm feeling more like myself."

Hunter grabbed the suitcase and set it on the floor. "The car is here. We need to go."

Minutes later, Hunter and I settled into the backseat of the Mercedes.

He patted the driver on the shoulder as I buckled in. "Thanks, Zayne. The fans get crazy, so I want Teagan to have a bodyguard in case someone tries to get too close to her. I always appreciate when you're available."

"Pay me back with a good win, man." Zayne flashed us a smile before he put the car in gear and drove down the driveway.

Whenever Hunter got nervous about overzealous fans, he called Westbrook Security to hire one of the men who could fly out to a game and stay with me. Since I was pregnant, it comforted me, so I never argued with my hubs. Plus, Hunter needed a clear head to give a hundred percent on the field, which couldn't happen if he was worried about me.

An hour later, Zayne snuck us through the back entrance of a red brick building, then escorted us to the elevator and the third floor.

"Do you need me inside the doctor's office, or would you rather I remain in the hall?" Zayne asked, his green eyes scouring the area.

"The doctor took into consideration Hunter's celebrity status, so we're the only people here. I think we'll be fine going in alone. Thank you." I patted his arm.

Hunter opened the door and placed his hand on the small of my back while we walked into the empty waiting room.

Dr. Huber, a middle-aged blonde-haired woman with kind brown eyes, greeted us. "Hi, Teagan. How are you feeling?" She gave me a warm smile.

"Much better." I glanced at my husband, who was shifting from one foot to the next.

"Someone's eager." I giggled.

"Then let's get going." She led the way and continued with small chit-chat as Hunter grabbed my hand and we followed her into the exam room.

I climbed up on the table, and my husband stood next to me.

"Okay. Let's have a look."

Dr. Huber squeezed the gel onto the ultrasound probe before she gently lifted my shirt, exposing my belly.

The whoosh whoosh of the baby's heartbeat filled the small equipment speaker.

"There we go." The doctor moved the wand around, then smiled at us. She pointed at the screen. "Here's the head and arms ... the legs ... and ..."

"Yeah?" Hunter urged her.

"Do you want to know the sex of the baby?"

"Please," we both said at the same time.

"And there's a penis. You're having a boy."

"Hell yeah!" My husband whooped, beaming at me. "And everything looks good? My wife and kid are healthy?"

"Yes, they are both doing great. Congratulations, you two."

The doctor took pictures for us before she handed me some tissues to wipe off my belly.

"When you're ready, meet me up front." Dr. Huber excused herself, leaving us alone in the room.

The second the door closed, I burst into tears.

"Babe, what's wrong?" Hunter scooped me up in his arms, cradled me, then walked to the chair and sat down.

"I'm happy." Laughing through my cries, I kissed him hard. "What do you think about naming him Levi James Calloway?"

A flash of pain was quickly replaced with the joy that morphed over his face.

"I would love that."

"Good. I want to honor your brother's memory."

"Me too." Hunter brushed his lips against mine. "I love you, Teagan, and I'm so excited to start a family with you."

"Love you too, baby. Love you too."

***

Check out the **Ruthless Obsession bonus scene** that's *TOO STEAMY FOR AMAZON!* **Click here.**

Don't miss Kane in **Sinful Obsession**, a dark, enemies-to-lovers, second chance, secret society, sports standalone FREE in Kindle Unlimited. **Click Here! Turn the page for the Sample!**

Sinful Obsession Sample

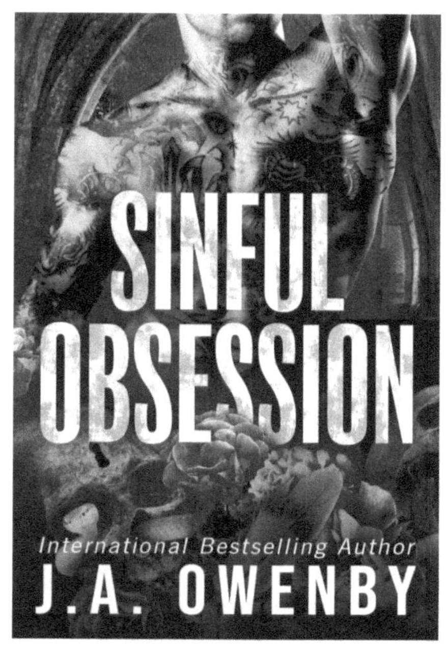

Brie

He's stalking me.
Someone has been in my home, left messages on my wall.
I've had dreams that a stranger in a mask touches me while I'm sleeping,
forcing my body to bend to his wicked ways.
But I want more. Crave more.
He has the key to release me from my prison.
Can I trust him, or will he be the end of me instead?

Kane
I'm playing a dangerous game. Stalking her. Breaking into her house while she's asleep.
Brie Langston left me for dead.
Years later, I see her face at Whitmore U.
Now, I'm the leader of a secret society,
And the star quarterback with a future in the NFL.
I'm king and it feels good ... and she could take it all away.

I know what happens when you mix fire and gasoline ...
The flames consume and destroy.
But I'm torn between the girl I used to love and the one I have a sinful obsession with now.

She ruined me once, but this time I know her secrets.
If I'm going down, I'm going to destroy her first.

Prepare to delve into the shadows of Kane's captivating journey, where his dark and kinky desires will leave you breathless! His story will take you on a wild ride full of jaw-dropping twists and turns that will keep you on the edge of your seat!

*Sinful Obsession is a full-length **dark, enemies-to-lovers, second chance, sports standalone** featuring a damaged hero, a* *strong heroine, and a lot of kinky, good times. No cheating, no cliffhanger, and a happily ever after guaranteed!*

Download Sinful Obsession on Amazon or **FREE** in Kindle Unlimited! **Click Here!**

Turn the page for the Sample of Sinful Obsession.

Prologue

I grabbed her shoulders, piercing her with an intense stare. "Run, Lyndsay!"

"I can't leave you, Jacob. I won't." Tears streamed down her pale cheeks as she clung to my arms. She shook her head, her blue eyes wide with fear.

I gathered her in for a hug, and her petite body trembled against mine. "You have to. We'll both die if you don't go. Now." I rubbed her back, hoping it would give her the courage she needed to save herself —to save us.

The dogs barking in the distance were closing in on us fast. Our time was running out.

She threw her arms around my neck and sobbed into my shirt. "I love you. I'll bring help and come back for you, I swear."

"I love you, too." I tilted her chin and placed a kiss to her mouth. "Go." A lump lodged itself in my throat as she turned and ran for her fucking life. She had to make it. She had to come back for me. She was my only hope, especially now that I'd helped her escape. But if we made one mistake ... our lives would be over.

Fear scraped its sharp talons down my spine as I whirled around on the heel of my black boot and ran in the opposite direction. I tried to pick up my pace, stumbling over the ground that was thick with brush and sticks, only the pale half-moon to light my way.

The sound of dogs barking pricked my ears. They were close. Too close. "Fuck," I breathed into the frigid air. I slowed and listened, then realized the best way for me to ensure Lyndsay's escape was to stop the guards. Sweat beaded on my forehead as I ran in the direction from which the mutts were barking.

It wasn't long before I met the three guards. This time, the dogs weren't hunting for food. They were hunting Lyndsay and me.

"It's just me, Jacob." I held my hands in the air, surrendering. "I took a walk when I couldn't sleep and got lost."

"Where's Lyndsay?" one of them asked, jerking on the leash as his overgrown pup snarled and jumped toward me.

I backed away slowly, not wanting to be shredded to death. "I don't know. I had no idea she was outside, I swear."

"You two stay with Jacob. I'm going to search for the girl," the dark-haired man said, eyeing me suspiciously.

Shit! I had to stop him from going after her.

"I fucked her," I spat, with more venom than I thought possible. "She's no longer a virgin."

Gilmore, the lead guard, growled. "What the hell did you say, boy?"

The three stepped toward me, and I backed away with my hands still in the air. I had to keep stalling, even if it cost me my life. I would gladly give mine for Lyndsay's freedom.

"Lyndsay and I love each other, and there's no way I would let the elders fuck her. *She's mine.*"

One of the guards threw his head back, filling the air with his maniacal laughter.

"Boy, you're the one fucked now. You know the consequences for defiling a young girl."

My nostrils flared and my hands fisted. There was no way this would end well for me.

"I love her." My voice held steady, even though my legs were anything but.

Another guard gave his leash to the other, then approached me.

"We're taking you to the elders, and they can decide your punishment for disobeying the law," he snarled.

"You have to catch me first, you fat piece of shit." A rush of adrenaline flooded my system. Not once in my fifteen years had I ever considered talking back.

Instinct kicked in, and I hightailed it away from the guards and in the opposite direction Lyndsay had run.

"Little punk." Footsteps followed me as the cursing drew nearer.

At least I had speed on my side. One of the elders loved a game called football, so he taught the kids how to play every day there wasn't rain or snow. I'd fallen in love with the sport, and he worked with me one-on-one. I was the running zigzag king, and if I could see where the fuck I was going, I could outrun anyone here. But the one thing I'd counted on to keep Lyndsay and me safe that night had just turned into my enemy. It was so dark I struggled to see more than a few feet ahead, which slowed me down.

A strong hand grabbed my arm and jerked me back. I glowered at him over my shoulder, projecting an air of confidence that wasn't feasibly possible at the moment.

"Have it your way." The guard raised his club, a devious grin on his ugly mug.

I attempted to cover my head as I saw him swing, bracing for the impact. The thud knocked me forward, and I stumbled, stars dancing before my eyes. My vision clouded, then turned as black as the night while I collapsed onto the frozen ground.

Chapter 1 ~ Brie

"Are you nervous?" my mother asked, clutching one of my many packed boxes in her arms as she hurried up the sidewalk behind me.

I bumped the door open with my hip, then entered the small living room. At least it was an open floor plan, so it felt bigger. I set a laundry basket full of clean clothes on top of the kitchen counter and turned to Mom. "A little. At least I have the other team members from the cheerleading squad. This summer gave me a chance to meet and get to know a few of them. Having some friends here already helps. Gabby and I hit it off immediately. It was almost as if we'd known each other for years instead of a few months before classes started."

Mom sat down the box she was carrying, then blew a wisp of hair out of her eyes while she planted her hands on her slender hips. A smile lit up her face.

"Brie!" My five-year-old brother called as he rushed into the living room full speed ahead. He abruptly stopped and gave me his bottle of bubbles. "Can you play with me?"

His sweet expression was full of love and trust. Since Mom and

Dad had Conner later in life, I'd had an opportunity to help take care of him and be a part of his everyday routine. I loved this little guy a ton, and I would miss him the most.

I reached down, grabbed him under his arms, and hauled him up, sitting him on top of the white kitchen counter. "As soon as we're done unloading, I'll take you outside, and we can play before you have to leave." I gently tapped the tip of his nose, adoring his dusting of freckles.

His lower lip formed a cute pout. "I don't want you to stay here. Come home, Brie." Tears welled in his eyes, and I wrapped him up in my arms.

"We will FaceTime every week. It will almost be like I'm still there with you."

"Promise?"

I kissed his forehead. "Buddy, I wouldn't miss it for the world." I glanced at Mom, her wistful expression tugging at my heartstrings.

"He's really going to miss you. We all are," Mom said softly.

"Son of a bitch!" Dad swore, as he stumbled through the doorway, the side of a large box bouncing off the door frame.

"Rodger, language." Mom shook her head, grinning while she grabbed one side of the heavy load and helped him. Once it was safe and sound on the black leather couch, Dad brushed off his hands.

"Sorry, bud. Don't say that word at school, okay?" Dad raised an eyebrow at my little brother, and I attempted to stifle my giggle.

Conner scrunched up his nose. "That was four words, Dad."

We broke into laughter, my heart singing. Shit, I was going to miss my family something awful. Unlike a lot of nineteen-year-olds, I was close to my parents. We traveled together, had movie nights, and shared our wins of the day every night at the dinner table. I cried on Mom's shoulder when my first major crush had rejected me, then laughed alongside her when, two years later, he had it so bad for me that he followed me around like a heartsick puppy.

"I'm so glad we hired movers to bring the furniture. Good grief, it's too hot to move today." Dad wiped the perspiration off his forehead with the back of his hand. His salt-and-pepper hair was slick with sweat, and his grey T-shirt was plastered against his body. Dad was in good shape for his fifty-six years but moving had kicked all our asses.

My cell buzzed, and I reached into the back pocket of my jean shorts to fish it out. I grinned as Gabrielle McCallister's message popped up. Gabby, as her friends called her, had welcomed me to the squad, along with her friends, Leighton and Everlee.

Are you moved in yet?

I tapped out a response: *Almost! A few more boxes to bring in.*

Sweet. Get your cute little ass to my place so we can catch up on all the things since we last saw you.

I snorted, then replied. *It was only three days ago. LOL.*

Gabby's message vibrated my phone. *Whatevs. Just hurry up.*

I set my cell on the counter next to Conner.

"You look happy," Mom said.

"Yeah, the girls I mentioned I'd made friends with want me to hang with them after we're done unloading. Gabby and Everlee are on the team and are also roomies."

Dad's expression faltered. "I'm sure it would have been easier if you had roommates, but ..."

"I know. I'll be fine. I promise. The privacy and quiet will help me study since I have my own place."

"Also, when you're ready, there is a box in the bottom drawer of your dresser."

"Okay." Mom didn't need to say anything else. I knew what she was implying. Whatever Mom had put together for me would have to wait until ...

Mom grabbed me for a quick hug. "You know if you need us for anything, we're only a call away." She smoothed my long, wavy blonde hair.

"I know." The air around us crackled with anticipation. My parents had been bound and determined to set me up for success and found a cute little house for me close to the Whitmore University campus. And even though we wouldn't speak it out loud, we were all holding our breath to see if I would stay. Some demons I could never get rid of. They rode me piggyback, whispering dark thoughts into my ear while they clawed at my soul.

"Well, if you have plans, we'd better finish up." Dad slid his arm around my shoulders.

"And play bubbles," Conner reminded, poking me in the side with his finger.

I giggled, then turned to him. "Tickle monster!" His fit of laughter filled the space and lit up my heart. At the same time, I'd spent the last several years helping out my parents with his care, and I desperately wanted to see what life was like outside of my family. Here at school, I was only responsible for myself.

"Why don't we wait on the boxes and take care of your room?" Dad gave my arm a gentle squeeze.

"Okay." My pulse hammered against my wrist. I hated this part, but it was necessary, especially while living alone.

I followed Dad down the hall, then closed the door behind us. He walked over to the dresser as I glanced at the queen-size bed and frame that were already put together. The area was actually a decent size, so my matching nightstand and dresser fit beautifully and left plenty of space to walk. Thankfully, the rustic brown furniture helped offset the stark white walls.

The sound of a box opening pulled my attention back to the job at hand.

"Are you ready?" Dad's voice was peppered with worry.

I gulped as I stared at the leather strap of the handcuff. "Yeah," I whispered.

Download Sinful Obsession on Amazon or **FREE** in Kindle Unlimited! **Click Here!**

FREE BOOK

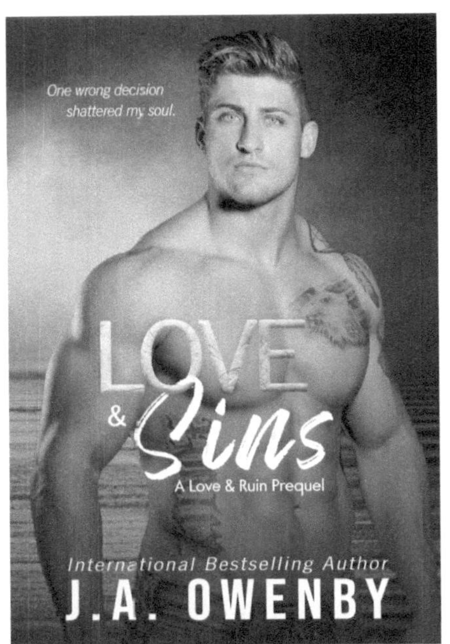

One wrong decision
shattered my soul.
LOVE
& Sins
A Love & Ruin Prequel
International Bestselling Author
J.A. OWENBY

Also by J.A. Owenby

The Whitmore Elite Series

Forbidden Obsession, a standalone novel

Ruthless Obsession, a standalone novel

Sinful Obsession, a standalone novel

Toxic Obsession, a standalone novel

The Beautifully Damaged Series

Beautifully Damaged

Beautifully Broken

Beautifully Shattered

The Love & Ruin Series

Love & Ruin

Love & Deception

Love & Redemption

Love & Consequences, a standalone novel

Love & Corruption, a standalone novel

Love & Revelations, a novella

Love & Seduction, a standalone novel

<u>Love & Vengeance</u>

<u>Love & Retaliation</u>

The Wicked Intentions Series

Dark Intentions

Fractured Intentions

About the Author

International bestselling author J.A. Owenby grew up in a small backwoods town in Arkansas where she learned how to swear like a sailor and spot water moccasins skimming across the lake.

She finally ditched the south and headed to Oregon. The first winter there, she was literally blown away a few times by ninety mile an hour winds and storms that rolled in off the ocean.

Eventually, she longed for quiet and headed up to snowier pastures. She now resides in Washington state with her hot nerdy husband and three purebred Siberian cats who insist on using her computer as their napping spot. She spends her days coming up with ways to torture characters in a way that either makes you want to throw your book down a flight of stairs or sob hysterically into a pillow.

J.A. Owenby writes new adult and romantic thriller novels. Her books ooze with emotion, angst, and twists that will leamazon.-com/J.A.-Owenby/e/B00J77KCFKave you breathless. Having battled her own demons, she's not afraid to tackle the secrets women are forced to hide. After all, the road to love is paved in the dark.

Her friends describe her as delightfully twisted. She loves fan mail and wine. Please send her all the wine.

You can follow the progress of her upcoming novel on Facebook at Author J.A. Owenby and on Twitter @jaowenby.

Sign up for J.A. Owenby's Newsletter at www.authorjaowenby.com

Like J.A. Owenby's Facebook:
https://www.facebook.com/JAOwenby

*J.A. Owenby's One Page At A Time reader group:*https://www.face
book.com/groups/JAOwenby